Her Father's Daughter

Cover Photography by TJ Drysdale

Cover Design by Matthew Weatherston

Griffith Cameron Publishing

ISBN - 978-1-955212-02-1

Her Father's Daughter

Eilidh Miller

Chapter 1

"Emi!"

The loud whispering of her name in a familiar voice caused Emi to pause in her work and smile because she knew the man to whom that voice belonged. She'd known him all her life, and the slight urgency that laced his tone meant he was up to something. Turning around, she saw him smile at her from the doorway to the kitchens where she worked.

"The weather is too fine to be indoors. Can ye nae come out for a time?" he whispered to her.

Emi turned back around, worrying her lip with her teeth for a moment before looking at the older woman beside her. Bridgette had taken her in as a child when Emi's mother and father — Helena and Darach — died, though Emi didn't remember them. She'd been just over a year old when they'd caught a fever and died within hours of each other, and as soon as they'd become ill, Bridgette had taken Emi into her care at Helena's request. When the worst happened, Bridgette and her husband Andrew kept Emi with them, unable to bear the thought of sending her away. Helena had entrusted Emi to them, and they refused to let that end just because Helena's life had.

"Maman, may I go outside for a little while as the dough sits?"

Bridgette offered her an amused smile. "Go on," she

said with a tip of her head toward the door as she gathered some bread and cheese into a towel. Wrapping it, she handed it to Emi. "And do not think I do not see you there, Alasdair Stewart. You are neither as clever nor as sneaky as you think you are."

Emi heard Alasdair laugh behind her, and she grinned, turning around and hurrying out of the door as Bridgette shook her head. If there was anyone who could pull Emi away from a task with extraordinarily little effort, it was Alasdair Stewart. A polite young man but a skilled warrior and horseman, he already had a reputation as one of the Stewart retainers others should do their best to avoid crossing. It wasn't for nothing, he'd proven that more than once, and he was given a wide berth by officers from other clans because of it. Tall and muscular, with a broad chest and shoulders, he could look quite intimidating if he chose to. Alasdair was also exceedingly handsome with his dark hair, blue eyes, and strong jawline, something Emi knew he was well aware of and used to his advantage as often as he was able.

He was a good friend of her brother Evander — a junior officer with the chief's men, along with many of the other young men both he and Emi had grown up with — but unlike Evander, Alasdair was a full officer in service to their chief, Crisdean Stewart. It was a high honor for one so young, and at only 21 he sat in an esteemed and influential place within the clan, though he certainly never let it go to his head. His job was his job, and that was all it was. It didn't make him special ... or at least that's what he always told Emi. Everyone else in the clan seemed to think otherwise, however.

Making the small jump from the stairs rather than taking them down, Emi landed next to Alasdair, the move making him grin. "There. I am outside. Now what?"

"Well, since ye were given a bite to eat, let us go sit by the river, so ye can enjoy it in the sunshine."

"I think that sounds perfect."

The two of them walked the short distance in silence, and Alasdair chose a spot for them to rest that was shielded from full view of the road by some trees. This ensured no one came around to bother them, and with time fully alone with each other a rarity, it seemed Alasdair had no intention of sharing it with someone else. Sitting down on the grass, Emi unwrapped the towel to find that Bridgette had also included two small pastries from the bunch she'd been preparing for that night's supper.

"I should tell Bridgette how much I love and adore her," Alasdair said as the treats were unveiled. Reaching for one, he found his hand promptly slapped, and he looked at Emi in confusion.

"Ye did nae ask if ye could have one. I thought the chief taught ye better manners? Besides, if I were to offer ye one, it should be at the end of my meal, nae the beginning."

"I did nae know I had to ask, as ye usually dinnae make me. Is life nae too short to save the best of things for the end?"

"I suppose that is true," she said, her expression thoughtful before her lips twisted in a wry smile. "Go on with ye, then."

Alasdair responded with a triumphant grin before he took the treat and popped it into his mouth with a happy sigh. As he closed his eyes and lay back on the grass, Emi watched the sun sparkle through the leaves of the trees and dance in bright spots across his face. Scottish summers could be so beautiful, and it often made the endurance of the rest of the year worth it.

"Are ye nae supposed to be with the chief?"

"I was," he replied once he'd finished chewing his food. "Released now."

"That is early, no?"

"Aye, but that is because we are leaving in the morning."

"Leaving? To where?"

"Inverness. The chief has business there."

"Oh. Is it as beautiful as they say?"

"Inverness? No. It is a city."

"I mean the journey, ye dolt," Emi said, laughing.

"Oh, aye, that part is."

"I wish I could go."

"What if ye could?" he asked, opening his eyes and turning his head to look at her.

She looked at him with genuine curiosity. "How could I?"

"Maybe I could convince him to let ye come along to restock some things for the kitchens."

"But that is Maman's job."

"She could always delegate it to ye."

"She will nae."

"Ye have nae ever asked, have ye?" Emi fell quiet and Alasdair sat up, propping himself on an elbow and watching her as she mulled the idea over. "Come with us, Em. I know I could get him to allow it. Ye have never gone anywhere farther than the village, and I know ye want to."

"I do," she admitted. "But then what about Arabella? What about yer mam and Fergus' mam?"

"Yers will still be here, and everyone will be fine. The clan and our families will nae collapse in yer absence."

Alasdair's persuasive ability drove her mad at times, but this wasn't one of those moments. She did want to go now that he'd offered it and was more than willing to let him talk her into it. "If ye can get him and Maman to agree, then I will go. But ye have to ask them both yerself."

"If that is the cost of ye coming along, I will gladly pay it and then some."

She smiled shyly at him and turned her eyes back to her food, eating a small piece of cheese as she watched the glittering water slide by. Going outside of the village on a new adventure with Alasdair, as well as spending so long a time with him, was an exciting and appealing opportunity. Though he was two years older than she was, the same age as Evander, it hadn't ever seemed to matter, and he'd been her friend from her earliest memories. When his own father had died when he was seven, she'd sat silent in a corner with him, holding his hand as he'd gone between wailing and staring blankly.

Emi had been the only soul he'd let near him those first few days, and it was Emi who had been able to coax him to eat or drink. He would sleep with his head in her lap while she stroked his hair, and through it all Emi hadn't left his side. She knew it was something he'd never forgotten, he'd said so many times, and he held her close because of it. She was his dearest friend, woman or no, and knew a great deal more about him than anyone else did. Other women were jealous of the high esteem and care he held for Emi, but none dared do or say anything, lest they ruin any chance they might have with him. To speak badly of or harm Emi was the surest way to earn Alasdair's permanent disdain.

The pair of them were well-suited friends, having similar minds, similar quick wits, and similar interests. He knew how to get a rise out of her and sometimes did so just because he could, though she was equally able to return the favor. Emi was one part of Alasdair's group of closest friends, the only female in the pack, and had earned her place there fairly. When they were all young, she'd been just as quick to get dirty, climb trees — and fall out of them — roughhouse, fish, or hunt as they had. They all adored her in their own ways and for their own reasons, as she did them, with Bridgette often worrying aloud that it would prevent Emi from ever courting or marrying because the young man would have to get through a thorough inspection and approval by half of Crisdean's officers and junior officers first.

"Je souhaite que vous ne souriez pas autant," he said to her, following the words with a small smile. *I do wish you would not smile so much.*

Alasdair could speak French fluently, the chief had made sure of it, and he enjoyed using it with Emi, who was the same because of Bridgette, who'd come to Stewart land with her husband after meeting him during a visit by the current chief's father to France. Doing so allowed him to keep in practice, and while he also spoke it with Evander, he seemed to use it more often with her.

"Pourquoi?" she asked, looking over at him as her brow knitted in a frown. *Why?*

"Parce que tu es beaucoup trop jolie quand tu le fais, et j'ai peur de devoir commencer à retenir les garçons bientôt," he replied. *Because you are far too pretty when you do, and I fear I am going to have to start holding lads back soon.*

Emi gave him a curious look. He'd never said anything like that before. "What a strange thing to say."

"Is it?"

"There is no one here to hold back, Alasdair, in case ye have suddenly gone blind. Besides, there are plenty of other lasses to go to before I am even noticed."

"Why would ye say something as daft as that?"

"It is nae daft!"

"Aye, it is. Maybe I should sneak ye into the private quarters so that ye can look in a mirror, Em."

She shrugged in response. "If they were going to do so, they would have already. Nae as though I care that they have nae."

"And why is that? Should ye nae be wanting such attention?" he asked. "Though I have a fairly good idea why they have nae, and it has naught to do with a lack of beauty, believe me."

"Then what *does* it have to do with?"

"Ye have heard yer mam. They would have to deal with us, and, so far, none of them are brave enough to dare try."

"Well, that is fine by me, thank ye. I dinnae know why I am nae interested, really. Nae something I am really thinking of just now."

Alasdair said nothing, though she could tell he was holding something back. She didn't ask, she knew he'd tell her when he was ready to do so, and pressing him would get her nothing but a stone-faced wall that went by the name of Alasdair. She had a feeling she knew what it was he was avoiding saying to her: that he had his eye on one of the lasses who clamored after him, with a more serious thought than to just an evening or two. She wasn't surprised by it, as he was getting to the age where he should have a wife and a family, like their friend and Alasdair's fellow officer, Cailean, though why he would hesitate to tell her was a mystery. Perhaps he thought she'd be hurt by their being able to spend less time together, though she knew full well such a thing was inevitable.

"I should go back," she said as she stood up, her statement and movement bringing a look of alarm to his face.

"I did nae mean to upset ye, Emi."

"Ye have nae," she said, offering him a reassuring smile. "But I have bread that needs baking for supper tonight. Nae all of us get dismissed early, ye know."

"Ah. Right," he said, his sheepish smile showing his momentary embarrassment.

"Finish the bread and cheese, and bring the towel back when ye are done," she said, turning to walk away from him.

"Emi."

"Aye?" she said, stopping and looking back at him over her shoulder.

"I … thank ye for the food," he said in a rush, though Emi didn't miss his hesitation at the beginning.

"Ye are welcome. See ye at supper."

"Aye, see ye at supper."

When she returned, Emi resumed her place in the kitchen and let her work take over her thoughts. She loved baking, it was one of her favorite tasks, and she was happy to do it here with the fine ingredients the chief could provide. It allowed her to experiment, and those things she made were generally quite well received. Venison pie was a favorite and her signature dish, one she was always requested to make when the chief was having a private supper with a guest or alone with his officers.

"Emilia."

The sound of Crisdean's voice behind her made her jump, and she whirled around to face him. She'd been so absorbed in her task she hadn't heard him come in, or even noticed other work stopping at his appearance. She also hadn't noticed Bridgette leave the kitchens, but clearly, she had since she was standing next to him now.

"Chief," she replied, lowering herself into a curtsy. "Were ye after a pie, sir? I think there is time enough to get it done for supper if ye need. I can start right now."

Crisdean shook his head with a gentle laugh. "No, lass, but thank ye. I am nae in need of a pie tonight, though perhaps we will want to ready one for the road."

"The road, sir?"

"Aye. Ye are coming with us to Inverness, are ye nae? The men and I will need to eat."

Emi's eyes widened. Alasdair had done it. He'd really done it! "Aye, of course! I will start straight away! It will be the best pie I have ever made! Thank ye, Chief!"

Her exuberance made him laugh outright now. "Easy with ye, child. It is just Inverness; it is nae as if I am taking ye to France. Bridgette, excuse her from the supper preparations, would ye? That way she has all of her time free to see to provisioning."

"Yes, of course, Chief."

"Emilia, be ready to leave at dawn."

"Aye, Chief!"

As Crisdean departed, Bridgette looked over at her with a smile and a raised eyebrow. "Alasdair must have really wanted you to go along."

"What makes ye say that?"

"Well, he promised to do whatever I needed of him if I let him tell the chief that I wanted you to go to Inverness for me. Then he promised the chief extra watch shifts and stable work if he would allow you to go."

The thought of him wanting her to go so badly made her smile. "Then I had better get to work, so he does nae regret it."

Emi hurried to the storerooms to gather what she'd need for the pie, but when she got there, she found Alasdair waiting for her, a victorious smile on his lips. "I told ye I could convince him."

"Ye did, and now I need to get to work to be ready for the journey," she replied as she started picking up items and putting them in one of the baskets left by the door.

"Aye, and I am looking forward to eating that work."

"I am sure ye are," she said before she stopped, looking at him curiously and narrowing her eyes. "Alasdair, come here."

"What is it?"

"I think ye have a bit of grass in yer hair from earlier."

"Oh," he said, coming toward her and leaning down so she could get it out.

As soon as he was close enough, Emi reached up with flour-covered hands and mussed his hair before he could react, bringing a loud gasp from him as she laughed. "Now ye look like one of those fancy powdered gentlemen!"

"Oh, ye are in for it now."

Emi stopped laughing, belatedly thinking better of her prank, and took a couple of steps back before she turned to run. In the small space, he caught her easily and dragged her backward, clutching her back to his chest. Alasdair wrapped an arm around her as she squirmed. "Let go!"

"Oh, no, no, no. Revenge is mine," he retorted. Without another word, he began tickling her side, bringing a squeal from her before she laughed.

"Alasdair!"

"Fancy powdered gentleman, eh?"

"Aye!"

"Ohh, wrong answer!" he said, laughing and upping the ferocity of his attack.

Emi let out a small shout, sagging in his arms as she laughed harder. "We can take some soot and put a spot near yer lips and powder yer face, too, before we sell ye to France!"

"Sell me!" he exclaimed, still laughing. "Ye would have to catch me first!"

Emi had tears in her eyes from laughing and shook her head. "Stop!"

The moment she said the word he stopped, and she turned around in his arms with the intent to playfully shove him away from her. He had, however, remained much closer to her than she'd realized, and when she turned around, they were nearly face-to-face. Her laughter ceased in a tiny gasp, and she looked up at him, breathing quickly and cheeks red from the teasing. Alasdair looked down at her for a moment before he immediately released her, both of them backing away a few steps.

"I should go," he said, the words tumbling out in a quiet rush. "I need to get things ready and let Mam know I am leaving."

"Aye," she said, her confusion making her just as quiet.

He said nothing else as he brushed past her and departed, leaving her to try to make sense of what had just happened, even if she didn't know what that was.

The rest of the day passed quickly as she busied herself getting things ready for four days on the road, and it left her with no time to ponder the moment in the storeroom. By the time supper was ready, she'd finished her work and, because she didn't have to serve tonight, was able to change into a dress more suited for dining in the hall than working in the kitchens. As she emerged into the roar of a full hall, she threaded her way through the crowd to the table where those who worked in the kitchens sat.

"Emi!" Evander called out as he hurried toward her. "Are ye really going to Inverness?"

"Aye! Can ye believe it?" she replied, unable to hide her excitement at the very thought even if she'd tried.

"No, but I am happy for ye all the same. It is about time ye went somewhere else, though I am nae going this time."

"Because of me? I am sorry, Evander."

"No, nae because of ye, daft lass. The fields need work, so I need to do that instead while the weather is fine."

"Ah, of course."

"Ye watch yerself with them."

Emi looked at him curiously, finding it a strange thing for Evander to say about his own friends, though had she been anyone else, there might have been those giving the same warning to her about *him*. She knew Evander saw her as his true sister, blood or not, and he was as protective of her as any blood brother would be. His desire to keep her close and protect her had only increased since his father's death two years prior, seeing it as his duty as the now head of their family.

"Why?"

"Just watch yerself, all right?" he said in a low voice before he departed.

She turned and watched him walk back across the hall to the table where Alasdair sat with the other officers, glancing at her as he took his seat, but Alasdair didn't acknowledge her at all. She stood still for a moment, hoping he'd at least look her way and smile, but she turned around and continued to the table when it was clear he wasn't going to. It bothered her more than it should, though she couldn't say why, and as she sat down, she cast a glance back at the officer's table to find him laughing with Cailean. Turning her gaze forward again, she clasped her hands together tightly in her lap.

"Emi, sweetness, are you all right?"

Bridgette's voice broke her thoughts, and Emi glanced over at her. Was she all right? No. No, she wasn't. "I … I have lost my appetite, Maman. Nerves about tomorrow probably. Excuse me, would ye?"

"Emi —"

Emi didn't wait to hear the rest of what Bridgette wanted to say, walking across the hall and out as fast as she could without running and picking up a lantern. Her desire to not remain there far outweighed any hunger she may have felt, and as she hurried down the path that would take her home, she wiped tears from her cheeks with her free hand. Why was she crying? It made no sense, really. Perhaps she was just over-tired, and her excitement was wearing off enough to show it.

After a night of restless sleep, Emi was at the castle before dawn, loading up the things she'd made and armed with a list from Bridgette of things she needed to get in Inverness. It wasn't long before Crisdean and his officers emerged, walking past her, and she watched them gather together to go through one final check on saddles, bags, and other things.

"Are we ready?" Crisdean called out.

Emi made her way toward the front of the cart, but Alasdair stopped her with a gentle hand on her arm, the first time he'd acknowledged her presence since the storeroom. "Ye are riding with us. Come, let me help ye," he said before he led her to the horse meant for her. "May I?"

"Aye, thank ye," she said.

With a nod, he lifted her by the waist and sat her atop the horse before mounting his own next to her. Fergus and Cailean were riding vanguard with Crisdean between them, while Alasdair stayed to her right, and another of the officers joined them on the left. The cart would come behind them, with two other officers following it. When Crisdean gave the signal to ride out, the group moved forward through the gates and onto the road that would take them through the village to the main road to Inverness. There was silence for now, and the sky was getting lighter, the deep pinks and purples of the horizon becoming softer. By the time they reached the main road, the sun was nearly up, and it wasn't long before they were on the other side of the village and into territory Emi had never seen before. Through the trees to her left, she could see a great loch, a layer of morning mist still hanging over its surface. The chirping and twittering of the birds was loud in the stillness of all else.

"Is it as beautiful as ye had hoped so far?" Alasdair asked, breaking the silence.

Emi looked over at him, her face half-hidden by the hood of her arasaid. "Oh, so ye wish to speak to me now?"

"What?" Alasdair asked, looking over at her in confusion.

"Ye have nae said a word to me since yesterday afternoon, but now ye want to speak to me as if that were nae so?" she said, her tone sharper than she'd intended, before turning her eyes forward again.

"I … I was busy, Em. I had things to do."

"Too busy to even say hello to me at supper?"

"Were ye there? I did nae see ye."

Emi looked over at him again, unable to keep the hurt out of her expression. "Ye did nae see me. Thank ye so very much, Alasdair. Good to know I am as invisible to ye as I told ye I was yesterday."

"Emi, I apologize; that was nae how I meant that. Ye are nae invisible; I must have just missed seeing ye before ye sat down. If I had seen ye, then ye know I would have spoken to ye, just as I always do."

Emi said nothing for a long moment, trying to understand why what he'd said even bothered her. It shouldn't, and normally wouldn't, but today it felt like rejection and the sting of it was vicious. "I know," she finally replied, though her voice was quiet. "I dinnae know why I said that or snapped at ye. Sorry, Alasdair."

Alasdair smiled reassuringly. "Dinnae fret. I should nae have said what I did, and I am sorry I missed speaking with ye. I guess I was just so tied up with getting ready, running everything through in my head, that I was nae really paying attention."

"It is beautiful, though," she said, changing the subject as she looked around her.

"We have nae even left our own lands yet."

"We have nae?"

Alasdair looked at her curiously. "No. How small do ye think our lands are, Em?"

"I dinnae know. I thought it was the castle and the surrounding area, the loch and the area around it, then up to the village."

He laughed and shook his head. "No. It is quite a bit larger than that. Perhaps one of these days, Evander, the lads, and I will take ye out to ride the boundaries so that ye can see just how much belongs to the chief and the clan."

"Would ye?" she asked, unable to suppress the bright smile the idea brought. "That sounds lovely."

"Aye, I will. I promise."

***

After his promise, Emi beamed and turned her face forward, riding in silence. When she'd looked away from him, Alasdair cursed himself silently. What he'd said hadn't been what he'd meant, and it had come out all wrong. Then again, he'd known full well she was there and was only trying to cover for his own behavior toward her last night. He shouldn't have ignored her; it was a cruel thing to do to someone he cared so much about. The excuse he'd given as to why he'd done it was a plausible one, and at least partially true, which is why she'd believed him. That, too, made him feel cross with himself. He was lying to her, and she trusted him so much that she'd never think to question it. In reality he hadn't known what to say to her after the storeroom. It was a moment he hadn't expected to hit him as hard as it had, and he hadn't wanted her to see how conflicted he was or say the wrong thing — as he'd just done.

There were a few moments of silence between them before she started to sing. It was a child's song about making soup, and the fun was thinking of ever more crazy things to put in it, then repeating all else that had gone in before. The men all looked at each other, then glanced at her, until Alasdair joined the next verse. One by one, the men added their bits, laughing and trying to outdo each other with ridiculous items. Even Crisdean joined the fun, which took several of them by surprise. He'd made many of these journeys, but Alasdair couldn't think of one where everyone was laughing and singing so soon as this, and usually the songs were far less appropriate for a lady's ears. It was different when Bridgette came — she was a married woman and knew how things stood — but Emi didn't, and there had been some quiet questioning as to how much they'd need to restrain themselves. Emi, it seemed, had other ideas, and intended to make the most of her first foray out of the village.

When they stopped for dinner, the cheer that went up when Emi produced the venison pie made her laugh. Clearly, they had no idea what she would've packed, but judging by what she set out, she hadn't had any intention of letting them down. Aside from the pie, there was bread and fresh butter, cheese, berries, and tiny tarts she'd made the previous day. There were sounds of appreciation as she set each thing out, followed by silence because the men were too busy feasting to worry about talking, and Emi took up a place on a small rock just outside of the main group.

"Why are ye sitting over there, Emilia?" Crisdean asked. "Is there one of us who needs to bathe? If so, point him out, and I will send him to the river immediately."

The others laughed, and Emi smiled. "No, I think they have all had their baths if the amount of water being heated last night was anything to go by, sir. No, I just thought ye would nae want female company during yer dinner."

Crisdean gave her a quizzical look. "And why, exactly, would that be?"

"Dinnae ye usually only have just yerselves?"

"We do, which is all the more reason to have ye join us than nae, especially with this excellent meal ye have set out for us. Even Bridgette does nae feed us this well on the road. Come sit ye down over here with the rest of us."

Emi stood and dutifully made her way over to the group, sitting down in the empty space between Fergus and Cailean. "As ye wish it, Chief" she said before popping a berry into her mouth. "Dinnae ye even try it, Fergus."

Fergus paused, his hand halfway to the napkin holding her food, intending to playfully swipe an extra dessert. "How did ye even know?"

Emi gave him a look, and Alasdair buried a laugh in his hand. "Because I know ye, that is why."

"Ach, no, she is like all lasses by a certain age. They see all. It is how our mams know if we are up to something we should nae be," Cailean said, laughing.

Emi laughed with him and then picked up one of her tarts, holding it out to Fergus. "Here, ye can have it."

Fergus blinked. "No, it is yers. I was only playing with ye, Emi."

Emi placed it on his napkin anyway. "I want ye to. I know how much ye like sweets," she said, following her words with her typical kind smile before turning back to her meal.

There was a hush over them all as Fergus looked truly touched by the gesture. No one could say Emi wasn't kind or thoughtful — she was, to a fault. She'd give something to someone just to make them happy, even if it left her with nothing, just as she'd done a moment ago.

"Thank ye, Emi," Fergus said, his voice soft. "That is very sweet of ye."

She gave him a nod in reply and then looked at the others. "Why are ye lot all staring at me? Eat!"

Her directive brought more laughter as they all tucked into their meals once more. When dinner was over, everyone saw to packing things up so that they could set off on their way once more. As Emi turned her back to pick up the last things to return to the cart, Alasdair placed the tart he'd kept aside on the gate along with a small wildflower beside it. Standing beside his horse from a short distance away, he watched as she picked the flower up with a soft gasp and looked around her, no idea which of the men had been the one to leave it. She smiled and put the small treat in her mouth before she tucked the flower into the front of her bodice, behind her stays, where it sat on top like a lovely brooch. Shutting the gate of the cart, she made her way back to her horse, where Alasdair was waiting to help her up.

"That is a lovely flower ye found, Em," he said as he lifted her into the saddle.

"I did nae! One of the others left it for me along with one of their tarts. It was nae Fergus, for I saw him eat all of his, so that means someone held one back just for me. It was very kind, and I wish I knew who it was so I could thank them."

"I am sure they will know ye are thankful just by seeing ye with that wee flower tucked in yer bodice," he replied before he mounted his horse beside her.

As they made their way along Loch Oich in the late afternoon, their halfway point came into view: Invergarry Castle. Home of the MacDonell's of Glengarry, Invergarry sat on a strategic point on the loch, able to see great distances on all sides of it. As they came into the yard, Chief MacDonell came outside to greet them with some of his officers. There was no animosity to be seen in any of their faces, allies as they were.

"Crisdean!" Chief MacDonell called out. "Good to see ye, old friend."

Crisdean dismounted and met him halfway, shaking his hand. "John, a pleasure as always. Thank ye for once again offering yer hospitality in letting us stay with ye overnight."

"Happy to do so, as ye do the same for us when we must pass yer way."

"And always shall."

"Bring everyone in and take yer ease."

"Lads!" Crisdean called. "See to the horses and then make yer way inside. Emilia, ye come with me."

Alasdair was instantly there to help her down, and she walked to where Crisdean stood and curtsied to Chief MacDonell.

"John, this is Emilia, Bridgette's daughter. She has come for Bridgette instead this time."

"Hello, Emilia," Chief MacDonell said with a welcoming smile. "It is good to finally meet ye. Yer mother speaks so highly of ye when she is here."

"Thank ye, Chief," Emi said, returning the smile. "It is a pleasure to meet ye as well."

The two men turned and went inside while talking quietly with Emi trailing behind them, and Alasdair watched her pause in the doorway to look around the hall in slight awe before taking her horse and moving forward with both hers and his to the stables with the other men.

Chapter 2

After being shown to the kitchens, Emi returned to the hall and sat down at one of the tables, looking around her. It was slightly larger than their own, but quite a bit more ornate in its decoration. It was odd to be in a different hall and she felt keenly the sense of being a visitor here.

"Good afternoon to ye, lass."

Emi turned her eyes forward to find one of the young Glengarry men standing before her. "Good afternoon."

"Do ye mind if I sit with ye? Ye seem as though ye might like some company."

"Nae at all," she replied, gesturing to the bench.

"What is yer name?" he asked as he sat down.

"Emilia, and ye?"

"Dougal. A pleasure to meet ye, Emilia. A beautiful name for an equally beautiful lass."

Emi felt her cheeks heat at the compliment. "Thank ye for saying so."

"No need to thank me for speaking the truth. Here," he said, producing a flower. "I think ye should have this."

Emi couldn't help the small gasp that left her lips. "Oh, how lovely that is! Thank ye!"

"Ye are quite welcome, and I know just where it should

go," he replied, sliding closer to her as he reached out and tucked the flower into her hair behind her ear.

It was a liberty this man was taking, and there was an intimacy in the lack of distance between them, but it was easy to dismiss what seemed to her like an innocent gesture, so she didn't stop him.

"What are ye doing?"

Both of them jumped at the sound of someone else's voice, the tone commanding and tinged with displeasure. The young man looked nervous while Emi looked at Alasdair, confused as to why he was using such a tone for no reason.

"I was talking to her is all," the young man said.

"Aye, well, stop talking to her."

"Why? Is she married? If nae, she is as free for me to speak to as any, and if I wish to give a pretty lass a flower, then I will."

"She is nae married, and while ye may be free to speak to her, ye should keep yer distance while doing so."

"I dinnae have to listen to ye. Ye are on *our* land, if ye remember, nae Stewart. Ye are nae in charge here."

"And unless ye wish to be buried on yer land before the dawn, I suggest ye do as I say," Alasdair said, his voice calm but full of warning.

"She is nae worth it anyway," the young man said in irritation before he stood up and left the hall.

Emi watched him leave, her face a mask of confusion and hurt before she looked back to Alasdair. "Why did ye do that?"

"He had no business speaking to ye, much less touching ye so closely."

"Why? He was only putting a flower in my hair that he gave me. Were ye nae just saying yesterday that I should be thinking of such things?"

"Nae with him."

Emi stood up, glaring at him, before she turned on her heel and stormed out of the hall and into the woods. She didn't know where she was going, but that didn't matter right now. Alasdair followed close behind her, grabbing her arm only for her to yank it free and turn on him. "Dinnae touch me!" she hissed.

"Emi, stop!"

"No! Who are ye to say who I can speak to and nae? Ye are nae my father or my brother, Alasdair. Ye have *no* say!"

"No, I am nae, but —"

"But naught!" she shouted at him. "Ye leave me alone and let me make my own choices! I dinnae need yer help!"

She turned again to go farther into the woods to get away from him, but he grabbed her wrist and pulled her back. Her body turned with the force, and before she could do anything, his free hand cupped her cheek and his lips were on hers. She inhaled sharply, and for a brief second, she considered pulling away, but that was washed away in the flood of what she felt. It was unexpected and overwhelming, but she also didn't want it to stop.

"Dinnae think of such things with him, because ye are *mine*," he whispered after he pulled away from her just enough to speak. "Think them of me, as I think them of ye."

"Alasdair ... I —"

"If ye dinnae feel the same, I will leave ye be but, I swear to Christ, I would sell my soul if it meant ye would say otherwise."

Her eyes widened at his blasphemy. "Ye should nae say that!"

"Then tell me otherwise."

"I —"

"Tell me yer heart is nae mine, Emi, that it has nae been. That ye dinnae want me as I want ye. Say it and I will walk away from ye this very moment."

She felt as though she could hardly breathe, much less think. Was her heart his? Had it always been? Had she not, in that most secret of places, always known it? Always wanted it? Wanted him? Wished he would say to her what he was saying now?

"I cannae," she whispered.

Alasdair released her wrist and brought that hand to rest on her other cheek. "Let me court ye, Emi. It is all I want."

"But the others —"

"What others?"

"The other women ye —"

He shook his head. "There are none. I have done naught since I realized how I truly felt for ye. I could nae, for they were nae ye and ye were what I wanted. It held no appeal."

"How do I know ye are nae just saying so to get what ye really want?"

The hurt that entered his eyes at those words surprised her. "Why would ye say something like that? Why would ye *ever* think that of me? Ye are my dearest friend, the one closest to my heart; why would I risk the loss of ye and all ye represent to me for a night in yer bed?"

She shook her head gently. "Sorry," she whispered. "I just dinnae understand what is happening or why now?"

"Because I know if I remain silent any longer, I will lose ye, and I cannae," he replied, stroking her cheeks with his thumbs. "Please," he whispered, closing his eyes and resting his forehead against hers.

The swirl of emotions felt almost paralyzing. She'd never kissed a man, and that contact all on its own had been dizzying, but his words made it even more so. She'd never heard him speak this way, never heard his voice the way it was now, never heard him almost plead in such a manner. He wanted her, but he wanted her for something more than what he might have been inclined to with others. Emi struggled to make sense of any of it, but she gave up and found the courage to kiss him this time, hearing him take in a sharp breath of surprise. Alasdair didn't hesitate to respond to her boldness, his hands moving away from her face so that he could wrap his arms around her and hold her against him. He pulled back from her only to press a fevered kiss to her neck where it met her shoulder. Emi let go of a loud gasp and gripped his coat, her head dropping back involuntarily, and he rewarded the granted access with another kiss and the smallest of bites. He brought his lips back to hers for a long moment before he stopped and took a step back.

Emi looked at him in utter confusion. Why had he stopped? Had she done something wrong? "Alasdair?"

When he saw her confusion, he spoke quickly. "No, it is nae ye. I just … I need a moment."

"Why?"

"Because right now all I want to do is find a more secluded spot farther away so we can continue, but that is nae right. It will come in its own time, but nae now."

"What if I agreed to it?"

Alasdair looked at her, shocked for a moment, before he gave a gentle shake of his head. "No. Nae here, nae this way. Trust me," he said as he came closer to her again. "Ye deserve better than this, and when it is time for such things, ye shall have it. Ye need nae promise such to keep me here."

"But ye are used to —"

He placed a gentle finger against her lips. "Aye, but that is nae ye, Emi. Dinnae try to become someone ye are nae just because ye think it is what I want. Be ye, be my Emi, the one I know. I want no other but her."

"What will we tell the chief?"

"We will nae. I wish to speak to Evander first."

"Evander? Why?"

"He is the closest ye have to a brother, Em. I owe him that, and his father is dead. As much as I hate to say it, this must remain between us for a while. I dinnae know how long, but I want no one to interfere. No jealous women, no kin, no one. Just ye and me until we reach a point together where no one can tear us apart no matter how they might try."

Emi responded with a soft nod, understanding the logic in what he was saying. "It will be hard to hide."

"Aye, it will, but we will do our best. If, on this trip, I keep my distance from ye, know it is because all I want in that moment is to be with ye. I will find a way whenever I can to be near ye or come to ye."

"Especially if ye need to murder a Glengarry?"

Alasdair's laugh was soft. "If I must do so, I will nae care for secrecy about my feelings for ye."

"Je souhaite que vous ne souriez pas autant, parce que tu es beaucoup trop beau quand tu le fais," she whispered, placing her hand on his cheek. *I do wish you would not smile so much because you are far too handsome when you do.*

When she echoed his own words back to him, he covered her small hand with his own. After a moment, he pulled it away from his cheek to kiss her palm and then her wrist. Emi shivered, and he placed her hand back on his cheek.

"Cannae do that," he replied. "It is all I can do when I am with ye."

"I never thought ye would think of such a thing, at least nae with me."

"Why nae?"

"Ye have yer pick, Alasdair, and I am naught special. Ye were always my friend."

"Aye, for a long time I was, ye are right. I remember when that changed for me, when I saw ye differently suddenly. It was almost a year ago, and ye came to the cottage with yer mam to sit and mix remedies with mine. Ye came through the door and pushed the hood of yer arasaid back, the chill of the fall air left yer cheeks pink and yer eyes bright, and I just ..." he shook his head gently. "Ye were stunning to me in that moment, and I realized ye were no longer the little lass I had known so long."

"So long ago. Why did ye say naught?"

"I was worried ye would be opposed to it because ye did nae feel the same way, or ye found me objectionable as a suitor in some way."

It was Emi's turn to laugh now. "Ye are ridiculous. Whatever made ye think I would find ye objectionable? Ye are the most beautiful man on Stewart land, and ye think I would find something wrong with ye?"

"Ah, but ye know me deeper than my face, lass. Ye know who I truly am; ye know so many of my secrets. So many I trusted only to ye. It was those things that concerned me."

"Well, ye are wrong."

"Did ye feel the same then?"

Had she? Emi took a moment, thinking about it. She knew she must've, or the other night wouldn't have hurt her as much as it had, and the feeling of rejection in his words the following morning wouldn't have cut so deeply. "Deep down I suppose I did but would nae admit it because I felt ye would nae even look my way for such a thing."

"Now, who is the ridiculous one? I saw no one but ye; any others would need to live up to ye, and they could nae." Alasdair stroked her cheek. "My intentions toward ye are serious, Em. It is why I want to do this the right way. I want to talk to Evander and yer mam so that when the time comes, I have their support when I go to the chief."

Emi gasped. To go to the chief meant to ask his permission to marry. He wanted to marry her. "Alasdair, I —"

"Only if ye want to, of course."

"No!"

Alasdair's eyes went wide.

"I mean, I do! When I said no, I meant to say I did nae wish for ye to think I did nae."

A small smile turned into a laugh. "We are both nervous. I understand ye now."

"Are ye calm enough yet?"

Alasdair grinned for a moment before kissing her again, this time in a far different manner. He took the urgency out of it, replacing it with deeper feeling, and it immediately made her lean into him. Her hand still on his cheek, she felt his hands on her back, pressing her against his body, and the contact made her heart and mind race.

"Alasdair!"

Hearing his name called out parted them in an instant, and he looked back the way they'd come before he brought his gaze back to her. Alasdair stroked her cheek with the backs of his fingers, gave her a last, small kiss, and then departed. Emi stood there and watched him go, trying to get a handle on her thoughts. Had that really just happened? Everything coursing through her said it had. Alasdair had just told her he wanted her and no other, that he had serious intentions, and had just kissed her in a way she'd always wished he would but never realized she'd wanted. The memory of it made her smile, and she placed her fingertips against her lips even as her stomach twisted ever so slightly and demanded she run after him to pull him back. She couldn't, of course, but it didn't mean she didn't want to. Closing her eyes, she took a few deep breaths to calm herself, and then started back, picking up some wood sorrel and a few other things to add to the morning oats for the men so it wouldn't seem odd that she was coming back after he was.

"Ah, there ye are Emilia!" Crisdean called out as she entered the hall. "We were wondering if ye were picked up by the fae, going out at dusk!"

Behind him, a sly smile formed on Alasdair's lips, and he followed it with a wink, but she somehow managed not to blush. "No, sir, they would want naught of me. I simply went out to pick a few things to mix with yer breakfasts is all."

"Naught of ye? I was always told they were fond of pretty maids," Crisdean said.

"Thank ye for the compliment, Chief, but I saw none on my walk; what a shame. I did find some lovely wood sorrel and some berries, however," she replied, flashing him a triumphant look that made Crisdean laugh, and Alasdair, too, though for different reasons.

"I suppose ye found the flower out there as well?"

The flower. She'd forgotten about that. "No, that was given to me by one of the Glengarry men."

There was a collective sound of amusement from the Stewart men at her proclamation, all except Alasdair, whose expression darkened. "Which one, lass? We shall inspect him for his worth!"

Emi's lips curled into an amused smile as she pulled the flower from behind her ear. "Thank ye, Chief, but no need. It would take more than a flower to interest me." Stepping forward, she tucked it behind Fergus' ear. "Looks quite fetching on Fergus, though."

Fergus blinked in confusion, but the other men laughed uproariously, as did Emi. It brought a slow smile and then laughter from Fergus himself. "Is nae my color, I dinnae think."

"Put those bits ye collected where ye need them, Emilia, and come have yer supper with us," Crisdean said, wiping his eyes.

"Aye, Chief," Emi replied with a smile and a curtsy before making her way to where her things were stored.

Supper passed merrily, with the Stewarts considered honored guests and thus offered finer wine and whisky, with richer food prepared than might normally be served. Emi sat and quietly observed everyone from her seat at the table. To her right were the quiet voices of the two chiefs and to her left the chatter of his wife and daughters commenting on the Stewart officers. It was hard to miss their talk of Alasdair, and though their mother chastised them for it, their musings on what it might be like to be near him or alone with him. Emi hid her smile in her cup because she knew the answers to those questions now, and the memory of those stolen moments brought butterflies to life in her stomach.

When instruments came out, music was played for dancing, and she watched those same girls angle to get him to dance with them and he did, of course. He had to, and Emi knew that perfectly well, but it was a relief when he also extended his hand to her for a dance. Alasdair reminded her of their earlier meeting in the subtlest of ways: holding her hand a little longer, pulling her closer to him in just enough of an increment not to be noticed, running his thumb across the top of her hand when he kissed it at the end of the dance.

With supper over, and as the others readied their pallets in the hall, Emi hummed the song they'd been dancing to as she put the last bits together to ensure all was ready for her to make quick work of the breakfast preparation and allow them to get underway. When she was satisfied, she turned to head into the hall to ready her own bed. There'd been a suggestion she sleep away from them, but that idea had been immediately dismissed. She was safer amongst her own so that they could protect her if necessary. As she passed an open door, her arm was seized, and she was pulled into a darkened storeroom and pinned to the wall by another body. Before she could scream for Alasdair, a hand covered her mouth, and she heard his voice in her ear.

"The gathering bits for the porridge was clever of ye," he whispered against her ear.

Emi's stomach tightened to have him near her again so un-expectedly, and she closed her eyes, her body almost sagging against his for a brief moment. "I could nae very well tell the truth, could I?" she replied when he removed his hand.

"No, though part of me wished ye would."

"Ye said nae to."

"I rather like a bit of defiance, but I am glad ye did nae."

"Ye cannae have it both ways, Alasdair."

"Oh, I assure ye I can, but nae yet," he said, the words followed by a soft chuckle she could feel against her own chest.

There was something in the sound of his voice, a dark promise of sorts, and it made her long to know what he meant by it. "This will be torture, this game."

"Aye, and I am sorry for it. Know it will be hard on me, too."

"I dinnae know about that. Ye have plenty of flirting to do, as ye so capably demonstrated after supper."

"Perhaps, but ye will be the one in my mind. All I will want is to be with ye. The memory of how ye feel in my arms, the softness of yer lips and yer hands, the smell of ye … it will all surround me and make me long for ye, crave ye. I already am."

Dear God, what was she getting into? Those words and the way he said them made her heart race and her skin become so hot she could swear he must feel it, and it was as astonishing as it was terrifying. How could he do this to her so easily? An idea took root in her mind then: two could play at this game. She wouldn't be the only one left with this feeling tonight. Placing her hands against his stomach, she gripped his shirt and pulled it up in the front until it finally came free of his kilt.

"Emi —" he began before the words were cut off by the small moan he smothered as she placed her hands on the now bare skin of his abdomen. "Jesus," he whispered.

She smiled in the darkness and slid her hands up, hearing his breath catch. He was so much softer and smoother than she'd anticipated, though the muscles beneath her hands were solid, and she very much wished she could feel his hands on her in a similar manner. Leaning up, she placed a soft kiss against the skin of his neck as her hands slid over his chest, and she heard him draw a breath in through his teeth. This time he couldn't silence himself, though he did manage to keep it low.

"Christ, Em …"

She remembered the small bite he'd given her and mimicked it, feeling him shudder and hearing his hand land hard against the wall near her to support himself. She stepped back from him then, removing her hands. "Goodnight," she whispered, brushing her lips just barely across his before turning and leaving the room.

Alasdair wanted to grab her and pull her back with every ounce of himself so that he could show her exactly what she'd done to him and what such games could earn her but refrained. He wanted her so badly he could scream, and he rested his forehead against the cool stone of the wall to try and regain control. The memory of the warmth and softness of those hands against his skin, the intimacy of it, would drive him mad, but he wouldn't have it any other way. He wanted her as his wife, he knew that and had known that for quite some time, but dear God, he wanted her this way, too. It was going to be a *very* long night.

Once he felt collected enough, he tucked his shirt back in and returned to the hall. Emi lay in her pallet, her back to where he would be, and he wondered if she was already asleep. Somehow, he doubted it. He spread out on the floor, covering himself with his plaid, and watched the fire dancing in the hall's fireplace, the reds and yellows and oranges swirling around each other, fighting the urge to pick up his things and set up beside her instead. He wanted to be near her so badly now that this had all come to light, but it was now also the last thing he could do. His eyes grew heavy and slowly slid closed as sleep claimed him at last.

Chapter 3

Emi rose as soon as she heard the men beside her stirring and the Glengarry household awakening. Sitting up, she rubbed her bleary eyes before she stood and stretched. With a yawn, she returned to the kitchens, passing the storeroom he'd pulled her into the night before. The memory made her smile, and she gave her head a quick shake to clear it as she hurried past. She brought some water to a boil and made the porridge, adding a bit of the butter she'd made, then mashing some of the berries and stirring it into each bowl. This would give it the richness of the butter, the sweetness of the berries, and the slight zest of the wood sorrel. She topped them with whole berries, then set them on a tray along with tea, carrying it out to the hall where the Stewart men were just sitting up from their sleep now that their chief had joined them.

"Good morning, Chief. Good morning, lads," Emi said brightly. "I have yer breakfast and yer tea," she continued as she went to each man to let him take a bowl and a cup of tea, starting with Crisdean.

"Why is the porridge pink?" Cailean asked.

"Because I mixed berries into it."

"Oh," he said before he took a bite and paused. "Ohhh," he said again, digging into it.

With that reaction the others wasted no time in trying Emi's concoction, and Crisdean nodded. "Emilia, this is wonderful!"

"Thank ye, sir. I am glad ye like it."

"I think normal porridge will be quite disappointing now."

"Aye," responded a chorus of male voices.

Emi laughed a bit. "Well, then I suppose I will have to make sure they know my recipe in the kitchens so that they can feed ye."

"Or I can give ye a better position," he said, "and ye can make it for me yerself."

"I … sir, it … I mean …" Emi stammered, shocked.

The position he was offering her was an important one, higher than even her mother's. To be the personal cook for the chief was an honor, and it would mean that while Bridgette and the rest of the kitchens cooked for everyone else, Emi alone would cook for the head table. Such a position also came with a room in the castle so that she could be there whenever he requested something or, at the very least, be there to make and serve breakfast to the chief and his family. Other than Alasdair, she would be the only one so young in such a position.

"It is an aye or no question, Emilia, but ye think about it. Talk it over with Bridgette when we return. For now, I still get the benefit of having ye in that position on this trip. Now, have yer own breakfast while the lads get the horses ready."

"Aye, sir," Emi said with a curtsy. As she turned around, Alasdair caught her eye and smiled at her, and she did blush this time.

When Emi emerged into the courtyard, Alasdair was there to help her onto her horse. When he put his hands on her waist, it brought back the memory of his arms around her yesterday and she felt flustered.

"I love ye," he whispered as he lifted her and sat her atop the horse, then handed her the reins.

The words sobered her, and her eyes widened. She looked at him in shock, only to have him wink at her before walking away to mount his own horse. The young man who'd been speaking to her yesterday glared at Alasdair, and the look Alasdair gave him in return was as threatening as it was withering. Emi understood why now and forced herself not to smile at his display of protectiveness as well as possessiveness. She was *his* intended, and there was no one who would make any sort of overtures toward her without him stopping it, whether they knew the truth or not.

"John, thank ye again for yer hospitality," Crisdean said as he and Chief MacDonell exited the hall.

"Ye are quite welcome, and I expect to see ye the day after tomorrow," Chief MacDonell replied as Crisdean mounted his waiting horse.

"Aye, ye shall. Right, lads, let us be on our way. Inverness awaits."

With that command the party left the courtyard and Glengarry castle behind. When, after a time, the road came out along Loch Ness, Emi gasped and pulled her horse to a stop, staring at the beauty of it as it sparkled in the morning sun. Her stopping brought the entire party to a halt, and they looked at her with curiosity.

"Ye well, Emi?" Cailean asked.

"Aye. Just look at it, Cailean," she breathed. "I dinnae know where this is, but it is so beautiful and I wish I could take the image with me forever."

All of them looked out at the great expanse of water. They'd all seen it so many times before it was easy to forget that Emi hadn't. It truly was beautiful, the breeze rippling the water and making it glitter like a thousand tiny stars. The green of the hills beyond peeked out from behind the morning mist still clinging to them, beckoning with the promise of hidden magic and waiting fae.

"Ye are right, Emilia, it is," Crisdean said. "This is Loch Ness."

"Loch Ness," she repeated in a soft voice.

"Ye will be seeing much of it, as we are traveling along it for the rest of the journey. Come, let us all be on our way," he said as they started forward again.

Alasdair was riding vanguard today, leaving him up front with the other officer who'd been riding next to her yesterday. Fergus and Cailean were Emi's company now, and she didn't mind it a bit. Emi helped to care for Fergus' younger sister, Arabella, whenever he was away. Arabella had been born too soon, and though she'd survived, she was delicate and often sickly. Emi would sit with her and entertain her so that Fergus' mother could take a break, be it going to the village for supplies, needing to see someone who was ill, or delivering a baby. Ealasaid was one of the most trusted midwives and healers on Stewart land, and she'd taught Emi how to mix certain remedies and what they were used for. She'd spent many happy hours with Bridgette, Ealasaid, and Alasdair's mother Coira, sorting ingredients and grinding them to store away for use when those herbs and plants were not in season. Listening in silence, she'd learned much from women's talk around those tables. Talk of families and what problems they might have, women married to men who harmed them, standing up for herself and speaking her mind, never simply marrying just to do so, and to be wary of young men and their promises. She knew it was part of what had made her question Alasdair's words yesterday even though she knew he'd never do such a thing to her.

At 25, Cailean was the oldest of the friends, though Fergus was not far behind him at 23. Cailean had a wife and three children, all of whom he adored. His wife Anna had served in the castle until her marriage, after which time she'd decided to leave to tend the house and small farm Cailean rented from Crisdean. Emi often wondered if she'd be able to do such a thing when she finally married. What if she didn't wish to leave her position? There were plenty of women who didn't, of course, so it wasn't as though she had no choice. She wondered now what Alasdair would wish her to do. She knew she ought to discuss Crisdean's offer with him as well as with Bridgette, for it would affect him, too.

"Emi!"

Emi jumped, snapped out of her thoughts by Cailean's raised voice. "Aye?"

"Where is yer head at, lass?" he asked, laughing at her reaction.

"Far and away, it seems," Fergus said, joining him in laughter.

"Oh, I was thinking about the chief's offer."

"Ye should take it!" Fergus exclaimed. "It is quite an honor, Emi."

"Aye, I agree," Cailean said. "Yer mam will be so proud of ye when ye tell her."

"I am certainly leaning toward taking it."

"Ye would be daft nae to," Cailean countered.

"He is right, Emi," Fergus continued. "Ye have earned such a place, and taking it would set ye up for a very nice life all on yer own. Ye would nae need to settle for a husband just so ye had someone to support ye."

"Aye, I suppose ye are right about that, but it would leave me less time to help yer mam, Fergus."

"Aye, but for good reason. It would have happened sometime, be it this or ye having yer own family to tend to."

"I know ye could nae see him, but Alasdair was beaming he was so proud of ye," Cailean added.

"Was he?"

"Of course he was! Ye know ye are his favorite! Why would he nae be pleased for yer good fortune?"

Emi smiled. "I will have to ask him."

The rest of the trip passed with ease, and when they came over the rise that brought Inverness into view, Emi pulled sharply to stop. The city looked huge to her, and she'd never seen anything like it. There were buildings everywhere, it seemed — how did anyone find anything? She didn't stop long, not wanting to hold up the group, and as they entered town, it was a cacophony of noise. Carts, mongers, horses, and more people than she'd ever seen in her life. When they arrived at the inn they were to reside at for the next two nights, Fergus helped her down from her horse. Stretching, she walked toward the front of the court-yard just to move her legs before seeing something move in a doorway as she reached the street. Peering at it curiously, she walked toward it with slow steps, only to have it skitter away. Only when it ran from a cart did she realize what it was: a little orange kitten! With a gasp, Emi hurried forward, reaching for it, only to have it run.

"No! Stop! I just want to help ye!" she said as she hurried after it, following it into a small close. Cornered, the kitten hissed and spit at her, but she smiled at it in amusement. "Ye are nae at all frightening, ye know that, dinnae ye?"

Squatting down, she picked it up in her apron, holding tight to it for a few moments while it struggled and tried to bite her. When it stopped, she opened her apron and looked down at it, its blue eyes wide and its breathing heavy.

"Ach, look at ye. Ye are terrified, ye poor wee thing. And a lad, too! Well, ye will be at home with this lot then, all lads like ye. Come on, we will figure out what to do with ye."

Emi reached out a finger and stroked the bridge of its nose, and the kitten closed its eyes before it started purring. She laughed and turned around, making her way back out to the street. Starting back the way she thought she'd come, nothing looked familiar to her, and she stopped, turning a small circle. Heart pounding, she realized she had no idea where she was or how far back the inn was. She didn't even know the name of it. The bustle of carts and people became louder and more overwhelming, and she had no idea what to do.

"Fergus! Cailean!" she called out, though her voice was drowned out by the sounds of the city. "Alasdair!"

Walking forward, she looked around her, trying to make some sort of sense of where she was, but the more she looked, the stranger it seemed, and her eyes filled with tears. What if she couldn't find them? What would happen to her? How would she get home?

"Alasdair!" she called out again, looking around, praying he or one of the others had noticed she was missing and gone in search of her. The faces around her seemed to grow unfriendly, and she backed up until she hit a wall.

"Emi!"

Hearing her name called, she turned to find Alasdair threading through the crowds as he strode toward her, and she thought she might weep in relief. "Alasdair!"

"What are ye doing wandering away like that? Are ye mad?" he said when he reached her.

"I did nae … I just …"

Alasdair paused, able to see her fright. "All right," he said, softening as he pulled her close and embraced her. "I found ye."

Emi let herself cry in relief for a few moments. "I was only trying to help it, and I did nae realize how far away I had gone!"

"Help what?"

Emi produced the kitten, who let out a tiny mew as it stared at Alasdair, who blinked and looked back at it in surprise. "He is lost, ye see? He almost got himself run over by a cart!"

"Ye … ye wandered away … for a kitten?"

"I could nae let him get smashed, could I?"

Alasdair pressed his lips together in an attempt to keep from laughing but failed. "Christ, Em, if that is nae just like ye, I dinnae know what is. Come on, let us go back. Ye can put him back down where ye found him."

"No," Emi said, frowning and pulling the kitten close to her in a protective gesture as though Alasdair might take him. "I cannae just leave him here this way!"

"What are ye going to do with him? Take him home?"

She hadn't really thought that far ahead, but this felt like a challenge she wasn't about to let Alasdair win. "Aye," she said, resolute. "I am. He can chase mice in the kitchens."

"Em —"

"I am nae putting him back, Alasdair Stewart."

Alasdair looked at her, and a smile made its slow way

across his lips before he shook his head. "Fine. Ye can ask the chief, come on."

Emi followed Alasdair back down the street, everything seeming far less frightening with him there. "There are so many people here!"

"Aye, there is. I dinnae care for it."

"Nor I," she said in agreement as they entered the courtyard of the inn.

"Found her," Alasdair announced.

"Emilia! What in God's name are ye doing walking away from here and —" but Crisdean's words ceased as Emi held up the little orange ball of fur. "Why do ye have that?"

"I saw him almost get run over by a cart, sir, and I could nae just let him alone. He would die for certain! Poor wee lamb does nae have a family, so someone had to rescue him."

"And what is it ye intend to do with it now that ye have saved it from death on the street?"

"If ye dinnae mind, sir, I want to take him home so he can keep the kitchens and castle free of mice."

Crisdean smiled. "Why does that answer nae surprise me? All right, ye can bring him back."

"Thank ye, sir!" Emi said, excited, as she cuddled the kitten to her chest. "Did ye hear that, lamb? Ye get to come home with me! Oh, it is so much better there than this scary place."

The men laughed at her enthusiasm as she talked to the kitten. "That is what ye ought to name him," Cailean said. "Lamb."

"Ye think so? What do ye think, hm?" The kitten mewed, and she nodded. "Lamb it is then. Let us get ye some milk, shall we?" she said as she followed Crisdean and the others inside.

"Ah, Chief Stewart, welcome back. Good to see ye, as always. Lads," the landlord said with a nod to the officers.

"Mr. MacRae," they all said in return.

"Good to see ye as well, MacRae," Crisdean said.

"Yer normal rooms are ready for ye, and my staff are

seeing yer things there now," he said as his gaze fell on Emi. "And who is this?"

"This is Emilia, who has come in place of Bridgette this time. Emilia, this is Mr. MacRae, the landlord."

"Sir," she said with a small curtsy.

"What have ye got there, lass?"

"I found this poor wee soul on the street outside, sir. He is coming home with us to keep the kitchens free from mice."

MacRae chuckled. "A soft heart, just like my own daughter. I will send a saucer of cream up and some table scraps. It will need meat. I will also send up a bowl of warm water, so ye can bathe the filthy wee mite."

"Thank ye, MacRae, that is very kind of ye. Come along, ye lot."

They followed the chief up the stairs, Emi looking around her and trying to take it all in. She'd never been in an inn, and this was yet another experience to be savored. When they reached the top of the stairs and walked down the hall, a set of doors stood open, and some of their things were being set inside. Emi stopped in the middle of the room to look around her in awe. It was a beautiful room with lovely furnishings, nothing at all like her cottage at home. The floors here were wood and covered with rugs, whereas her home had floors that were packed earth. The walls were paneled with wood, and lanthorns were spaced along the walls, their mirrored backs reflecting the candlelight to make it brighter.

"Emilia, ye will be staying in that room over there," Crisdean said, gesturing to a door.

Emi nodded and went to it, opening the door and then turning around in confusion. The room was small, and she couldn't imagine how the other six would fit in it with her. "But where will the others sleep?"

"Whatever do ye mean, child?" Crisdean asked her with a curious expression.

"I dinnae think there is room for all of us there."

"Why in the world would all of these lads be in there with ye?"

"Ye said it was where we were staying, sir."

"I said it was where *ye* are staying, Emilia. The lads will sleep out here, as they always do."

Emi looked at the room and then back to him. "I will be there alone?"

"Aye, why would … oh," he said, seeming to understand her confusion. "Ye have never had a room to yerself, have ye."

"No, sir. To tell truth, we dinnae have but the one room."

"Well, now ye get to have one for two nights."

A room to herself. An entire room. This was a luxury she could never have conceived of. "Thank ye, sir," she said, unable to keep herself from smiling.

A knock sounded at the door and Fergus opened it to find one of the staff waiting with a small box of earth tucked under one arm and a tray with a saucer of cream and some meat scraps, along with a small basin of water balanced in his other hand.

"Pardon the interruption, but Mr. MacRae sent this up for the lass," he said.

"Aye, thank ye, come in and set it down upon the table," Crisdean said.

The young man nodded and did as directed. "He wished me to tell her the earth in the box is for it to relieve itself."

"Thank ye," Emi said.

The young man looked at her and was momentarily flustered before he bowed and departed, bringing laughter from Crisdean and the other men. "Seems he was a bit taken by ye, Emilia."

"Dinnae know why," she said as she brought Lamb to the table and set him before the food. The kitten wasted no time, making little growling sounds as he worked on the meat scraps. Emi chuckled and shook her head. "Starving, ye were. Ye eat up, and then when ye are fat and sleepy, we will bathe ye."

"Sounds like a good evening to me," Fergus joked.

"Aye, well, dinnae be getting ideas about receiving any such treatment from Emi," Cailean said.

"As if I would?" Fergus said. "No offense meant to ye, Emi, but ye are like a sister to me."

"Indeed nae," Crisdean said. "But ye all know better than that."

"No offense taken, Fergus," Emi replied, forcing herself not to look at Alasdair but instead focus on Lamb. How she wished they could just tell the chief now! But she knew Alasdair had his reasons and she needed to trust him.

"Tomorrow, Alasdair, I want ye to accompany Emilia to the market for her protection. Ye know how things work, so ye will be able to assist her if needed. Ye have the leave to show her the rest of the city if ye have time left. The rest of ye can stick with me."

"Aye, Chief," Alasdair said.

After Lamb had stuffed himself, Emi bathed him without him putting up much of a fuss, cleaning the mud and grime from his fur. She dried him in her apron and took a seat on the hearth by the fire so that he could be warm, and it instantly turned him into a sleeping, purring lump in her lap. There was a pamphlet on a nearby table, and she picked it up, but though she could read the words on the page, as a whole it made very little sense to her. There was a war somewhere far away, and the English were part of it, but she didn't know where Austria was or why France wanted to be at war with them anyway, so she set it aside and Fergus picked it up moments later. She was fortunate to be able to read at all, but Bridgette felt it was important so she'd taught Emi. She listened to the men talking quietly amongst themselves about what it said, but the warmth of the fire made her eyes feel heavy.

"Emilia, why dinnae ye turn in, lass. Ye are about to fall asleep there, and ye have had a long couple of days," Crisdean said.

"Aye, thank ye, Chief," Emi said as she stood up. Lamb mewed in irritation at being roused, which made her smile and the men chuckle as she entered the room and shut the door behind her.

Setting Lamb on the pillow, she undressed herself and used the warm water in the basin near the fire to wash herself down before putting on a fresh shift. It was odd to be in here alone after spending her whole life without this sort of privacy. In a way it was almost a bit uncomfortable, knowing that Alasdair and the others would be sleeping on the floor outside. Alasdair. She smiled the moment the thought of him surfaced in her mind. For a moment there was the wicked thought of wishing he were in here with her for some reason just so that she could spend the night near him. The memory of his kissing her, of the sound he'd made in the storeroom, floated to the surface, and she closed her eyes with a sigh. She very much wished she could kiss him now, but it was impossible. At least she would get to spend the day with him tomorrow.

Climbing into the bed, she made a happy sound as she sank into the feather mattress. What a divine thing this was! She wondered how many feathers one would need for such a bed. Probably a great many more than she could get her hands on. Lamb made his sleepy, stumbling way across the pillow to snuggle up under her chin with his little head on her neck, and began purring away. Emi smiled and reached up to give his head a little stroke. First Alasdair and now this little creature. This trip was turning out to be even better than she could've imagined.

Chapter 4

"Emi?" Alasdair called out as he gently knocked on the closed door. He could hear a rustling that let him know she'd at least heard him.

"Hm?"

"Ye well in there, lass?"

"Aye, fine. Better if ye would let me sleep," she groused.

Alasdair bit his lip hard to keep from laughing at her grumpy tone. Clearly, she'd slept well and resented his intrusion. "Emi, it is nigh eight," he said after clearing his throat.

He heard her gasp in shock, followed by the sound of her feet hitting the floor as she scrambled from bed. In the next moment the door flew open, Emi nearly bowling him over as she dashed from the room, tying her apron.

"Why did ye nae wake me sooner!" she said to him as she moved past. "Oh, I am so very sorry, Chief. I dinnae know what happened!"

"Um … Emilia, lass?" Crisdean said, clearing his throat to avoid laughing, just as Alasdair had done.

"Aye, sir?"

"Ye may want to take yer time and go put a dress on."

"What?" she asked in confusion before she noticed that all of the men were staring at her with wide eyes. Only then did she realize she'd come out in just a shift and an apron, hair down, feet bare. She let out an embarrassed squeak just before Alasdair hurriedly threw his plaid around her shoulders and turned her away from them, ushering her back to the room as the rest of the men laughed.

"And ye need nae fret about breakfast, lass!" Crisdean called out. "MacRae sent up the morning meal as always, and yers is waiting for ye."

Alasdair closed the door behind her, taking a very brief moment to collect himself before turning around with an amused smile. "Clearly nae awake," he said, letting go of the laugh he'd been holding.

"Aye," Crisdean said. "Alasdair, I am going to leave ye with her. The rest of us need to make our way."

"Aye, Chief," Alasdair said with a small bow.

He knew perfectly well that this was highly unusual, leaving an unmarried man and woman alone, but he also knew it was because Crisdean trusted him. An entire day alone with Emi was the biggest gift Crisdean could have unknowingly given him, and if he knew the truth, there was no way this would be happening. As tempting as it was, he wasn't going to take as much advantage of it as he'd want to. *As much.*

"Ye make sure the lass gets about safely and be sure it is obvious ye are on duty and guarding her, so no one gets the wrong idea about the pair of ye. Understood?"

"Aye, Chief."

"Good. Let us be off, men," Crisdean said before they all stood up from the table.

Alasdair watched as they all slid broadswords back into baldrics, checked the locations of any concealed weapons, and made themselves ready to leave. As Crisdean passed him, Alasdair bowed, nodding to the others as they passed. The door shut behind them, and he heard the sound of their boots on the stairs. Moving quickly, he took up a position against the wall next to one of the windows, watching the courtyard below but keeping his face out of sight. When he saw them mount up and leave, he grinned and made his way back across the room. Opening the door to the room Emi was in, he saw her turn around in surprise, and before she could say a word, his lips were on hers. She made a small sound against his lips, placing her hands on his cheeks and kissing him in return until he parted from her.

"Good morning," he whispered, following the words with a sly smile.

"Alasdair! What are ye doing in here!" she replied in a scandalized whisper. "They are going to see ye!"

"No, they will nae. They have all left, and it is just ye and me."

"What? No, that is nae —"

"Proper?"

"Aye!"

"Nae generally, but this is a bit of a different circumstance. He trusts me and has no idea what is between us, so he would nae think much of it," he said before placing a kiss near her ear and hearing her sigh. "I will nae make him regret it, but I cannae help taking the chance to at least kiss ye again. I wanted to do so all day yesterday and could nae. It was maddening."

"I wanted ye to as well. I was thinking last night as I fell asleep that I wished ye were here with me so I could be near ye."

"Did ye now?" he asked with a wicked little smile even though he knew she wasn't thinking of that statement in the same way he was.

"I will take this, though."

He laughed and then kissed the length of her neck as he drew the back of a finger along her skin where the shift ended just above the top of her stays. She took a gentle breath in before he returned his lips to hers and buried his hands in the back of her hair to gently pull her head back. Her lips pulled away from his, and he kissed down her throat and followed them with kisses along the same line his finger had just taken. Emi shivered in his arms and made a tiny sound he knew she stifled. Alasdair removed his hands from her hair and slid them down her sides, placing them on her hips to pull them against his own as he once again kissed her lips. When Emi immediately deepened that kiss, his fingers tightened on her hips, and he fought the urge to pull her down onto the bed, earlier intentions be damned.

"No," he whispered, pulling back from her. "We have to stop now, or I —"

"Ye what?"

"I will want to do what I should nae, and I will nae betray his trust in such a way."

There was disappointment on her face for a moment, but he knew she understood. "Aye, ye are right."

"I know," he said, offering a gentle smile. "I am as disappointed as ye are."

"I was rather hoping I would hear ye make that sound again."

"Which one?" he asked, looking at her with a raised eyebrow.

Emi rose up on her toes to place her lips near his ear. "The one ye made in the storeroom the other night," she whispered, placing her hand against his abdomen.

The way she said it, the way she whispered it against his ear while placing her hand in the same place, brought a sharp breath from him, and he closed his eyes. Even though it was through his clothing now, it brought him back there in an instant, reminding him of how her hands felt on his skin. He covered her hand with one of his own, pressing it against him.

"Soon," he replied. "Hopefully soon."

"Ye liked it then?"

"Would nae have made that sound if I did nae."

Emi smiled up at him. "Ye said something yesterday that I found curious."

"Aye? What was that?"

"Ye told me ye loved me."

"Because I do?"

"Do ye?"

"I want to marry ye, so, aye, I should love ye, dinnae ye think?"

"Say it again."

Alasdair smiled before he pressed his lips to hers for a moment. "I love ye, Emi."

"Hearing ye say it out loud, nae in a whisper, makes me want to cry. I love ye, too, Alasdair."

The impact hearing those words had on him was unexpected. She'd never said them until now, not that he'd ever given her a reason to, but he hadn't realized until she'd said them just how desperately he'd wanted to hear them. It made his heart ache, but in the best way possible. Pulling her close, he held her for a few moments before stepping back and kissing her forehead.

"Ye should get dressed," he said, sitting down on the bed. "Ach, Christ, no wonder ye slept so long!"

Emi laughed. "Aye, it is glorious, is it nae?"

"I am a wee bit jealous now."

"You should be a little more so."

"Should I? And why is that?"

"I had another lad in my bed." Alasdair stared at her, and she started to laugh. "Lamb slept against my neck all night."

"Oh," he said, chuckling. Lamb made his way into Alasdair's lap, as it was stationary and warm. "Hello to ye, wee one," he said as he rubbed a fingertip behind one of Lamb's ears. "Ye are quite soft, are ye nae? Ye will be a spoiled wee thing before we get ye back, nae inclined to catch mice when there is a warm lap for ye to be in."

"Cannae he do both?"

Alasdair laughed. "Aye, I suppose he could," he replied, watching her start to pin up her hair. "I wish ye did nae have to do that."

"Why?" she asked, pausing and glancing at him over her shoulder through the window her arm made.

"Because ye are so beautiful with it down. Nae that ye are nae always, ye are, but this morning and just now ..." he began before he paused, smiling and looking down at Lamb. "Ye looked such a picture with it wild over yer shoulders as it was, the way it framed yer face. I look forward to mornings beside ye when I get to see ye that way, smiling at me."

"Thank ye," she said in a soft voice, showing she was touched by his words. "I look forward to them, too. Though I still dinnae know why ye think such, as there are far prettier lasses than I."

Alasdair looked up and put Lamb back on the bed before he stood up, taking her hand. "Come with me."

"But I am nae through!"

"Ye can go back to it in a moment," he said, striding out of the room while pulling her behind him. Opening the door to the other room, it would be clear to her thatyt this was where the chief was sleeping. Alasdair stopped in front of the looking glass, placing her before it. "Look. Look at yerself."

He knew Emi had never seen a looking glass before, and she stood before it with a sense of wonder. Staring back at her was a young woman with dark hair, half of it pinned up while the other half fell in gentle curls over her shoulders and down her back. Her eyes were green, her skin fair, and she looked almost dainty with a delicate neck and features. Stepping forward, she reached out and touched her reflection.

"This is me?" she asked, staring at herself in the mirror. "This is what I look like?"

"Aye, it is ye. Look at how beautiful ye are, Em. Look at what everyone else sees when they look at ye, and then ye ask me again why I think what I do. Try to tell me again that there are lasses far prettier than ye are. It is nae so, Emi, and every man with us here would say the same."

"Thank ye for showing me," she said, her voice still soft with the astonishment of seeing her own reflection for the first time. "How does this work?"

"What do ye mean?"

"How does my image show up here?"

"There is silver painted behind the glass, and it is that which shows ye the image."

"What an amazing thing."

"Aye," he replied. "But ye should finish getting dressed, so ye can eat and we can be on our way. There is much for ye to do, and no matter how I might wish to keep ye here all day, I must make sure ye accomplish all of it."

Emi nodded and turned away from the glass, leaving the room and going back to her own to finish dressing. Once done, she had a quick breakfast, leaving the meat scraps and cream for Lamb before shutting him inside the room with his earth box. Alasdair followed behind her as they left the rooms they were staying in, Emi carrying a large basket over one arm. No one seemed to bat an eye as they entered the main rooms downstairs and then went out, and it was clear it was because Alasdair was doing as he was instructed and making it obvious he was on duty with her.

Stepping out onto the street, Alasdair closed the distance a bit and was now just slightly in front of her so that she could follow him to the market and no one could come near her. Weaving in and out of the crowd, they finally reached the market, and Emi pulled the list Bridgette had sent from her apron pocket. On it were the names of certain stores and sellers, along with what was needed and what the normal cost was so that Emi would know if they were trying to cheat her. She made her way through, looking at varying things set out even if they weren't what she was there for.

A store window selling ladies' items caught her attention, and she stopped to inspect it. From near her, Alasdair watched her admiring the hats, gloves, trims, and notions behind the glass, wishing more than anything that he could buy any of them for her. She deserved one of those fine hats as much as any lady, but such things were far beyond his means. It made him wish he were some great and grand man so that he might bring her stacks of hats in shining boxes, all of them decorated with obscene amounts of silk ribbon or laces. Boxes and boxes of gloves, a pair for every hour of the day, painted fans, spools of ribbon and lace, shining buttons, heeled shoes made of silk damask dyed to match any number of gowns he would give her. Though it was quite a fantasy, it made him smile to think of. What would she say, he wondered. He watched her eyes wander to a spool of wide ribbon in the loveliest shade of pale pink, her fingertips touching the glass for a moment before she turned away from the window and made her way along the street once again.

"Hello," Emi said as they stopped in front of a store where a man was working out front and stacking some root vegetables. "My mother Bridgette usually comes here. Might ye help me?"

"Yes! Is she unwell and sent ye in her place?"

"No, sir, she just thought I would enjoy a trip to see Inverness for myself."

"How kind of her. Come inside," he said, and they followed him in. "Hello again, Alasdair."

"Hello, Mr. MacMillan," Alasdair said with a nod.

"Now, did she need the same as before?"

Emi held out the list to him. "This is what she needs."

MacMillan took it and looked it over, then nodded. "Almost the same. Placing her order for the winter, I see. I will make sure to have it for ye next week."

"Next week! But, sir, we are only here until tomorrow!"

"Mr. MacMillan sends his orders by cart directly to us," Alasdair explained. "We cannae carry that much on our own."

"Ah, right," Emi said, sheepish. "I apologize."

MacMillan chuckled. "Dinnae fret, lass, ye are new at this. Now ye will know for next time."

"Aye, thank ye," Emi said, looking relieved.

"There are a few more here who will be the same, as Alasdair can tell ye. He knows the system well enough, as he is usually the one who goes along with yer mother," he said, studying the list and writing down his part of the order. "Ah, Mr. Gunn has died since last yer mother was here, but I know where ye can get the goods listed here for the same price. Ye will want to be sure to tell her."

"Thank ye, sir," Emi replied, taking back the list when he offered it to her.

Alasdair and Emi stepped back out onto the street, following the directions to the new seller who, indeed, had what was needed at the same cost. He was more than happy to accept the terms of payment upon delivery, and with that done they set out to get the other, smaller things they'd be taking back with them. As they emerged from the market, Emi's basket was overflowing, and Alasdair took it from her so that she didn't have to carry it. He was still just ahead of her as they came into an area with fine houses.

"Would ye ever wish to live in the city if doing so meant ye lived in one of these houses?" Alasdair asked, breaking the silence.

"I dinnae know," Emi said. "It would be nice to live so richly, but to do so I would need to trade the beauty of home. The woods, the loch, the river. I dinnae feel as though I would like that trade for long."

"Nae even if some grand fop came and swept ye away?"

Emi gave him a look. "Aye, I am sure there are grand fops all over Inverness just waiting to sweep out into the Highlands in search of common lasses to bring back here instead of finding lasses of their own station."

"I would step back if one ever did."

Emi stopped and looked at him. "Why would ye say something like that?"

"I would want ye to have a fine life, Emi. If some man came to offer it to ye, I would nae stop him. I love ye too much to keep ye from all of the beautiful things such a man could give ye."

"Alasdair, I dinnae want *things*; I want *ye*. What good is any of that if ye are nae there to share it with me? I am quite content where I am, thank ye, as long as I get to have ye by my side every day for the rest of our lives."

He smiled at her, though there was a sadness in it he couldn't hide. "I wish I could give ye more."

"Dinnae fret about it, please. Ye are that 'more,' and I am

the luckiest lass in Scotland for it. I dinnae feel as though I am missing out on anything."

"I make ye that happy?"

"Of course ye do, ye dolt. Ye have been my best friend all my life, and someday soon we get to spend the rest of that life together. I will get to love and be loved by ye, the only thing I have ever really wanted even if I would nae have admitted it before. I have never wished for fine frocks or dishes made of silver. All I wanted was to have love, and I do."

He took her free hand in his and kissed it. Mindful of the public nature of their surroundings, he didn't keep hold of it as he wanted to. "Aye, ye do have love: mine. Ye always have and ye always will. I am certain my heart was yers long before I admitted it to myself."

"As mine likely was yers," she replied, starting to walk again. "I did want to speak with ye on something."

"Aye?"

"The chief's offer to me: I am nae sure what I want to do."

"Ye are asking me what I think ye should do?"

"Aye, for it does nae have an effect just on me, but on ye, too. Especially where we now stand."

Alasdair walked in silence for a moment before speaking. "I think ye should take it. It is a high honor, Em, something to be proud of. Ye would be earning a bit of money besides, and such a thing would put ye in a better place if ye ever needed to support yerself."

"Support myself?"

"None of us can promise tomorrow, love," he said, his voice quiet. "If something ever happened to me, ye would be able to care for yerself."

"Alasdair, dinnae say things like that."

"I have to, Emi. Ye need to understand that the man ye will marry is a soldier, that his job is full of danger, always. There is a higher chance of my nae coming home to ye than there would be with someone else."

Emi sighed. "I know, but I try nae to think about it."

"I understand ye."

"If I took this position, it would make things harder for us."

"How so?"

"I would be living in the castle. Nae exactly easy to see each other."

"It is nae required for ye to do so as long as ye are there to see to his breakfast or for someone to fetch ye if he requires something of ye. It is nae as though he orders things in the night unless he is unwell and wishes some warmed wine or something like that. Trust me, I know, for I have been on the night watch plenty of times. Ye could even do it some nights and nae others."

"Aye, I suppose ye are right there."

"I will see ye often, for ye will be there as much as I am, more than ye are now. It is likely ye would be making these trips more often as well so that he always has food he knows is nae tampered with."

"What does he do about that now?"

"Did ye nae notice Fergus tasted both his wine and his food at Glengarry? Each time they filled his cup, he passed it to Fergus to taste first. They may be our allies, but anyone would check. Chief MacDonell does the same when he passes through our hall."

"I had nae, though the thought of something happening to Fergus because of something like that is distressing. I will look now, though. Cailean said ye were proud of me when I was asked."

Alasdair smiled. "I was, I am. That *my* lass should be elevated so, that she should join me at such a young age in a position of esteem is something to be proud of. Ye are only 19, Em, and here ye are being offered the position to be the chief's personal cook!"

"Ye were younger when ye became an officer."

"Aye, I was, but the difference is that I was nae the only

one in my position, as ye are. Ye are nae even taking over the post from someone, it is being offered to ye outright."

"That is true, aye." They stopped at a bluff overlooking the sea, spreading vast and blue to the horizon, the wind ruffling her skirts, apron, and hair. "Oh, how beautiful it is," she whispered. "Is this the sea, Alasdair?"

"Aye, it is. If ye sail from out of the firth, it will take ye to the Continent or to the Nordic countries."

"I wonder what it is like to sail on a ship."

"Dinnae know. It is something I have nae actually done."

"Would ye want to?"

"Sometimes I think I would. It would be grand to see the wider world beyond Scotland, but I know I would miss my home and everyone in it."

"Is Austria out there?"

Alasdair looked at her curiously. "Aye, but why do ye ask?"

"I saw it in the pamphlet at the inn, but I dinnae know where it is. It said there was a war there."

"There is a war on the whole of the Continent," Alasdair said. "I fear it will be here soon enough."

"Why? We have nae got anything any of those places would want, have we?"

"Nae exactly, but they could land here for an English invasion to avoid the English navy. If that happens, we will have a choice to make; do we support the English, or do we support everyone else?"

"What are they fighting over?"

"Succession, who will rule next and where. It is complicated and I am nae sure even I understand it."

"Well, they can stay over there and fight, for there is naught here to rule anyway except midges, sheep, and cattle."

Alasdair laughed and couldn't stop, laughing so hard it brought tears to his eyes. "From yer lips to the Lord's ear, my lass. Come on, let us get back."

***

The two of them walked back, joking and laughing, and when they entered the rooms at the inn, they found that the rest of the group had returned. Lamb had been let out and had taken up a place on Crisdean's shoulder while he read over some documents, and it made Emi laugh to see him there, snuggled in amongst the folds of the chief's plaid.

"Ah! There ye are," Crisdean said. "Did ye see to all ye needed?"

"Aye, sir," Emi replied as Alasdair placed her basket on the table. "We even got a new supplier for the things Mr. Gunn sold. Mr. MacMillan said he died nae long ago."

"That is a shame," Crisdean said. "He was a good man. I know we did nae have an outstanding bill with him, but here, Alasdair," he continued, pulling out some coins. "Be a good lad and take that to his widow with the clan's best wishes."

"Aye, Chief," Alasdair said with a bow, taking the coins and departing immediately.

"Yer little lad here was crying up a storm the moment he heard us all come in, so we opened the door for him. He has spent time with all of us, and I am his current choice," Crisdean said.

Emi laughed. "Ah, but he does look very well and happy there, sir."

"I must say I dinnae mind him there. He is a sweet little thing, are ye nae, Lamb?" Crisdean asked as he stroked the kitten's head with a fingertip.

"Sir," Emi began, trying to force herself not to fidget and betray her nerves. "I was thinking today about the offer ye made me."

Crisdean stopped what he was doing and looked up, as did the rest of the men, the room going silent in a way Emi found disquieting. "Aye?"

"I have decided to accept it, and I thank ye for the confidence ye have in me to make such an offer to someone my age."

Crisdean smiled broadly, as did Fergus and Cailean. "I am very happy to hear it, Emilia, and no matter yer age, ye have earned it with what ye have shown us on the trip so far. I welcome ye to my personal staff."

"Thank ye, sir," Emi said, her tone brightening once the knot in her stomach untangled. "Ye will nae regret it. I know that the position comes with a room in the castle, but I only ask that I be able to go back and forth, depending on my needs. If Ealasaid and Arabella need me, I would like to be able to stay with them, or if Maman needs me. I would be back to make sure yer breakfast awaited ye and see to all else."

"I think that is a reasonable thing to ask and am happy to grant ye that leave. I suppose ye had better get used to coming to Inverness, lass, as this will be yer job, now. Yer mother will see to sending a list along with ye of what the main kitchens need while ye come here with us to see to my personal stores."

"Aye, Chief," she said with a small curtsy. "Is there anything ye would wish me to fetch along those lines before we leave? There is still plenty of time, and ye can send one of the other officers with me."

"Now that ye mention it, aye," he said, pulling coins out of his sporran and handing them to her. "If this is nae enough, have them send a bill with ye, and it will be paid. Cailean, go with Emilia."

"Aye, Chief," Cailean said, standing and preparing to leave.

Emi handed Crisdean the slip of parchment Bridgette had given her, taking the things in her basket out as he wrote some things down for her and handed it back. "If ye see anything else ye think would be of interest, go ahead and purchase it."

"Aye, Chief," she said with another small curtsy as Cailean came up beside her and took the basket.

Cailean and Emi departed, though once they reached the street, Emi found it somehow less intimidating than it had been previously. Perhaps it was because she'd already seen it and navigated it with Alasdair's assistance that she felt far calmer.

"It is hard to imagine that what I saw yesterday when we arrived was the 'quiet' time in this place, though that seems to be the case," Emi said, breaking the silence between them.

"Aye, is it nae? So many people bustling about at all times, and ye wonder where they come from. I know Alasdair does nae care for it."

"Nor I, but that is why we dinnae live here."

"Aye, too true, lass," Cailean said, chuckling.

Inverness Castle loomed large in the near distance, and to Emi there was a sense of foreboding around it. "Such a place would be where spirits dwelled, I am sure of it," Emi said, inclining her head toward the castle.

Cailean followed her gaze and nodded. "I agree with ye. I would nae want to go there if I could help it. Nae that we can anyway."

"Fine by me," Emi said, which made Cailean laugh.

This trip, Emi took her time studying what was on offer, paying special attention to the fresh ingredients. She picked up the things the chief had requested for himself, along with as many sacks of berries as she could carry, even passing a few to Cailean. There were spices and herbs, different seasoning ingredients, and vegetables. Once she had what she wanted, they returned to the inn, and she sent Cailean ahead with the basket.

"Mr. MacRae?"

"Hello, Emilia," MacRae said from behind his desk. "How are ye finding Inverness so far?"

"Too large and too busy," she said, smiling when MacRae laughed at her comment. "I was hoping I might be able to beg a favor of ye?"

"Perhaps. What is it?"

"I purchased some oysters when I was at the market," Emi explained, holding up the sack they were in. "I wanted to prepare them for the chief, but I have nae the tools to do so. Might I make use of yer kitchens?"

"Aye, I dinnae see why nae. Come this way," he said, and Emi followed him back to the kitchens. "Morag, would ye be so kind as to help Emilia? She wants to use a wee bit of space here to prepare something for Chief Stewart."

"Of course," Morag said, her face ruddy but her smile kind. "What is it ye need to make?" she asked as MacRae departed.

"I purchased some oysters in the market so that I can prepare something special for the chief as a thanks for my promotion."

"A promotion! Ye cannae be but a bairn!"

"I am 19," Emi said, laughing.

"As I said, a bairn," Morag replied, her lips twisting in a wry smile. "Well done, ye. Have ye made them before?"

"I assisted once, but I admit I dinnae know how to get them started."

"Easy once ye get the hang of it. Come, let me show ye."

Morag showed her how to carefully clean and shuck the oysters, and Emi made up a sauce to go with them using a bit of vinegar, wine, and a hint of garlic along with some lemon juice she was able to squeeze out of a half Morag had given her after she'd used it for her own recipe. Placing it all on a borrowed platter, she thanked Morag profusely before taking her surprise upstairs. Balancing the tray with care, she walked inside to find all of the men sitting at the table talking, including Alasdair. They all looked up at her curiously as she came inside and placed the platter in the center of the table with a triumphant smile.

"For ye and the lads, Chief, as a thank ye."

"What … oh, Emilia lass, this looks wonderful!" Crisdean said in surprise.

"I hope it tastes as good as it looks, and since I was the one who made it, no one else needs to try it first," she said with a nod that made Alasdair smile.

Crisdean picked up one of the oyster shells and dumped

the contents into his mouth, his eyes widening before he swallowed it and grinned. "That, my lass, is magnificent. What did ye put in it?"

"Vinegar, red wine, garlic, and a wee bit of lemon I managed to find," she said, ticking it off on her fingers.

"Ye managed to get a lemon!"

"Well, nae exactly. The kitchen had one, and I managed to get enough out of it for this after they had used it. I could have, but I did nae want to make such a purchase without yer approval, sir."

He shook his head and then picked up another oyster. "Ye are a marvel. Go ahead, lads, these are for ye as much as for me!"

The officers didn't need to be asked twice, each of them grabbing one and eating it, savoring it, and then going for another. Emi smiled as they enjoyed her handiwork and sat down at the table with them.

"We are all going to be great, fat men before long with her in charge," Fergus mumbled before he ate another oyster.

"Worth every button I pop," Cailean said, which made Crisdean laugh.

Emi watched Alasdair enjoy the food, happy to see the pleasure on his face as he ate the special dish she'd provided. Their supper arrived not long afterward, and the tray of empty oyster shells was cleared away. There was laughter and conversation over food and wine, and Lamb took up his place in Emi's lap for the duration, purring away. After supper it was time to turn in, so they could rise early for the journey home.

When Emi entered her room, she noticed something sitting atop the pillow. Raising an eyebrow as she put Lamb down, she went to pick it up and then gasped: waiting for her was a length of the pink satin ribbon she'd so admired earlier in the day. A sprig of heather sat upon it, and she picked both up. The ribbon was so unbelievably soft and smooth, a length just long enough for her to tie in her hair. There was only one person who could've done this, and she clutched the ribbon to her heart while trying not to cry. Alasdair was the only one who would have seen her looking at this, and she knew even this small length would've cost him dearly, a month's wages at the very least. Turning back to look at him through the doorway, his smile told her how pleased he was to see he'd made her so happy with his gift.

As the party departed Inverness the following morning, the ribbon was tied in her hair, Lamb rode in her apron pocket, Alasdair was beside her once more, and a new life awaited.

Chapter 5

One month. It had been nearly one month since he'd seen her last, and now that they were so near to home, everything in him screamed to break formation, to hell with the others, and ride full speed for the castle and for her. Of course, he couldn't do that for many reasons, first among them his duty and the simple fact that their relationship was still between them alone. He'd missed her desperately but had no one to confide in, and it had made him short-tempered and ill-humored. The others knew something was wrong but were unable to get it out of him.

When they'd returned from Inverness several months ago, there was a great deal of surprise at Emi's promotion, but Bridgette was thrilled for her. She knew as well as Alasdair did that such a position would set Emi up for life no matter what happened to any of the rest of them. Crisdean presented Emi with an officer's badge as a sign of her new rank, since there wasn't anything precisely for what she was doing, and he wanted to mark her out somehow. She wore it proudly and had yet to give Crisdean a reason to regret having elevated her. The meals she served him, his family, and his officers were all exemplary and creative, making something wonderful out of seemingly very little.

As they rode into the yard, those who were working in the castle came out to greet them, and his eyes scanned for the one person he wanted to see. He found her standing toward the back, away from everyone, and when he caught her eye, she smiled at him. He smiled in return, fighting the urge to leap from his horse, shove his way through the small crowd, and hold her in his arms. After a moment, she made her way toward them, and his heart was pounding.

"Evander!" she called out. "Welcome home!"

It caught Alasdair off guard for a moment as she ignored him completely, hugging Evander, who was just as happy to see her as she was to see him. He understood, of course, but that didn't make it hurt less. She was playing the game he'd forced her into, and he suddenly hated himself for having done it. Near him, Alasdair missed the eagle-eyed and curious glance from Cailean.

"Ach, hello Em. Are ye well? Is Mam?"

"Oh, aye, we are all fine here," she replied before she smiled at Alasdair as though she'd just noticed him standing there. "Hello, Alasdair."

"Emi," he said, trying to keep his voice as neutral as possible.

"Lads," she said with a nod to Cailean and Fergus.

"Emi," they both replied.

"I should get back to work, especially now that ye are all back, but I will send Mam out with bread and such for ye."

"Thank ye, lass," Evander said as she turned and departed.

Alasdair's hands tightened on the reins, his jaw tighter, before he turned without a word and led his horse to the stables. Ushering the horse into his stall, Alasdair took a moment to close his eyes and try to hold his heart together. That greeting had pained him more than he'd thought it would. He'd longed to see her, excited by the very thought of it, but she'd been so indifferent, and that indifference was like a cold knife in his heart. He couldn't help but wonder if it was true indifference and she no longer loved him as he loved her, or if it was the deception required of her.

"When were ye planning on telling us?"

Alasdair jumped, opening his eyes and turning around to look at Cailean, who leaned against the stall door, arms folded across his chest.

"Tell ye what?"

"Dinnae play the idiot, Alasdair, for I know ye far too well for that particular game. When were ye planning on telling us ye are in love with Emi? Does she know?"

"I … well …" he stammered before he stopped, able to offer only a dejected sigh. "Aye, she knows. We have been courting since she came with us to Inverness."

Cailean's eyes widened. "Alasdair, that is nearly five months gone!"

"Aye, I know."

"Why have ye said naught?"

"I just did nae feel everyone needed to know. I wanted to make sure we were on solid ground because ye know there will be those who try to stop us for whatever reason. Nae only that, but I simply wanted her for myself. This is something of my own, something I dinnae have to share for the first time in my life."

Cailean's expression saddened. "Aye, I understand ye. No wonder ye were a miserable sod this whole month. Ye missed her."

"More than anything," Alasdair said.

"But ye are home now, so why are ye so glum still?"

"Ye saw how she greeted us, aye?"

"What did ye expect? If ye have made her keep it a secret, what did ye want her to do?"

"I dinnae know, really, but it hurt all the same. All I want is her and to go to her, but I cannae."

"That time will come, I am sure. At least we are here and nae on the road."

"Aye."

"Alasdair?"

Both men looked up to find Emi standing there, a mug of

ale in one hand and something wrapped in cloth in her other.

"Hello," he said, unable to get his voice to rise above anything but soft.

"If ye will excuse me, I need to go see to some things at the barracks. See ye at supper, Alasdair."

"Aye, Cailean."

Cailean smiled at Emi as he went past and left them alone.

"I brought ye some ale and some fresh bread," she said, her own voice quiet and almost shy.

"Thank ye."

She nodded and set it on a small shelf, folding her hands and looking sad. "I am sure ye have a lot of work to do, so I will leave ye to it."

Leave. The word snapped Alasdair out of it, and he stepped forward to stop her by grabbing her hand. "No, please, dinnae leave."

Emi looked up at him with teary eyes. "Why? So ye can tell me yer feelings have changed? Ye dinnae have to say the words; I can see it plain enough."

"Wait, what? No! They have nae at all! I thought yers had!"

"Why would ye think that?"

"Ye were so cold just now, Emi."

"What did ye want me to do, Alasdair? I cannae very well do what I want to, can I?"

Alasdair sighed. "No, nor can I," he said, lifting her hand to his lips before he pulled her into his arms and hugged her tight. "God help me, I have missed ye terribly."

Emi's arms were around him in an instant as she cried into his chest. "I missed ye, too."

"Dinnae ever think, even for a moment, that I dinnae love ye with every scrap of me. I thought of ye all the time, longed for ye, and I am so glad I am home."

Emi looked up before she cupped his face in her hands and kissed him hard. It took him by surprise, but only for a second before he responded, wishing he could drop everything right now and spend some time alone in her company. Time doing this, in particular. To be able to physically connect with her again fed his soul, bringing it back from the darkness that had beckoned only moments before.

"I love ye," she whispered to him when they parted. "Meet me tonight at the hunting lodge."

Alasdair looked at her with a quizzical expression. "Tonight? But what about —"

"I dinnae care about day or night, I just want ye to myself. Please?"

He smiled and gave a small nod. "Aye, I will. When?"

"Come when the chief releases ye after supper."

"Will ye nae be there as well?"

"No, but that will be because I am waiting for ye at the lodge. I am nae serving tonight and will plead ill to avoid eating in the hall," she said, winking and making him laugh.

"Very well."

"See ye then," she whispered before giving him another quick kiss and departing.

She couldn't stay, he knew that, but he wished she could all the same. She'd ostensibly come only to give him the bread and ale, which wouldn't take her long. Alasdair grinned and patted his horse, who huffed in response. Going over to the shelf, he unfolded the cloth to find buttered bread, cheese, and a small tart she'd snuck in. It made him chuckle before he happily tucked into the snack.

Over the last months, they'd managed to find time together when they could, late-night rendezvous where he'd left the barracks and she'd slipped out of the castle. The times she was at home with Bridgette, they'd sometimes meet in the woods. It was only ever talking, kissing, dreaming of what their lives might be like when they married. He'd loved every moment of it, and it was one of the things he'd very much missed while he was away, the memories both paining him and getting him through the separation.

It was a long evening at supper, his mind on one thing only and not at all where it should be. He was distracted, he couldn't help it, and when they were finally dismissed, he was beyond relieved. As the officers made their way back to the barracks, Alasdair fell into step alongside Cailean, who was on the chief's watch tonight even though he'd only just returned.

"I need yer help," he whispered.

"For what?"

"Would ye cover for me tonight? If anyone wants to come to get me at home, dinnae let them, for I will nae be there."

"Where wi — OH."

"Will ye?"

"Aye, go on with ye," Cailean said, a knowing smile on his lips.

Alasdair grinned, clapped him on the back, and hurried off. Thankfully, the direction he needed to go was in the same direction home was, so no one would think it strange. Instead of turning left to follow the path at the loch, he went straight across the bridge at the ford, taking him to the other side of the loch. Though the walk wasn't really that long, tonight it felt interminable as he made his way down the road and up to where the hunting lodge was. As he neared it on the path through the woods, he saw the windows alight and smiled; she was here, just as she'd said she'd be. He knocked on the door, and it opened in seconds, Emi reaching out and grabbing his arm to pull him inside. The moment the door was shut, she pressed his back against it and kissed him deeply. There was a sharp inhale of surprise from him before his hands flattened on her back and pressed her into him while a moan escaped his lips. When she pulled back, they both laughed.

"Hello to ye, too," he said.

"Mmm, hello."

Alasdair kissed her again before he released her, and she stepped away from him to gesture to the table, where she had some wine set out. He noticed she was also wearing the finest frock she had, with the ribbon from Inverness in her hair, and it touched him that she'd gone to such trouble. He stood up straight, going to the table and sitting down.

"Ye look lovely," he said as she sat down across from him.

"Thank ye. I thought I should nae look like I just came out of the kitchen."

Alasdair chuckled. "Would nae have mattered to me if ye had. I am just glad to see ye," he said before he noticed something and looked at her with a raised eyebrow. "What is wrong?"

"Naught, why?"

"Ye are lying to me. Ye look nervous and are fidgeting … what is wrong?"

"I …" she began before she sighed, and he knew she was annoyed that he knew her so well. "I was hoping ye might nae go home tonight."

It took him a moment to understand what she was saying, and his eyes widened for a moment. "Oh."

"If ye wish to go, ye can, of course."

"No, but are ye sure?" he asked as he reached across the table and took her hand in his. "Ye dinnae have to do this just because ye think it is what I want."

"I am nae. I am doing it because it is what *I* want. I long for more of ye than what I have even if I dinnae know exactly what that is. When ye kiss me, I feel so much, and it only makes me want to be closer to ye, but I dinnae know how to be. I know I have dreamt of ye because I have woken up feeling the way only ye have made me. I want to know what comes next. I want to know what it feels like to have yer hands on me the way I had them on ye in that storeroom at Glengarry. I love ye, and I want all that comes with it."

Alasdair sat in silence, considering her words. He couldn't blame her, he felt it too, but he knew what he was missing, and she didn't. He'd wanted to leave it until she wanted to take that step or until they were married, but was she not asking him now? Was she not sitting here, bold and clear, telling him what she wanted from him? She was, and he had no intention of denying her. He rose slowly from the chair, looking down at her.

"I am more than willing to do as ye are asking of me, but I want to do something else first."

"What is that?"

"Stand up, please."

Emi stood up, eyeing him with curiosity, and he reached out and took the white flowers she'd placed in a cup, tucking them into her hair to make a crown. Once he'd finished, he pulled a long strip of Stewart tartan from his sporran, something they all carried in case they needed to mark their way while they were out somewhere. He took her hand in his, and with the other he wrapped the cloth around their hands once.

"Emilia, while I cannae yet marry ye properly in a church, I can do it in the old way."

"Alasdair," she whispered.

"No, please," he said. "Just listen. This moment will mean just as much to me, if nae more, and will be just as binding in my heart. I love ye, truly and deeply, and I want no other but ye for the rest of my days. Emilia Cairistiona Stewart, I take ye for my wife, in the presence of God, who sees all, and our ancestors who walk these lands. Do ye consent?"

Emi looked down at their hands, and he could feel the warmth of her tears as they hit his skin. They weren't tears of sadness; he knew there was no way they could be.

"Aye, I consent," she said as she lifted her eyes to meet his.

Alasdair reached out to brush tears from her cheeks. "Then ye are Emilia Stewart, forevermore my wife, from this moment on." Emi broke down for a moment, and he wrapped his free arm around her to hold her close to him. "May I kiss my bride, or will she be spending our wedding night crying like a bairn?" Alasdair asked, his tone making it clear he was teasing her.

His words made her laugh, and she wiped her eyes with her sleeve. "Kiss me then and seal it before I change my mind."

Alasdair laughed with her, following it with the requested kiss, but it was soft and slow, making her melt into his arms. He unwrapped their hands and pulled her fully into his arms, deepening the kiss as he walked her backward toward the small room usually left for the chief when he stayed here during a hunt. There was a basic bed with a straw mattress, and while it wasn't quite what he'd hoped to give her for this moment, it would do. Breaking the kiss, he took off his boots, baldric, and sword, before he unfastened his plaid for them to use as a blanket and pulled her close once more. His lips went to her neck, and she sighed, tilting her head back to allow him access. His hands went to work unpinning her from the dress she wore, and he could feel her trembling, but he expected that from a woman who had no idea what was coming. Alasdair's lips slid over her shoulders as his hands pushed her over gown from them before moving to untie her skirts and let them puddle at her feet.

Emi got the idea and pushed his coat from his shoulders, and he helped her by shrugging out of it. As he loosened her stays, she removed the sporran and the belt which held his kilt, tossing them aside and allowing the heavy wool to fall to the floor. This left him in just his long shirt, and he rewarded her decision with a kiss of a type he'd never allowed himself to give her before, lest it lead to this moment sooner than they wanted to get there. He broke it to pull her stays over her head, throwing them aside, and before she could think about it, he removed her shift, too. She gasped at the chilly air and the surprise of suddenly being all but naked before him, and he chuckled before he kissed her again.

Emi felt the sound rumble in his chest where her hands rested as he slowly moved her backward and onto the bed, dragging his fingertips down her spine, making her shiver against him. Alasdair broke the kiss to once more place kisses on her neck and shoulders as he ran a hand over her body. Emi gasped; the sensation better than she'd imagined it might be. Alasdair moved down, his lips following the path of his hand, and her back arched into him as she groaned softly with the pleasure of it, her fingers twining in his hair. There was a small sound of disappointment when he sat up, but his smile was wolfish as he lifted one leg and untied the garter before kissing his way down her leg as he rolled the stocking down. When he reached her foot, he pulled her shoe off and tossed it aside, kissing the top of her foot before removing the stocking and dropping it to the floor. He repeated the process with the other leg, and by the end of it, she was squirming in anticipation of his next kiss.

Removing his shirt and sliding himself back up beside her, he kissed her lips again as he slid a hand down her side and over her hip. She inhaled sharply against his lips when she felt his fingers touch her in a place no one else ever had, but he didn't give her time to be self-conscious. Alasdair was fighting himself, making himself take his time, but every reaction from her stoked the fire within him to have her. Her body was beautiful, and it deserved to be lavished with all the attention he could give it.

Dear Lord, no wonder this was considered sinful! Emi felt like her insides were twisting themselves into tighter and tighter knots, and there was a desperation to release them before she went mad. Within a moment she felt as though she were no longer in control of anything as a strong wave of pleasure swept through her, making her cry out loudly and repeatedly. In the sheer relief of the moment, Alasdair moved quickly, and Emi let out a small sound of pain. She was momentarily confused by it, but the quickness with which it faded made her wonder if she'd felt it at all. He groaned in her ear, and it made her stomach knot again in an instant, even as her body moved by itself, moving with him, wanting to keep him where he was. She ran her hands up his back and slid one leg over his hip, the movement bringing a loud moan from him before one of his strong hands gripped her thigh, pinning it in place to keep her from removing it.

"Emi," he groaned into her ear.

"Dinnae stop, Alasdair," she breathed, feeling that maddening desperation building before it again released itself, and she felt as though she actually *did* scream this time.

Her release pulled his from him, and he buried his moan against the skin of her neck, gripping her leg just a little harder as his other hand gripped the plaid beneath them. He stayed there, unmoving, trying to catch his breath, trying to think, and finding he could do neither. When he felt he could speak, he looked at her and smiled, reaching out to stroke her cheek.

"Are ye well?"

"More than," she said, a grin spreading across her beautiful face. "That was what I have been wanting and missing all this time?"

"Aye," he replied, laughing softly.

"Well, this certainly will nae help me nae do either of those things. In fact, it may be worse now."

"Oh, it will be," he said, still laughing. "And nae just for ye."

"That was … I did nae realize I could … I mean …"

"I think it very much depends on who ye are with, but ye can trust that I will always make sure ye do. I would be a poor lover if ye did nae."

"Ye are nae my lover; ye are my husband."

"I am both."

"I suppose ye are right, ye are."

"But ye are well and truly wed to me now. No giving me back."

"Dinnae want to, thank ye."

Alasdair laughed and then nuzzled her cheek. "I do love ye, always and forever."

"And I love ye the same."

"Do ye remember that night at Invergarry, when ye told me I could nae have both defiance and obedience, and I told ye I could?"

"Aye?"

"Ye are about to find out what I meant by that," he said with a devilish smile as he produced the strip of tartan he'd handfasted them with.

"What?"

Moving quickly, he tied her wrists together with it. "Ye are my prisoner now, and ye will do as I tell ye … unless ye want to tell me no so I can torture ye into obedience with pleasure."

Emi's eyes went wide. "Alasdair!" she said in a scandalized tone before she surprised him with a smile as dark as his own. "When do we start?"

"Christ, I am going to spend every day from now on thanking the Almighty for ye," he said, his voice now deeper with desire.

"Maybe if I do this right, ye will be thanking him before we are through."

"Sweet Christ, Em," he breathed. "Just when I thought ye could nae be more perfect."

"Perfect? But I have done wrong if I am yer prisoner, and perhaps ye need to punish me for it."

Alasdair groaned, beyond turned on by her words. "Aye, indeed."

Chapter 6

Alasdair was loath to leave her in the early hours before dawn, but it had to be done. She had work to do to prepare breakfast for the returned chief, and he wouldn't keep her from it. There were no tears, they would see each other daily, but there was a promise to meet here as often as they could. At least then, for a few hours, they could be the newlyweds they considered themselves to be. Alasdair stopped on his way back to wash up in the loch before returning to the barracks to freshen up his clothes and hair. Entering the hall for breakfast with the others, only Cailean was present at the officer's table, and he chuckled when Alasdair sat down beside him.

"Ye look bonnie and bright this morning."

"Have all the reason in the world to," Alasdair said, grinning.

"Went that well, did it?"

He laughed and shook his head. "Oh, aye, it did, but …" he paused and looked around before lowering his voice and continuing. "She is also my wife."

"What!" Cailean exclaimed in a whisper. "When!"

"Last night. I did it the old way, binding our hands with tartan, stating my intention, and getting her consent."

Cailean's grin was wide. "Congratulations to ye, lad. Never thought I would see the day."

"Never thought it would come, but I was wrong."

"She was the only one who probably could have proved ye wrong anyway."

Alasdair chuckled. "Aye, but that has always been true with her, has it nae?"

"Oh, aye. Are ye going to tell everyone?"

"No. Just ye, Fergus, and Evander. I am nae ready to go to the chief yet. I want to make sure I have everything in place."

"Fair enough, but ye should tell yer mam and Bridgette. It will make it easier for the pair of ye to be together."

"Ye think I should?"

"Aye. It would allow ye to use that deserted cottage near yers to make a home even if no one knows yet. Ye could spend yer nights there, go home to her like a proper husband, and all of us would cover for ye."

"I worry about how Evander will take it."

"Make sure we are all there when ye tell him, including her. Even better if ye make sure Bridgette is there, too."

"Aye. I dinnae have duty until after dinner, so I will talk to her, then our mams. After that I will tell a few of the others."

Once breakfast was finished and the morning meeting for the officers was released, Alasdair headed to the kitchens. Catching Emi's eye, he gestured for her to follow him, though she looked concerned when she reached him.

"What is wrong?" she asked, her brow furrowed.

"Naught," he said. "I just wanted to see ye. Good morning, Wife."

Emi shushed him, looking around with a grin. "Ye are mad."

Out of nowhere, Alasdair felt something hit his boot and looked down to find Lamb wrapped around his ankle, trying to bite it through the thick leather. "Lamb!" Alasdair said, picking up the kitten and giving it a cuddle. "I was wondering when ye would launch yer offensive. Ye are getting much better at it."

Emi laughed as Lamb began purring madly when Alasdair

picked him up. "Ye may be his favorite target, but he does love it when ye give him a cuddle and ye were gone for so long."

"Cailean knows."

She blinked and looked at him in surprise at his sudden declaration. "How?"

"He figured it out yesterday before ye came to give me the bread and ale. He is my best friend, my brother, he knows me better than anyone except for ye. He had a good idea, and I wanted to see what ye thought about it."

"What idea is that?"

"He thinks we should tell our mams and a few others, for it would make it easier for ye and I to be together. We could use the abandoned cottage near mine at night, so I could go home and spend it with ye like a proper husband should. He said they would all cover for me. If Bridgette knows, it will be easier to tell Evander."

Emi seemed to consider it and then nodded. "Aye, I think he is right."

"Where is Bridgette now?"

"In the kitchen office, come on," Emi said.

Alasdair put Lamb down and followed Emi to the small room she and Bridgette used as an office of sorts. Bridgette looked up from an account book when the pair of them came in together, raising an eyebrow when Emi shut the door.

"What is this?"

"Maman, Alasdair has something he would like to tell ye," Emi said.

"Bridgette, I —"

"You have been courting Emi since Inverness." She laughed as both of them looked at her in shock. "I am not blind."

"Maman, last night Alasdair handfasted us and asked for my consent to be his wife. I gave it."

It was Bridgette's turn to look shocked. "You married in the old way?"

"Aye," Alasdair said, nodding. "I am nae ready to go to the

chief, but I did nae wish to wait to make her my wife. It was all I wanted."

"Ah, Alasdair, such a romantic, just like your father," Bridgette said as she stood and walked around the desk. "Welcome then to my family, dearest boy. There is no one better I could have wished for her," she said as she kissed his cheeks.

Emi tried not to cry, and Alasdair beamed. "I will nae hurt her."

"I know you will not, at least not purposefully."

"There is an empty cottage by mine, and I was hoping to use it at night, so I might spend my evenings with Emi, as I would do if everyone knew and we had done it in church."

"You have my blessing to do so, and I will make sure she is able to join you there without interference."

"I was hoping ye would say that."

"I am sure you were. Emi, love, you had best get back to that dough, hm?"

"Of course, Maman," Emi said before daring to give Alasdair a parting kiss on her way out.

Once the door shut, Bridgette looked at him. "There is a reason I have not yet dismissed you. There is something I think you should know."

Alasdair was instantly wary. "What is it?"

"What do you know of Emi's birth parents?"

"Same as we all know; that they were farmers on the outskirts of Stewart land, they died when she was wee, and she came to ye."

"Yes, all of that is true, but there is more to it than that." Bridgette sighed. "The man we have always said was Emi's father was actually not. He knew it, we all did. It was a bit of an open secret."

"Then who was?"

"The chief," she replied in a quiet voice.

"Wait … Emi is …"

"The natural daughter of the chief, yes."

Alasdair's head spun as he tried to make sense of it. Emi, his

Emi, was the daughter of his master. "Did the chief know?"

"Yes, he did. Her mother worked here, and, well, things happened. The man who claimed Emi married Helena because he had always loved her from afar. Helena was happy to marry him, for she cared a great deal about him, and I do believe she loved him by the end. The chief, in private, acknowledged Emi to his wife, and because of that, he would send them a small sum for her upkeep. It was also why she came here when they died. He gives that bit to me now, but he also cares for her in his own way, as you have seen. He makes sure she is safe here, employed, loved. She will always have a place here because she is his acknowledged child, no matter what happens. It means nothing as far as dowry or inheritance are concerned."

"Does she know?"

"No, she does not, and it has been preferred that it be kept that way. The knowledge would serve her no purpose. I wanted you to know because when you go to him, his reaction will be coming from a different place. It will be from a father, and you should approach it with that in mind."

"Thank ye for telling me."

"Do not let it change anything, Alasdair. It means nothing in the end."

"Bridgette, she is my master's daughter. I … he never would have allowed it, and he may nae."

"He will because he loves you, and there is no better match for her than you. She is not legitimate, Alasdair. If she were, things might be different, but she is not. She is free to marry where her heart bids her, just like any other young woman here."

Alasdair nodded, knowing she was right. Natural children could be acknowledged, but they never were in line for anything, never lived the lives they might have if they were legitimate children. It was even more true for daughters.

"Where are you going next?"

"To my mam."

"Go on, then," Bridgette said with a smile. "I am sure she will be as overjoyed by the news as I am. Give Coira my love, hm?"

Alasdair smiled, bowed, and left. As he passed, Emi caught his eye and smiled at him. He couldn't believe he hadn't seen it before now: she had Crisdean's eyes and smile. Alasdair winked at her and made his way out and homeward.

"Mam!" he called out as he came to the clearing their cottage occupied.

"Alasdair! Ye are home!" Coira said as she came out and embraced her son.

"Aye, got home last evening."

"Where have ye been, then?"

"Come inside, there is something I want to tell ye."

"What is it?" she asked as they went in and Alasdair shut the door.

"Mam, I am married."

"What! Alasdair! Dinnae make such jests!"

"I am nae jesting," he said, laughing. "Ye asked where I was last night, and I am telling ye. I was with Emi, and I married her in the old way, in secret. Emilia is my wife."

Coira's eyes widened. "Christ above, Alasdair!"

"I am sorry ye were nae there but —"

"Ach, dinnae ye fret about that," Coira interrupted. "I will be there when ye do it in church, though as far as I am concerned, and as ye clearly are, it is a done deed."

"Bridgette feels so, too."

"Ye told her then?"

"Aye. I needed her blessing, and yers, to do what I am thinking of."

"Which is?"

"Ye know the cottage near here?"

"Aye."

"I want to use it to spend my evenings with Emi, as I should do."

"Ah, well, ye certainly have mine. I can make excuses for ye if someone comes here looking for ye."

"Cailean and a few of the lads will know, so that will help. When I feel I have everything ready, I will go to the chief."

"About that —"

"Aye, I know. Bridgette told me."

Coira smiled with a sort of dark amusement. "Look at ye, secretly married to the chief's daughter. Yer father would be proud."

"Why?"

"That is a level of romance he could never *dream* of meeting."

Alasdair laughed. "I will accept that compliment then," he said before he hugged her. "Thank ye, Mam."

"Ach, I am so happy for ye, Alasdair. Ye have chosen a wonderful lass, and I know ye will be happy together. How long have ye been courting?"

"Almost half a year."

"But ye have been in love with her far longer than that. Bridgette and I could see it even if ye could nae."

Alasdair smiled. "I am nae needed at the castle until dinner. Let me help ye with what ye need here."

"Oh no, lad, we are going to the cottage and making it suitable, which is yer job as a husband now. Change yer clothes and let us be off."

***

"Congratulations to ye, Alasdair," Fergus said, embracing his friend as they stood in the barracks later that afternoon. "An excellent choice, though I never thought I would see ye do it."

"Do what?"

Cailean, Alasdair, and Fergus turned to see Evander standing there in the doorway. This was *not* the way Alasdair had intended for this to go, but it seemed he'd have no choice now.

"Evander, shut the door," Cailean said.

"What is going on?" Evander asked even as he complied, coming inside and shutting the door.

"Alasdair has something he needs to tell ye."

"Evander, I —" he began, but then paused. "I married Emi."

Evander started laughing. "Aye, sure. What did ye really get into?" When he noticed none of the others were laughing, he stopped. "Wait …"

"She and I married last night, the ancient way."

"Ye what? Without even talking to me! Ye bastard!" Evander shouted, starting toward Alasdair before Cailean stopped him.

"Evander, calm down," Cailean said.

"That is my sister!"

"Aye, and she willingly gave her consent," Cailean replied in his usual calm manner.

"It was nae planned ahead of time, or I would have said something. I wanted to be ready, which is why we had nae even been public about our courtship," Alasdair said.

"How long!"

"Ever since the trip to Inverness, but Evander, I have loved her longer, far longer. She is everything to me. Yer mam has given her blessing."

Evander stopped struggling against Cailean, though his expression was still angry. "If ye hurt her or dinnae make good on properly wedding her, I will end ye," he hissed.

Alasdair shoved back the urge to tell him he could try, knowing that this was a mix of Evander's protectiveness as Emi's brother along with feeling betrayed by a friend. "I will nae. Ye have my word."

"Come on, Evander," Fergus said. "Ye should be happy! Alasdair is yer friend and a fine match for Emi. Ye have known him yer whole life, and ye know that if he took this step, he is serious. Sometimes things just happen, and this was one of those. We will all be in the church when it happens again."

Evander sighed. "I just wish ye would have at least spoken to me about courting her."

"I intended to, but it was never the right time. I *am* sorry, Evander," Alasdair said in a soft voice, truly feeling bad about upsetting him. "I know ye only want to protect her, and so do I."

With a small nod, Evander held out his hand. "Then I am glad to now call ye brother," he said.

Alasdair sighed in relief and shook his hand. "Thank ye. We are going to be staying at the old cottage near mine in the evenings. If anyone needs me, ye can find me there, but dinnae tell them so. Tell them ye found me at my mam's."

"Of course," Evander said. "I know it will make Emi happy, and that is all I want. I will help ye how I can."

Later that evening, Alasdair made his way home after dismissal with a lighter step, knowing that he was going home to *her*. To Emi. To his wife. As he neared the cottage, he heard Emi singing, and it brought a smile to his lips. Opening the door, he joined her in the song, and she turned around with a bright smile.

"Hello," she said as he shut the door.

Alasdair gathered her into his arms and kissed her. "Hello to ye as well, sweet Wife."

"I love to hear ye say that," she said as he released her to return to the pot she'd been stirring.

"Aye? Well, plan on hearing it often."

"I came to spruce things up here, and when I arrived, I found it all done! I wonder how that happened," she said, shooting him a wry smile over her shoulder.

"Did ye? The fae must have been pleased by our marriage."

Emi laughed and shook her head. "Sit down, ye ridiculous man."

Alasdair laughed and sat down by the fire with a happy sigh. "I still cannae believe this is happening, but I am beyond happy it is."

"So am I," she said as she handed him a cup of warmed wine. "How did the lads take it?"

"They were happy, even yer brother."

Emi grinned as she sat in a chair across from him. "Good. Does it sound strange to ye that I am excited to sleep beside ye tonight? It was so wonderful last night."

"Does nae sound strange at all. I am looking forward to it as well."

"Even if it is just sleep?"

"Aye, even then, ye daft lass. There will always be days when we dinnae feel up to sport, and that is perfectly fine. We went all these months without it, a day or two here and there will nae kill us."

"True," she said. "But tonight will nae be one of those."

Alasdair laughed. "Well, then what are we waiting for?" he asked as he set his cup aside and stood, scooping her up into his arms as she made a sound of surprise before she started laughing as he carried her to the bed.

Alasdair woke later with a small start, forgetting where he was for a moment and feeling panicked until he saw Emi next to him, sleeping peacefully and bathed in the light from the fire. He smiled and placed a kiss on her temple before leaving the bed to stoke the fire. Emi snuggled into him when he returned, and he held her close to him. It still felt like a dream to him. He was a husband with a wife to return to at night, and best of all, it was his beloved Emi. He combed his fingers through her long hair slowly, watching her sleep, hardly feeling as though he deserved her. Yet, here she was in his arms, his forever. With a happy smile, he closed his eyes and went back to sleep.

Chapter 7

The hall was filled with music and merriment, another Hogmanay. The chief held a party each year for those who worked at the castle, the officers, and their families as a thank you for all their hard work through the previous year. Crisdean brought out whisky and wine, provided a fine meal, music for dancing, and small gifts for the children. It was something looked forward to by all of them, and for one night, everyone within was equal.

In a small anteroom, Fergus, Cailean, Evander, Alasdair, and Emi sat alone at a table, while Cailean's wife visited with Coira and Bridgette in the hall and his children were off dancing. Whisky warmed them all, making laughter easier and spirits lighter. Emi sat on Alasdair's lap, his arms around her. In such an intimate setting, there was no need to hide, and everyone seated here knew. It was nice to be with him in such a way, so publicly, not hiding for once.

Alasdair nuzzled Emi's cheek, and she closed her eyes. "I love ye so," he whispered in her ear.

Smiling, she turned her face toward him. "And I love ye."

"Ach, stop it the pair of ye," Cailean grumbled, his tone as playful as his expression.

"Aye, I have something to give to Emi for Hogmanay, but ye have to release her first," Fergus said.

Alasdair and Emi both raised an eyebrow, but she sat up and returned to the chair she'd been seated in. "You did nae have to get me anything, Fergus."

"Aye, but I felt ye deserved it, so I did," he said as he placed a parcel wrapped in fabric on the table.

Emi smiled and reached out, pulling back the fabric. Within was a beautiful cloak in dark green wool, woven so finely it felt almost like silk. There was black trim around the hood, the shoulders, and where it came together at the neck, as well as the bottom. It was sewn in such a way as to look like lace, even though it wasn't. On top of it sat a pair of mittens in the same wool and a pair of doe skin gloves. She gasped and looked up at him in shock, and even the other men were surprised by such a gift.

"Fergus, this is —"

"Before ye say it is too much, it is nae. Ye help my mam take such good care of Arabella when I am away, and I know she would be lost without ye; they both would. This is naught less than ye deserve. Ye may have been born to a farmer, but ye are the finest lady I know, and I want ye to feel like one. I made it all myself, even the trim and the wool fabric. I looked for some trim in Edinburgh but could nae find any that suited that was nae also ridiculously expensive, so I set to making my own instead. I made the mittens and gloves, too, and I took the doe myself. I made sure it was done with care, as I knew ye would never abide it if ye knew she had suffered even a little."

Fergus had, as Alasdair and the others had also done, learned a trade for his life after service. Cailean and Evander learned about farming, Alasdair trained in caring for horses, and Fergus was an excellent tailor. No one could cut a waistcoat like Fergus, and he often made them for his friends and their uniforms. He'd even made a fancy embroidered one for Alasdair to wear when he was in more formal settings with the chief, as he often was because of how highly Crisdean held him in his esteem. It was no secret to anyone that Alasdair was the most valued and trusted of Crisdean's officers.

Emi's eyes filled with tears, and it left her unable to speak. She ran a gentle hand over the cloak, knowing this had taken a great deal of work on his part, and how much love and care had gone into the making of it. All of the others were just as moved by Fergus' loving gesture.

"Try it on! I want to see it on ye! I hope I got the right length."

Emi stood and so did Fergus, lifting the cloak from the table and draping it across her shoulders before he came around and fastened the button in the front. The length was perfect, and he stood back and admired his handiwork.

"Christ, Fergus, that is the finest work I have ever seen," Cailean said. "Ye have outdone yerself."

"Ye look gorgeous, love," Alasdair said. "The color suits ye and brings out the green in yer eyes."

"She will be the envy of every Stewart lass with such finery!" Evander said.

"As well she should," Fergus countered. "She deserves every bit, and they should all strive to be like our Emi, always thinking of others and caring for them."

"Well-said, Fergus," Cailean agreed.

"The button is the same as the ones we wear on our uniforms," he continued. "I paid a few pence for an old one from our supplies, but it is a solid silver button all the same. It is actually one of Alasdair's old ones, Mary was taking them off of his old coat when I came in, and I thought it would mean so much to ye to have a something he wore to keep with ye whenever we are away."

Emi knew the button alone would be worth a small fortune, and she placed a hand over it, smiling through tears. "What a beautiful thought and gesture, Fergus. I absolutely love it."

"I am glad for it," Fergus said, still smiling. "Here, try on the gloves."

Emi slipped on the doe skin gloves, and they were the softest things she'd ever felt. "They fit perfectly!"

"Good. Now, when ye go riding with us to Inverness, ye can do so looking like a fine lady. The mittens," he said, picking them up, "are special though. I have included a pocket in the palm where ye can put a hot stone, so yer hands dinnae freeze."

Rising up on her toes, she hugged him tightly. "Thank ye for such a precious gift, Fergus. It does nae seem enough to say for all of this, but it is all I can think of. I will treasure these always."

"I know ye will, and that is why ye deserve it all the more."

"Come let us see it," Cailean said, beckoning her closer so that they could inspect the fineness of the Fergus' work.

"I have something for all of ye, too," Emi said once they'd all had a close look at the cloak, gloves, and mittens. Picking up a basket she'd set aside, she placed a small parcel in front of each man. "Go on," she said, smiling as she gestured at them to open the small bundles.

Fergus opened his first and then grinned. In his hands he held a handkerchief, embroidered with his name, his rank, and the Stewart badge in one corner. "Ach, this is lovely work, Emi!"

All of the others had the same, but Evander also got a wallet. It was Cailean who noticed the extra piece in their parcels first. "Emi … is this what I think it is?" he asked reverently.

"Tablet? Aye." The gasps from the other men at the table before they reached out and opened the small bag made her laugh. Tablet was a rare treat, the cost of the ingredients dear. "I asked the chief to hold back my pay to cover the cost of the sugar."

Fergus stuffed a piece in his mouth and sighed. "Heaven."

"I will have to share this with the bairns," Cailean said.

"No, ye will nae. That one is yers; I have small bags for them as well, and one for Arabella, Fergus."

"That is really very sweet of ye, Emi. They will be so excited," Cailean said.

"I am glad! It is Hogmanay; everyone deserves something special, aye?"

Alasdair pulled her back down into his lap and kissed her. "Aye, they do. What a wonderful thing for ye to do."

"Tell me again why ye dinnae think ye deserved a fine gift, Emi?" Fergus said, teasing her.

As the night wore on, Emi was able to get in at least a dance or two with Alasdair before having to dance with others as though she were not married to the handsome young officer who danced across the room with other women as though he were free. She didn't let it bother her, she knew that it was what had to be done, and his heart was with her even if his body wasn't. His behavior was courteous, but she didn't miss the behavior of the women, all of them trying to touch him in daring ways or get closer to him than they should be. It was this that troubled her, and both Cailean and Fergus did their best to distract her from it by dancing with her or entertaining her in some way. Along with wine and whisky, such merriment made it easy to push away any dark thoughts creeping at the edge of her mind. It was a new year, she was forever linked to the man she adored, and all was right in her own little world.

***

When the party ended, they all walked back together, snow crunching beneath their feet. The officers were given leave to spend the next day with their families, so there was no need to be at the barracks. Emi was on Evander's arm, talking quietly and laughing, while Alasdair walked with Coira. Fergus escorted Bridgette, and Cailean was with his family. His wife and his children didn't know the truth, so such pretenses were still necessary around them. As they branched off toward their respective homes, Evander took Bridgette's arm and kissed Emi's cheek in farewell before she took Alasdair's other arm. Once Coira was home, Emi and Alasdair walked together, her head against his shoulder. He opened the door and lit the candle there before he made his way across and stoked the fire back to life. When that was done, he pulled Emi close to him.

"A blessed Hogmanay to ye, my beautiful wee wife," he whispered.

"And to ye," she said, nuzzling his chest. "I have something else to give ye."

"Oh?"

"Mhm," she said, going to their bed and reaching beneath it to produce another larger parcel that she placed on the table.

Alasdair opened it to reveal two new shirts, lovingly made by Emi. Along one of the seams at the chest, she'd stitched her name, and he ran his finger over it. A shirt was always an intimate gift to give, something so close to the skin. "Thank ye, love, they are beautiful."

"I wish I could have got ye something more."

"More? Why? Ye have given so much already."

"Nae as much as I would like."

"Ye hush with that nonsense," he said. "I need no more than this, and they all mean a great deal because ye made them for me."

"I am glad ye like them. I stitched my name to keep me close to ye whenever ye are away."

"And that is just what it shall do. I will think of ye each time I see it, and whenever I run a finger over it, I will be wishing it was yer beautiful face I was touching. I did nae forget about ye, though," he said.

"What do ye mean?"

From his sporran, he pulled out a small, paper-wrapped parcel and placed it on the table in front of her. She looked at it and then looked at him with a wary sort of curiosity.

"Go on," he said, chuckling. "I wanted to wait to give it to ye until we were alone."

Emi carefully opened it and let out a small sound of shock at what she found inside. "Oh, Alasdair," she breathed as she picked it up in her hands. A length of green velvet ribbon rested in them, delicate and soft. "Ye should nae have!"

"Aye, I should," he said. "Ye deserve beautiful things,

Em, and I saw this in a window while we were away. When I told them why I was buying it, they gave me a very fair price. So, now, ye have satin and velvet. If I could afford a jewel, I would give it to ye so that the world could see ye as the princess ye are."

"Thank ye so very much," she said, leaning across the table to kiss him. "I love it, though I think I would be afraid to wear it."

"Dinnae be. Wear it to church or to a ceilidh, or whenever it strikes yer fancy."

Emi was quiet for a moment, shifting nervously on her feet before she spoke again. "Alasdair … do ye think perhaps ye could speak to the chief now?"

"No, nae yet. I am still trying to get things in order."

"What things?"

"I want to show him I have the means to support ye, for one. I will need to have an idea of what I want to do, ask him about renting this cottage and some land, that kind of thing."

"It has been almost three months and —"

"Emi, please. Just trust me and let me do this the way I feel I should."

"I am just so tired of pretending I dinnae love ye or that we are nae together. I am tired of watching others flirt with ye and try to catch yer eye, tired of watching ye pretend to entertain it. *All* I have done is pretend for months now, since Inverness!"

"And I have nae? Do ye think it has been easy on me?"

"Ye are the one who has the power to end it, though, nae me! If ye dinnae want to pretend any longer, then stop!"

"It is nae that easy!"

"Aye, it is! I am afraid I will forget one of these times."

Alasdair looked at her, eyes narrowed. "Dinnae ye dare."

"What?"

"If ye think pretending to slip up will help —"

"That is nae what I said!"

"Is it nae?"

"Dinnae ye put words in my mouth, Alasdair!"

"Then ye need to make sure ye watch yer tongue, as I have to do."

"Are ye ashamed of me? Is that it?"

"What? No!" Alasdair replied, taken aback by the question.

"Aye, happy to play my husband here at night when there is no one to see ye, but nae in the light, is that it?"

"Emi!"

"Just say it!" she shouted at him, tears in her eyes. "There is something more holding ye back, so what is it? Tell me the truth, Alasdair!"

"Emi, stop."

She shook her head. "What am I supposed to think?"

"That it is precisely what I told ye!"

"No," she said. "It is nae. It was one thing when ye were courting me, but it is different now. What is it ye are so worried about if someone does find out?"

"That the chief will be angry I did nae speak to him!"

"Then do it."

"I cannae."

"More like ye dinnae want to. Goodnight, Alasdair," she said, storming to the door and yanking it open.

Alasdair stood up and hurried after. "Emi, please!"

"No!" she snapped. "I am tired of being hidden like I am some terrible secret ye need to keep! If I am yer wife and ye are happy about it, then ye should want *everyone* to know, but ye dinnae! Instead, ye want to play games so that ye can have the best of both, aye? Me in yer bed and other lasses to play with."

He gasped, feeling like she'd slapped him. To hear her say those words hurt him in ways he couldn't begin to describe. It wasn't like that at all, but he could see where she might think so and he hated it. "Em, that was … why would ye say that?"

"Because that is what it feels like to *me*!" she sobbed out.

"But ye know that it is nae like that!"

"No, I dinnae! Stop telling me how I should feel, Alasdair! I am trying to tell ye, and ye dinnae care or want to hear me!"

Alasdair sighed. "I dinnae know what ye want me to say other than the thing I cannae."

In the darkness he heard a soft sob before she turned and ran from him.

"Emi!" he called out, chasing after her.

"Stay away from me!" she spat once they reached the road, the fury and hurt in her voice unmistakable.

Alasdair stopped, watching her run back toward the castle. She was going to stay there tonight instead of at home with him. Chest aching, he made his way back home and sat down at the table, burying his face in his hands. There *was* a reason, a good one, but it was a reason he didn't want to tell her about; he hardly wanted to admit it to himself. War was coming, he was sure of it. All those meetings in Inverness, all of the places they'd gone in the last month; something was happening, but he couldn't tell her. How could he? It would upset her, frighten her, and in the end maybe he'd be wrong, and he would've done that to her for nothing. He hated the thought of the tears he knew it would bring, the pain, not just for her, but for him, too.

"I am sorry, Emi," he whispered before he lost his composure.

Alasdair wasn't sure what time it was when he opened his eyes and lifted his head from the table, and for a moment he was confused as to why he was sleeping here. Where was Emi? It didn't take long for the memory of last night to crash over him like icy water from the loch. Remembering her words, the sound of her crying, made his heart hurt, and he stood up. Picking up the two buckets, he made his way to the loch for water, feeling as though he were moving through a fog that made his limbs as heavy as his heart and mind. Coming back through the door, he stopped short, not sure if what he was seeing was real or just what he wanted to see.

"Emi," he whispered.

She was sitting at the table and looked up when he said her name, pushing back the hood of the cloak she'd been given last night. The pain in her face, the red in her eyes, broke his heart.

"Alasdair, I —" but she stopped, shaking her head. Her lower lip trembled, and she covered her face with her hands, sobbing softly.

He put the buckets down and went to her, pulling her close to him. "Shh, it is all right."

"I am so sorry for the things I said!"

"I cannae blame ye for saying them or feeling them," he said. "Emi, I am nae ashamed of ye; I never could be. I would never do any of what ye accused me of."

"I know, I just … I dinnae understand!"

Alasdair sighed. "I do have a reason. One I have nae told ye, but if it means ye will understand, then I will tell ye now."

Emi lifted her head from her hands and looked at him.

"I am fairly certain war is coming," he said. "I dinnae know for sure, but that is what it seems like to me. The meetings in Inverness, the meetings we traveled to, they are all about a rising against the Hanovers and the return of the Stuarts. I did nae want to tell ye in case it did nae happen, but this is why I have nae spoken to him. He is nae in the right mind for it; he cannae think of it now. I have nae let the world know because I dinnae want to give them a chance to poison anything, as I know they would. I have seen what they do to each other, these lasses, when they are vying for a lad's attention. They are cruel and do their best to pull each other down, and that is nae what I want for ye. I told Cailean once that ye were something that was mine alone, something I did nae have to share for the first time in my life, and that is still true."

"War?" she whispered, as if she were afraid saying the word any louder would bring it to bear right this moment.

"Aye. There is a chance I am wrong, and I hope I am. If I discover that I am, I will ask him right that moment. Please dinnae be afraid or let yerself fret; just know that my holding back has naught to do with ye. I love ye more than my own life. Please, tell me ye understand."

"I do," she said before she burst into tears, putting her arms around his neck. "But, Alasdair, if ye must go —"

Alasdair placed a gentle finger against her lips. "I dinnae wish ye to fret. Let us nae think about it before we must. For now, let us just enjoy the day together, aye?"

"Aye, of course," she said, wiping her eyes on her sleeve before she smiled. "I brought something special to make for ye."

"Aye? I can hardly wait to eat whatever it is. First, would my wife be so kind as to grant me her forgiveness with a kiss?"

Emi laughed and then kissed him. "I am so sorry, Alasdair. I should nae doubt ye."

His whole body relaxed when she kissed him, and he sighed. "I am sorry, too. I should have explained it to ye from the start, should have known ye would understand." Reaching up, he gently pulled the pins from her hair and set them aside.

Emi gave him a curious look as her hair fell onto her shoulders. "I cannae cook this way, love."

"Of course nae," he said with a smile. From the table, he picked up the ribbon he'd bought for her, gathered her hair back behind her neck, and used the ribbon to tie it there much the same way he did his own. "Beautiful."

Emi kissed his forehead, and stood up. From the floor, she picked up the basket she'd brought with her. "Would ye fetch two more buckets of water for me, please?"

"Aye," he said, standing and dumping the water he'd brought into the larger bucket before going to fetch more.

When he returned, he could smell the food cooking as he neared the cottage, and his stomach rumbled, reminding him of just how hungry he was. He transferred the water, and Emi placed a cup of hot tea before him to ward off the January chill. Alasdair accepted it with gratitude, warming his hands on it, before he realized it was one of the chief's fine china cups. His eyes widened for a moment, realizing she must have gotten his permission to use them, but letting her take them showed the great deal of trust he had in her. He'd used them before, of course, but they seemed particularly luxurious in their humble surroundings. Alasdair wondered what she'd told him she was using them for or where she was taking them. A few moments later, she placed a matching china plate in front of him. On it were two large sausages, eggs, bread fried in the pan with the sausage drippings, and some parsnips, mushrooms, and turnips cooked in the same, along with a little bit of garlic and butter. It was a feast fit for a chief, and Alasdair was almost salivating at the sight of it all.

"Emi, this … what a fine meal ye have laid for us this morn!"

"Aye? Then stop talking to me and eat, ye silly man," she said, chuckling, before she kissed the top of his head. "I have some for yer mam, as well. We can take it to her after we eat."

He didn't need to be told twice, tucking into it as Emi sat down across from him with her own smaller version of the same meal. All was right in his world again, and it was easy to let all of last night's hurtful words slip away into nothingness, burned away with the wintry morning light of the first day of a new year, to leave only this moment and the two of them.

Chapter 8

As Alasdair and the others rode into the courtyard with Crisdean, he was full of anxiety over the moment he knew was coming. There was no way around it, no matter how much he might wish otherwise, and he knew his wasn't the only glum face in the group. It wasn't that he wasn't desperate to see Emi after having been gone for the last few weeks, but he was dreading the conversation he'd need to have with her and he had been for months. It had been a year since that first trip to Inverness, six months since he'd married her, and not one of those days had gone by where he didn't love her more than the last. It was all of those things that combined to make him loathe what was about to happen.

As they dismounted, he saw her step outside to stretch, and he caught her eye. The smile that appeared on her face the instant she saw him broke his heart, as he knew he was about to take it away. He smiled at her and nodded toward the river before handing the reins of his horse to one of the stable lads and walking that way, knowing full well she would make her excuses and join him there. He did his best to steel himself as he walked, to will himself the strength he'd need to say the words he must, but his stomach was in painful knots, reminding him that no matter what he was trying to act like, he was shattered.

It didn't take her long to arrive, and she flung her arms around him with a happy laugh. "Alasdair! Ah, I am glad ye have come home! I missed ye."

Alasdair held her tightly, perhaps tighter, and longer than he would normally do. "I missed ye, too," he whispered, unable to raise his voice without her hearing the emotion that choked it.

Emi, however, knew him better than that. With a frown, she stepped back and looked at him. "Alasdair, what is wrong?"

He could only look at her, wondering how he could say it in a way that wouldn't break her. He didn't want to tell her, didn't want to say the words, but he knew he must. It had to come from him and no one else. He couldn't leave her to find out with all the others.

"Alasdair …" she repeated, her voice apprehensive now.

"Emi, we …" he began and then sighed. "We are to war."

"No," Emi whispered, the color draining from her face.

"We are to meet the prince in Glenfinnan in a few weeks' time with a regiment of Stewart men."

She shook her head as if to deny what she'd just heard. "Ye cannae. Alasdair, ye cannae go!"

"I have to. I dinnae have a choice, Em."

"Ye do! Say no!"

"I cannae tell the chief no, and ye know that perfectly well. This is my job."

"I will tell him! I will tell him ye cannae go because … because …" she faltered, searching for something, anything. "Because ye have to wed me and I am —"

"No," he said, voice firm. "Dinnae even *think* about doing such a thing. If ye think that will keep me here, ye are wrong. He would tell ye the women will still be here to help ye through it, and that is all. Ye cannae stop this, Em."

"I can go to the prince myself!" she shouted at him before she burst into tears. "He does nae know ye, so he would nae care if ye were there or nae! Tell me where he is, and I will leave right this moment! I will walk the whole of the way to tell him he cannae have ye!"

Alasdair pulled her back into his arms and held her there even though she struggled before she gave up and just sobbed against his chest. "I am so sorry," he whispered. "Ye knew this was a possibility when all of it began. Ye were tying yerself to a soldier, and I told ye I was afraid this was coming."

"I never thought —"

"I know, and I had hoped ye never would have to experience it, but we do."

"How long will ye be away?"

"I cannae say." He couldn't even say if he would ever return, though he wouldn't dare say that to her. "I wanted to tell ye myself so that ye heard it from no other. I want ye to know I love ye even though I may nae have as much time for ye from now until we depart. I will do my best, but it is nae as though I am coming home to ye each night a husband in the way the chief knows. I have no excuse to leave the barracks."

"Ye could tell him; we could do it before ye leave."

Alasdair sighed. "There is nae time now, love. Ye are a wife to me in all ways but that, and that is what truly matters. When this is all over, I swear to ye we will make it final."

Emi stepped back from him and wiped her eyes on her sleeve, but Alasdair could tell she was heartbroken even if she would try to put on a brave face. "I will come up with a reason to explain my tears when I go back inside."

"No, dinnae," he said. "No more hiding. To ask ye to do so is unfair, and the time for such a thing has passed, along with the peace that held it."

She leaned up and wrapped her arms around his shoulders, and he held her close as he felt her body shake with sobs. He wanted to give over to tears as well, the pain in his chest was acute and unrelenting. He hated to leave her, and if he could find any way around it, he would take it. It was a thought he never would've entertained before, but the thought of being without her for God knew how long was almost too much to bear. Once they left, who could say when he would see her again, or if he would. It was that thought, along with hearing her cry, that brought his own tears. With her he didn't have to pretend that he wasn't upset or afraid, and he was both of those things. He might be a trained soldier, but war meant facing the very real possibility of his own death and the thought was terrifying.

Once they'd both calmed themselves a bit, it was time to go back, and they walked farther down the river and then up onto the road so that it wouldn't look like they were coming back from a tryst. That wasn't what he wanted others to see and think; he wanted them to see and know the truth of it. Her arm in his, they walked in silence, as there was nothing left to say now. When they reached the yard, he turned to her and pulled her into a kiss there in front of everyone. When he parted from her, he lifted her hand and kissed it before bowing and gently pressing it to his forehead in love and devotion, the same as one would do for a sovereign. The gesture left absolutely no doubt that the pair were in a serious courtship, and though people stared in shock, none of them would or could challenge it. From where they stood behind him, Fergus and Cailean stopped working and grinned.

Alasdair smiled at Emi and gave her hand a gentle squeeze before he kissed her forehead. "Tonight," he whispered against her skin. He felt the almost imperceptible nod of agreement before he parted from her to rejoin the others in their work.

***

Emi wanted to smile, wanted to be happy at his public display of affection and no longer having to hide her feelings for him, but she found she couldn't. She felt numb, wishing none of this was real. She would hide her feelings forever if it meant he wouldn't go, but she knew he would. He had to, just as Fergus did, Cailean did, and Evander did.

Evander.

Emi gasped softly before she turned and ran back to the kitchens. "Maman!" Emi shouted breathlessly as she threw open the door to the kitchen's parlor.

Bridgette looked up from her seat, eyes red and swollen, while Evander knelt at her feet, holding her hand. Seeing Emi, she fell into fresh tears.

"Emi," Evander said, the pain clear in his hoarse voice. "I … we are …"

"I know," Emi said, shutting the door behind her. "Evander, I …" she whispered, unable to get further without dissolving in tears.

Evander stood up and embraced her, the two of them crying together, equally as frightened by what this could all mean and all they might lose. Emi stood to lose both a brother and a husband in the coming conflict, and there was nothing she could do to stop it. She was as powerless as either of the men were, more so even, and all she could do, all any of them could do now, was pray. Pray for the men about to leave for an uncertain future, for the lives and families they would leave behind, for the souls of the ones who would inevitably not return.

The door opened again, and Crisdean entered, momentarily startled by the scene he'd just walked in on before recovering himself. "Emilia, I need ye to set to work immediately. My wife and sons are leaving for France as soon as they can pack. I need ye to prepare food for them to take on their journey."

"Yes, Chief," Emi said, and Crisdean's face saddened for a moment before he departed.

Emi left the room and went to her area of the kitchen, getting to work on preparing baskets for the party to travel with. There had to be food that wouldn't spoil, but she could send other things for them to eat before they boarded the ship for France. She let herself get lost in the task so that she wouldn't have to think about anything else, about any of the people she loved never coming home again once they left this place in a few weeks' time. Lamb curled himself in and out around her legs, seeming to sense that she needed him, and she allowed herself a moment to pick him up and cuddle him against her. His purring brought her to tears again, but these were silent, and Lamb made no effort to get away as they dropped from her cheeks into his orange fur.

Once the baskets were packed and ready, she took them out to where the carriage was already waiting and being loaded. She handed them off as Crisdean hugged his two young sons, Alexander and James, goodbye. The boys were too young to go to war, but not by much, and he was sending them to where they'd be safe in case the worst happened. Even if he fell, the clan would still have a leader, even if it were in exile. At 16, Alexander looked every bit his father, with his height, green eyes, light brown hair, and infectious smile. James, who was 15, favored his mother far more with his fair hair and blue eyes, along with his quiet nature. Both were maturing into fine-looking young men who were both educated and kind, aware of the duties that would one day be theirs and learning from their father since their earliest days.

Alexander paused, his foot on the step of the carriage, and turned toward Emi, looking at her with a sort of sadness that surprised her. "Goodbye, Emilia," he said, his voice quiet. "I will miss …" he began before he stopped, seeming to change what he'd wanted to say mid-sentence. "I will miss seeing ye and miss all of yer wonderful food. Ye stay safe, aye?"

"Aye, I shall, Master Alexander. I will miss seeing yer smiling faces each morning. Thank ye for yer kind words, and I will keep ye all in my prayers."

Alexander nodded and climbed into the carriage, James offering a shy wave as he followed.

Crisdean's wife Màiri embraced him, weeping, and he held her tight against him. Emi took it in with curiosity, having never seen this much emotion displayed between the chief and his wife before. It wasn't that she thought it was impossible, but they usually weren't this public about it. She wasn't sure why it surprised her to see a wife weeping while saying goodbye to a husband she wasn't sure she'd ever see again, the same as she would soon do with Alasdair. Crisdean kissed her and whispered words of farewell before ushering her to the carriage and helping her inside. He shut the door and took her hand as she extended it through the lowered window, kissing it before nodding to the driver, who got the team underway with a click of his tongue and a snap of the reins. Crisdean held her hand until the carriage pulled them apart, then stood there watching his family depart, looking lost and desolate over not being with them.

When he noticed Emi standing, there was a sad, half-hearted smile and a nod before he turned and went back inside. Emi looked back at the road, where the dust kicked up by the carriage was already settling. Why could they also not go to France? They could do it, she and Alasdair. They could leave here at night and catch a ship from Inverness; she was sure they had enough money between them. But what would they do once they arrived? Knowing no one, no money, no home. Alasdair could tend horses somewhere, but that wouldn't start right away. With a sigh, she shook her head. It was nonsense to even think of it because Alasdair would never go, never abandon his chief, his clan, or his duty, no matter how much she pleaded with him.

Supper that night was quiet, everyone lost in their own thoughts as word spread across the estate that the Stewart men had been called to war against the English. There were also whispers about Alasdair Stewart kissing Emilia in front of everyone in the courtyard and how they surely were courting, but how serious was it really? Emi ignored all of it, serving at the high table and waiting for the moment where she might be dismissed. When the moment finally came, she wasted no time in hurrying back to the kitchens and taking off her apron before making her way to the cottage. It was dark when she arrived, as she'd known it would be, and she lit a candle before moving to the hearth to get a fire going before Alasdair arrived.

"Let me help ye," he said softly, suddenly appearing beside her like a phantom. Taking the flint in his hands, he got the fire going as Emi shut the door behind him.

The pair stood in silence for a moment before Emi ran into his arms and hugged him, burying her face against his chest, and letting go of the tears that had been threatening since she'd been tasked to pack the baskets. Alasdair said nothing, holding her close to him. They both knew without it needing to be said that this was the last night they'd be spending together in who knew how long, maybe even the last one ever. Emi lifted her face from his chest and looked up at him, finding his expression anxious and sad. Leaning up on her toes, she kissed him, her hands tightening on the front of his coat, feeling him press her against him as he returned it. If this was their last night together, she was going to make it count.

***

"Emilia."

Emi looked up from the vegetables she was cutting, curtsying when she saw Crisdean. "Aye, Chief?"

"I need to see ye in my study, please," Crisdean said before turning and walking away.

Emi's mind raced, wondering if she'd done something wrong. Did he know about her and Alasdair beyond what everyone else knew? She wiped her hands on her apron and then removed it before she hurried to the chief's study. Outside of the closed doors, she took a deep breath to calm herself and released it before knocking.

"Enter."

Emi opened the door and stepped inside, shutting it behind her. "Ye wished to see me, sir?" she asked with a small curtsy. "Did ye wish to go over provisioning for yerself? Or did ye need some tea or something special for supper?"

"None of that. Come sit down," he said as he gestured toward a chair in front of his desk.

"Aye, sir," she said, closing the distance and sitting as instructed, though she was wary. She'd never sat in this room, not once, and doing so now made her uneasy.

"Emilia," he began, looking a bit unsure, the first time she'd seen such a thing in his face. "What do ye remember of yer mother?"

"My mother? Naught, sir, only what Maman has told me."

"I assume that is the same about yer father, then."

"Aye, sir, maybe even less about him than about her."

"There is something ye need to know, Emilia, before I leave. It is something ye should have been told long ago, but it never seemed like it was necessary to upset the things ye knew about yer life. Now that I am facing the very real possibility of nae returning here, I cannae and will nae hold my tongue on it any longer."

"Ye should nae say that," Emi said. "Ye will come back. I believe it in my heart and so should ye."

"That may be, but it does nae change what I wish to say."

"All right, sir."

"What I am about to tell ye will come as a shock, I know, and I ask that ye simply let me finish before ye speak. Will ye?"

"Aye," Emi said, nodding to allow him to go on.

"Helena … yer mother …" He sighed and closed his eyes. "When I was a young man, no older than Alasdair is now, I was in love with yer mother. She felt the same for me, and we courted for a time until my father found out. She was nae what he considered 'suitable' for me, being the daughter of a tenant farmer. He desired me to marry a woman of higher birth from another clan for alliance, though I had leave to choose who might suit me that way. I was instructed to end my courtship with Helena immediately and, needless to say, I was devastated. So was she, but she also understood. She told me she had always suspected such a thing might happen, but that she loved me all the same and always would. Nae long after that, she came to me and told me she was with child. I knew the child was mine; I was the only one who had been with her, and I knew that for a fact. She said she was going to marry a young man who had always wanted to court her, and she was nae asking for me to do anything, she just wished for me to know."

Emi sat still as stone, hardly breathing.

"I was there as she stood in the church and wed him, my father forced me to be, and I wanted to scream. I knew she did nae love him, that she carried my bairn, and that he would accept it as his own even though he knew it was nae. It was the best thing she could do, I knew that, but oh, my heart broke into a thousand pieces that day, and I dinnae think it has ever truly recovered. I married Màiri nae long after, and while I cared for her, I did nae love her, at least nae then. Such has grown between us, and for that I am thankful. I told her about yer mother after we married, told her about the bairn. I wanted to acknowledge it when it was born but nae put it above any children we may have together. She accepted it with grace because it happened before we had even begun courting. By this time, my father was in France, exiled there, though I wrote and told him of my intention to acknowledge the child and provide Helena a small sum on a regular basis to assist her. This was agreed to as long as I did nae announce it or even tell the child it was mine."

"When the child was born," he continued, "Helena came to me so that I might meet my bairn and choose a name. I remember the moment still, how small and beautiful the child was, my first child. My daughter. Helena chose Emilia but yer middle name, Cairistiona, was for me. I wept as I held ye, Emilia, wanting naught more than to break every vow and keep ye as my own. I could nae bear the thought of watching Darach claim my child in the same way he had claimed the lass I loved, but in the end, I had no other choice. When Helena and Darach both died, there was a moment in my pure grief where I wanted to take ye in — I was yer father — but I knew I could nae. Bridgette and Andrew were well-suited to the task, yer mother trusted them, and so I gave the small sum once meant for yer mother to Bridgette for yer care. I have had the privilege of watching ye grow right before my eyes with ye in the kitchens, and as ye got older, I could see myself in ye. I cannae keep silent any longer, nae with what is coming. Ye have the right to know where ye came from, Emilia, *who* ye truly came from."

Emi sat in stunned silence, trying to take in all that he'd said. Her father was not her father. Her father lived and sat before her now, letting go of a secret he'd held for 20 years, asking for her to understand.

"Ye … are my father?" she finally said.

"Aye, lass. Ye are mine as surely as those two boys who left here in that carriage two days ago. I wanted to send ye with them, but Màiri would nae hear of it, and I cannae say I dinnae understand. Ye are a reminder that she has never held my whole heart, and to take ye with her was too much to ask. Nae only that, but I would nae part ye from Alasdair. Nae now."

"Sir, I —"

Crisdean held up a hand. "I know ye have begun courting recently, and I cannae say I am displeased by it. He is a fine lad, and I am sorry I must pull him away to war."

Emi closed her eyes, forcing the tears in her eyes down her cheeks. "I am sorry, too."

"I want ye to know that everything I have given ye here, ye have earned. It has nae come because of who ye are. In fact, ye had to work harder to overcome that in my mind."

Emi nodded. "I dinnae know what to think or say or how I should act."

"The same as ye always have, I am afraid. In the end, my being yer father means naught to anyone but me. I want ye to know ye have a father who loves ye and always has, who has watched ye grow from the moment ye entered this world and watched with pride as ye changed into the beautiful woman ye have become. Ye are the only piece of my sweet Helena that remains to me."

Emi broke down, covering her face with her hands, and Crisdean rose from his seat. Gently, he lifted her from the chair and hugged her, finally able to hold his own daughter for the first time since the day he'd named her and held her in his arms when she was but days old. Emi wrapped her arms around him and wept as he stroked her hair gently. Something felt right about this, about finally belonging. Though Bridgette and Andrew had loved and cared for her, she'd always known she wasn't theirs. The two to whom she truly belonged were buried in a churchyard, or so she'd thought. To know that her father had been here all along, watching over her and caring for her in silence, was as heartbreaking as it was comforting. How painful must it have been for him to see her each day and have her look at him without a shred of recognition?

"My own sweet bairn," he whispered, his voice choked with emotion. "I cannae tell ye what I feel to have ye know the truth, to be able to embrace ye like a father should. How many times I have imagined this and longed for it. Ye mean more to me than ye could ever possibly understand, and though I still have to reflect the old lie outwardly, I will know that ye know who ye are, who I am, and that I love ye beyond measure. Ye are born of a Stewart chief, and I can see that fire in ye and the iron in yer spine."

Born of a Stewart chief. Those ancestors whose portraits hung here were her own, her grandfathers and great grandfathers. The next chief would be her brother, and the blood of the men who had settled these lands, run them, fought and died leading them, ran through her veins just as much as it did his. It was hard to comprehend.

"I will nae let ye down," she whispered. "I will make ye proud, as well as the spirits of those who have gone before ye."

Crisdean pulled back and smiled down at her, smoothing some tears from her cheeks. "My darling, ye already have. Now come, how about we see to yer provisioning for yer old Da, hm?"

Emi summoned all of her courage to change her response to him for the first time in her life. "Aye, Father."

***

The courtyard bustled with men, horses, and carts. The officers were busy rounding up their men, while final preparations were being made for the provisions and weapons carts. Emi was there to help make sure all of the provisions were packed and accounted for, the green cloak around her shoulders to keep her warm from the early morning chill. She was exhausted, having worked all hours in order to make sure the regiment had as much bread and hardtack as the kitchens could send. She'd been able to convince Crisdean to spare one of the junior officers to ride to Inverness with a list for Mr. MacMillan so that they could also take dry ingredients with them. Flour, salt, oats, and anything else she could come up with.

Emi and Bridgette had already said goodbye to Evander, as difficult as it had been, and Bridgette had left the rest of the provision checks to Emi, unable to contain her emotion and watch her son leave. The call to form up came as Crisdean exited and his officers mounted up, and Emi ceased her final checks, looking for Alasdair. They'd been unable to spend any true time together after that first night, both of them busy seeing to what they had to, and that left very little time for anything else. From behind her, his arms slid around her, and she closed her eyes, drinking in her last feel of him for goodness knew how long. She turned around and looked up at him, eyes brimming with tears, and he sighed.

"I know. My heart is breaking, too. I never understood what the others felt when we left to go out against another clan, but I do now. I will miss ye terribly and be thinking of ye all the time. Be safe, for I cannae bear to lose ye. Keep a watchful eye, for who knows what might happen if anyone takes it into their heads to raid while we are gone. Ye know where to go if they do?"

"Aye," Emi nodded. "Ye be safe, too. Dinnae take risks and be a hero, Alasdair Stewart. Ye stay safe, and ye come home to me. Ye have a promise to keep."

"Aye, I do, and that is what will protect me."

"Let us be underway if we are ready!" Crisdean called out.

Emi's heart seized for a moment and then ached. Alasdair gave her no time to speak and gave her a long kiss instead, knowing it would have to sustain them both. "I love ye," he whispered.

"And I ye," she replied before she gave him another small kiss. "Now go before the chief drags ye away by yer ear."

Alasdair gave an amused half-smile, hugged her again, and then departed. Emi watched him mount his horse, looking so strong and regal, every bit the warrior he was. Crisdean glanced back at her and smiled, and Emi placed her hand over her heart in silent acknowledgment to a father's farewell, one only he could see. The order to march was called out, and the mass started forward down the road and away from home, and those left standing there couldn't help but wonder how many of them would never return.

Chapter 9

"Dinnae touch me! He will kill ye when he finds out!"

"He can do nothing because he is dead," the English officer said.

"No …" Emi choked out. "No, he cannae be! Ye are lying!"

"I most certainly am not," he said as he grabbed her arm and started to walk her backwards.

Emi struggled against him to no avail, and he reached out his free hand to lift something from her neck before grasping it and yanking hard, causing her to scream in pain and fear.

"This will make a lovely gift for my wife. Thank you," he said. "And *you* will make a lovely gift for *me*," he said as he shoved her forcefully through the door.

Emi screamed, and Alasdair sat up in the darkness, shaking, his breathing heavy, looking around him as the echoes of her screams rang in his ears. The other officers slept soundly around him, and he closed his eyes, trying to catch his breath. It was just a nightmare, thank God. Emi. His Emi. He missed her more than there were words for, and he prayed constantly for her safety. He hated that he wasn't there to protect her or his mother from anything that might happen, hated that he had no idea how they were or if they were safe, or how they were passing the winter. He laid back down, staring at the ceiling of the hall where they were sleeping. They were fortunate that, as part of the victorious regiments of Falkirk, they'd been allowed to remain at Callendar House to keep watch for Cumberland. This afforded them a warm and dry place to sleep for the first time in months, and there wasn't a one of them who wasn't thankful for it.

After the battle at Falkirk, he'd seen some of the women of the more local clans weeping over the bodies of their fallen, and it had broken his heart. That could've been Emi, and still could be, though his body would never be returned to her to mourn over. It would be buried in a pit with all the rest. He'd gotten lucky this time, the cut to his side he'd gotten during the battle had been glancing. It was painful and would leave a scar, but at least he was alive. It wasn't the first time during this campaign that he'd had a close call, but this was the first to leave what would become a permanent reminder.

Reaching out, he slipped a hand into his sporran where it rested near his head, and pulled out a small, carefully wrapped parcel. It was a gift for her if he ever made it home again. When they'd been in Glasgow, he was walking with the chief when he'd seen it in a shop window. A beautiful, small pendant, made up of tiny purple bluebells encased forever in glass, and he'd been taking the time to study it while Crisdean was speaking to someone.

"A lovely little bauble," Crisdean said. Alasdair jumped at the unexpected presence beside him and looked over. "I know just who ye have that in mind for."

Alasdair nodded. "Aye. I know she would love it and it would look so beautiful on her, but I dinnae have the money for such an item so here it will remain."

"Aye, ye do," Crisdean said, pressing some coins into his palm. "Go on. Ye have well earned this, lad. Consider it my reward to ye for all ye have done thus far."

Alasdair looked down at his hand and then up at Crisdean quickly. "No, I cannae …"

"Ye can, and ye will. I will brook no refusal from ye, and if ye dinnae go in and get it, I will buy it and give it to her myself just to spite ye."

Alasdair gave a small amused smile and then did as he was told. As expected, it was something far beyond his own means, but the money Crisdean gave him was more than enough. Now, here in this hall, he held it in his hand and thought of her. He so badly wished to give it to her, but who knew when they'd be home again? He could see her face, hear her voice and her laugh. With a sigh, he slipped it back inside and tried to force himself to go back to sleep.

***

Emi stood in the kitchens, kneading dough and trying to lose herself in it as she usually did so that she could keep her thoughts at bay. The men had been away for over six months now, and she was starting to wonder if she'd ever see any of them again. There had been no word, no idea of where they'd been or where they were now, or even how the war was going. A teardrop hit the dough, and seeing it made her slam her fist into it in anger before she stepped back from the counter. She didn't want to cry; it felt as though it was all any of them had been doing. The hall was quiet at dinner and supper without the men, filled with only the quiet talk of the elderly, the women, and children who worried about husbands, fathers, and brothers. She sat down against the wall, resting her forehead against her hands, and felt Lamb crawl into her lap. Sighing, she took one hand and gently stroked his fur, finding it at least a little soothing.

A faint sound got her attention, and she frowned, turning her head to look at the open door, left that way to keep the kitchens cool during the heat of baking. She wasn't sure if she was imagining it, but it came again on the wind, growing louder and clearer: pipes and drums. Her heart froze, and her breath caught. She put Lamb down in the next instant, scrambling up and running outside to the yard, joining the people coming out of the castle in just enough time to see the Stewart men march into the yard behind Crisdean and his officers. There were loud cheers, and Emi scanned the faces of the officers for Alasdair. When she saw him, she thought she might either faint, weep in relief, or both. He was clearly looking for her, too, because as soon as he saw her, he was off his horse. Emi shoved her way through the crowd, desperate to reach him.

"Alasdair!" she called out, frantic, and suddenly he was there and she was in his arms as she broke down in tears.

"Ach, Emi, my love. God, I have missed ye."

"Ye are home! Thank the Lord! Is it over?"

"No," he said. "Just a small respite, but we shall make the most of it and enjoy our good fortune to see each other."

"Aye, we will," she said, hugging him again.

He didn't let the hug last too long before he kissed her hungrily, craving that contact with her just as much as she did with him. When he parted from her, she bounced in excitement and laughed before embracing him again. Alasdair laughed as well, the relief and the sheer joy of having her near him again plain in his expression. In that brief moment when she'd seen him before he'd spotted her, he looked exhausted, haunted, older. He needed rest, that was clear to her, though with his happiness, it was all wiped away and forgotten, allowing him to be himself again.

"Emi!"

She looked over as the familiar voice of Evander called her name.

"Evander!" she squealed in delight as she ran to embrace him.

He caught her with a grin and hugged her tight. "Ach, there is my wee sister. It is so good to see ye, and I cannae tell ye how much I have missed ye. Where is Mam?"

"Here somewhere, I am sure." It was then she noticed the

addition of the badge to his hat and reached out to touch it. "Evander, ye were promoted!"

"Aye," he said with a proud smile. "Made a full officer in Glasgow."

"Oh! I am so proud of ye!"

"I knew ye would be. The others are all right too, ye know. Fergus, Cailean."

"Thank God for it. I dinnae know what I would have done if I had lost any of ye. I dinnae think I could have borne it!"

"Ye did almost lose Alasdair a few times, though."

"What?" Emi gasped, horrified.

"Aye, he was wounded at Prestonpans but recovered. He survived a battle with Cumberland's dragoons at Clifton Moor even though they faced 4,000 to their 1,000. Then, just recently, he took a nasty cut from a sword at Falkirk. He is the luckiest bastard I know."

Emi looked back at Alasdair, who waited patiently for her at a respectful distance, and smiled when she caught his eye.

"Go on with ye; I will see ye later at home. Yer husband waits for ye."

Emi nudged him with an elbow. "I shall see ye indeed," she replied before she rejoined Alasdair.

Alasdair gathered her into his arms again and held her close to him. "I have to go for a while, I need to help unpack things and stable the horses, but I will find ye the moment I am done."

"Of course," she said, kissing his cheek. "Go on, and I will see ye soon."

He nodded, and she watched him go back to his men and gather the reins of his horse to lead it off.

"When he comes for you, you are released to go," Bridgette said. "It has been so long since you have seen him, and who knows how long you will have before they leave again."

Emi turned and sighed. "Aye, thank ye, Maman," she said, hugging her in thanks.

"You deserve this time, and I know he will need the comfort of you near him. When he comes, and after he sees his mother, take him home and let him rest. I will let the chief know that I told you to do so and will be filling in for you. I do not think he will object."

"Likely nae. I appreciate it more than I can say."

"I know you do. Go on, finish up what you were doing so that you are ready to leave when he comes."

Emi nodded and headed back to the kitchens to continue her work, unable to stop smiling, until he came to collect her about an hour later. Hand in hand, they walked the road back toward the loch and their respective homes, though Emi had a basket over one arm. Alasdair was quiet, but Emi could tell it was because he was nearly asleep on his feet. Coira screamed in joy to see her son and hugged him, weeping. It was a sight that brought tears to Emi's eyes.

"Ach, Emi! And ye here, too! Of course ye are. He would have found ye first!"

"Aye, I did," Alasdair replied. "She was there when we came in."

"I was so happy to see him," Emi said. "Maman, she —" But she stopped, worrying her lip.

"She what, lass?" Coira asked.

"She has given me leave to stay with Alasdair for the next few days, I will nae have to go in, but I dinnae want to take him away from ye. I should have thought of that before."

"Dinnae be silly, lass. Ye are his wife; his home is with ye now. Alasdair, ye look exhausted. Ye go rest with yer bride, let her see to ye, and come back to me when ye are ready. To know ye are alive and safe here at home will sustain me."

Alasdair looked surprised. "Are ye sure?"

"Aye, I am. Go on with ye now."

Alasdair kissed her cheek and stepped outside with Emi. "Home?"

"Aye, home," she said, starting down the path toward the cottage they'd used before the world changed.

When Emi opened the door and stepped inside, Alasdair looked as though he might weep with relief. Everything was neat and tidy, all of it the same as he'd last seen it. Even though he'd been gone, Emi lived here on her own, keeping the house and waiting for him to return to her. With the chief gone, there was no reason for her to stay in her room at the castle.

"I know ye are exhausted, but could ye fetch water while I get the fire started?" she asked.

"Aye, of course. Now that I am here with ye, I feel as though I have more energy than I have had in days. I will need to make a few trips though; I need a bath desperately," he said, chuckling.

Emi grinned and turned toward the hearth as he picked up the water buckets and headed for the loch. As Alasdair returned with water, she set it to warm in several small pots, as it would be quicker that way. When he made the last trip, he set the buckets down and shut the door. "It is nice to be home but strange, too," he said.

"Strange how?"

He offered a gentle shrug. "I have been at war so long I almost forgot what this was like."

Emi stood, looking at him with sadness. "I am sorry; it must have been horrible."

"Aye, but I will nae trouble ye with that. That is for me to keep, nae ye," he replied as he reached out and stroked her cheek. "Ye feel like a dream to me."

"Do I?"

"I dreamt of ye so many times, love. Dreamt of ye just to wake up alone in some cold tent in who knows where."

Emi covered his hand with her own. "I am real this time."

"Aye, ye are, and I am thanking God for it over and over."

"Let us get ye cleaned up so that ye can sleep. No matter what ye said before getting the water, ye look as though ye are about to drop."

"Feel like it, too," he admitted.

Emi led him to a chair and sat him down before she turned

and grabbed a pot, a rag, and soap. She helped him to get his boots off, then turned away to work on preparing more water so he'd have enough. He could and would bathe himself. After a few moments, she heard him hiss in pain and turned around to see him gently smoothing the cloth over a still-healing cut on his side that went diagonally from the top of his ribs on his right and very nearly ended at the top of his hip.

"Alasdair!" she cried out as she got up and hurried over to him.

He looked up at her, seeming puzzled by her reaction. "It is naught. It is healing well."

"Naught! Someone tried to cut ye open!"

"Aye, and they failed."

She looked up at him, shocked and a little afraid. She'd hoped he would come out entirely unscathed, but that was impossible. "I really did almost lose ye," she said, tears in her eyes.

"But ye did nae, and that is what ye should remember," he said in a soothing but firm tone, letting her know he had no interest in speaking about it.

"Ye are right, of course. Ye finish up, and I will help ye wash yer hair."

"Thank ye," he said, offering her a tired smile.

"Did ye want something to eat?" she asked as she returned to the hearth. "I brought some venison stew we made for supper tonight and bread."

"Ach, venison stew sounds like a bit of heaven right now," he said. "Cannae remember the last time I had a proper meal."

"Did ye run out of supplies?"

"No, but the options are rather limited when we dinnae have an Emi to cook for us," he replied, following it with a gentle laugh.

"I will go with ye when ye leave again to make sure ye all eat properly then. That happens, aye? Some clans bring women along to cook and clean and the like?"

"No," Alasdair said, turning around and looking at her in panic. "Ye cannae go; ye must stay here."

"But —"

"No," he said again. "Emi, ye dinnae understand what it is like, how dangerous it is. As much as I hate being apart from ye, I know ye are safer here. Ye could die out there just as easily as I could," he said as he gestured to the doorway, "and I cannae have it. Please."

"All right," she said, trying to sound reassuring as she took his hand. "Dinnae fret, Alasdair."

"Sorry," he said as he relaxed a bit and sighed. "I just need ye to be safe."

"I am," she said, giving his hand a squeeze. "I will warm the stew as soon as ye step out, and it should be ready by the time we finish yer hair."

"Aye," he said, going back to scrubbing himself down.

While he resumed his task, Emi took a clean shirt she'd made him while he was away and hung it over a chair near the fire so that it would be warm, and draped toweling over another chair to do the same. When he stepped out, she was waiting, and he let out a happy sigh when the warm toweling covered him. Sitting him down in a chair, Emi pulled over the wash basin he'd used and put it behind him. With fresh, warm water, she wet his hair and then took the soap to it, though she was sure he fell asleep for a few moments while she was doing it. After she rinsed it out, she took some of the toweling and dried it before handing him the fresh shirt to put on.

"I cannae tell ye how grand it is to have clean clothing to put on."

"I can imagine," she said, chuckling as she set a bowl of stew in front of him.

"Oh, ye angel," he breathed before he picked up the spoon and took a bite, letting loose a small moan of happiness as though he hadn't eaten in years.

Emi could tell that even though he could eat it so fast he'd barely taste it, he'd decided to take his time and savor every bite of it. The bread and fresh butter got the same reaction from him, and she kissed the top of his head before she began to run the comb through his hair. By the time he'd finished eating, all she could do was help him collapse into bed, and he seemed to be asleep before she'd even drawn the blanket over him.

"My poor Alasdair," she whispered, stroking his cheek. "Rest well, ye are home now."

When she rose in the morning, Alasdair didn't stir. It had been so wonderful to sleep beside him once more, to know he was there and alive and not dead on some battlefield, staring up at a sky he could no longer see. She gathered his uniform up into her basket and walked to the castle where she could use the larger washtubs. The clothing was filthy and torn, still bloody in places where he'd not been able to wash it out, and it horrified her to see. What had happened to him? How much of this blood was his own? She scrubbed it out as best she could, thankful that she'd spent the time weaving fabric and tartan with Coira, Anna, and Ealasaid, and using that wool to sew new shirts, kilts, coats, and waistcoats for Alasdair, Cailean, and Fergus.

After setting the clothing out to dry, she decided to check the supply wagons to see what was left and what was needed. With no certainty as to how long they'd have until the regiment left again, it wouldn't do to leave it too long if they had to send to Inverness for supplies. Once she had the numbers, Emi sat down to write a letter to Mr. MacMillan with what they needed and called one of the older stable lads to ride with haste to Inverness and deliver it, then wait for his reply.

She gathered up the clothing, as well as the dry goods she'd put aside for herself while Alasdair was away and made her way back home. The clothing could dry before their own fire, and she didn't want to be gone too long in case he woke up. Her worries were for nothing, however, as he was still deeply asleep. She smiled to see him there and hung out his uniform pieces to dry before having a bit of bread. As she was finishing, she heard a yowling at the door and raised an eyebrow. Getting up, she went to the door and opened it to find Lamb, who prompt-ly made his way inside as soon as the door was open. Emi stared at him in surprise, as he'd never come here before.

"What are ye doing here, ye great lump?" she asked as she bent down to stroke him. He purred and pressed himself into her hand before making his way to the bed and jumping onto it. With even louder purrs, he rubbed his face against Alasdair's shoulder before curling up beside him and closing his eyes.

"Oh, I see," Emi said with a wry smile. "Ye are throwing me over for him, are ye? Well, ye have good taste."

Chapter 10

When Alasdair awoke the following morning, he yawned and stretched before he realized he wasn't in a tent. Blinking and rubbing the sleep from his eyes, he looked around and realized he was home. It hadn't been a dream; he really *was* here. He closed his eyes and let out a deep breath of relief. But if he was home, where was Emi? He didn't get much of a chance to finish the thought before a purring, furry orange face was pressed against his.

"Lamb?" Alasdair said in confusion and surprise, reaching up to find the cat on his chest. "Ach, it is ye! How are ye, eh? Keeping busy with those mice, I bet. It is good to see ye, ye know. I never thought I would miss a cat, but here ye are."

"He has nae moved since yesterday."

Alasdair turned his head to find Emi at the table, smiling at him. "No?"

"He found his way here somehow; he must have known ye had come back because he meowed at the door for me to let him in. He went right to ye and curled up, and he has nae left yer side. He never comes here, so I am surprised."

"Ah, ye softie," Alasdair said, smiling. "Yer a good lad, Lamb."

"Would ye like some breakfast?"

"Aye, please," Alasdair said, sitting up and shifting Lamb to the bed beside him. He was a bit stiff, but that wasn't a surprise. Standing, he stretched again and felt the stiffness ease as his muscles warmed up. "Be right back," he said as he realized just how badly he needed to relieve himself.

Lamb made his way to one of the chairs set by the fire as Alasdair headed for the door and hopped up onto it, curling up in a ball and going back to sleep, making Emi laugh. "Ye lazy thing."

"It is so good to see ye," Alasdair said when he returned.

"And I feel the same," she said, giving him a gentle kiss. "Ye need nae worry about reporting for duty. Yer mam came to tell me that someone stopped to tell ye that ye had the week on leave to get some rest."

"Thank Christ," he said, sitting down. "God knows we could all use it. I dinnae think we have stopped moving since November."

"So long!" she said as she put a cup of tea down in front of him before going back to the hearth to work on his breakfast.

"Aye. Ye cannae imagine all of the places I have been."

"Tell me?"

"Edinburgh, Glasgow, Stirling … England."

Emi fumbled the spoon she was using and turned around to look at him, wide-eyed. "England!"

"Aye. We made it as far as Derby before we turned back."

"Where is that?"

"Four days' march from London."

"Ye were that close!"

"Aye."

"Then why did ye turn back?"

"We had nae the numbers for it. Five thousand against thirty thousand are impossible odds, and none of us felt like dying."

"Thirty thousand," Emi repeated, trying to imagine the number. "I am glad ye lot had some sense then."

Alasdair laughed. "Aye, well, it was nae our choice; we just went where we were told." Emi made a face and turned back to her cooking, which only made him laugh harder. "I feel the same, love."

"What was England like?"

"Flat," he replied before taking a drink of his tea. "But also cold and miserable in the winter, just like here."

"It does nae seem to make a bit of sense to go there in the winter when they are surely resting their men rather than marching all around the place."

"I tend to agree with ye. I would think they would be more ready for us in winter with nowhere else to go. I am sure that is part of the reason we turned back."

"Again, at least someone had some sense."

"Someone in command did, aye."

"Nae the prince? Is he nae in charge?"

"Aye, but he has advisors and the chiefs to help him."

"Did ye see him?"

"I have, aye, and have spoken with him."

"Really!" Emi exclaimed, turning around with an excited expression. "What was he like?"

"Rather friendly, believe it or nae. He saw me with the chief and spoke to me for a bit, asking me about myself. I told him about ye, my darling one who was waiting for me at home, and about how fair ye were. He told me he wished he could see such a beauty for himself, and the chief told him I spoke true and ye were as fair as I said."

"He said that about me?"

"Aye," Alasdair said, laughing at her incredulity. "Then he told me he would do his best to make sure I returned home to ye."

"That is very good of him. Tell him I said thank ye, if ye have the occasion to speak to him again."

"I shall. Ye would have been in pieces over his clothing. Silk, gilt embroidery, lace."

"Gilt embroidery on silk! What a picture he must make!"

"Aye, indeed. But, Em, I got to go inside Holyrood Palace."

"Did ye?" she asked as she placed a bowl of porridge in front of him and refilled his tea before taking a seat across from him. "Tell me all about it."

"It was so beautiful, love. I wish ye could see it. There are tapestries the size of three walls, so full of color. Gold everywhere, colored glass in the windows. Staircases as wide as this cottage. It would amaze ye how the finer folk live, and what I would nae give to see ye there dressed like a fine lady."

"If I were a fine lady, I would nae know ye, Alasdair, and I would nae trade ye for any of it."

He smiled and kissed her hand before taking a bite of the porridge. "Even porridge made by ye tastes like heaven. I dinnae know what ye do differently, but I am glad ye do it."

"It is a secret," she replied, winking at him. "Ah, but ye look better now that ye have had some rest."

"I feel a great deal better after a night's sleep."

"A night's sleep? Alasdair, ye slept for two days straight."

"What? Christ, I had no idea! Ye should have woken me!"

"Whatever for? Ye needed the rest and it helped, so that is what matters. I tried to wash yer uniform, but I could only do so much. It is a good thing I made ye a new set of clothing while ye were away."

"Did ye? Thank ye, love. Though, I think I will leave the clean set with ye until we are back for good."

"Do ye think that will be soon?"

"Cannae say," he said, finishing his porridge. "I hope so."

"So do I."

Reaching out, he stroked her cheek. "I missed ye so much, Em. I dreamt of ye often and prayed for ye every night."

"I prayed for ye all the time," she said. "Ye were never far from my thoughts no matter how I might try to distract myself."

Alasdair stood, making his way to where his sporran sat and picking it up, bringing it back to the table. Opening it, he pulled out a tiny package. "Almost forgot," he said, grinning.

Emi took it from him and opened it, before gasping and covering her mouth with her hand. "Alasdair," she whispered behind it. "Where did ye get this?"

"Glasgow. I saw it in a window, and I knew it was for ye. Do ye like it?"

"I love it! It is so beautiful!" she said as she reached out and picked it up to examine it. "The glass is so clear, and look at the flowers! The chain is so delicate."

Alasdair took it from her hand, stepping behind her and fastening the chain around her neck before coming back around to admire her. "Perfect, just as I knew it would be."

Emi covered it with a hand. "I never thought I would own anything so elegant as this."

"Now ye do. And dinnae fret about the money I paid or that I got it any way but honestly."

Emi smiled at him. "Thank ye, Alasdair. I will never take it off."

"It is a good thing I have more leave."

"Aye, ye need it."

"I do," he said, taking her hands and pulling her up in one swift movement, wrapping an arm around her to press her against him. "I have much missed time to make up for."

Alasdair didn't leave time for her to think about what he might mean before he kissed her in a way that told her exactly what that was.

***

At the end of the week, life resumed as normal at the castle. The officers returned to work, and the regiment gathered each day to drill. The hall was once again full of conversation and families, and Emi was thankful for it. When Crisdean sent for her, she was relieved, not having wanted to intrude upon his rest. She took herself to his study and knocked on the door, account books in hand.

"Enter."

Emi stepped inside and shut the door, then smiled at him, setting the books on a table. He smiled widely and stood, coming around the desk and opening his arms as Emi hurried to hug him. "Thank God ye are returned to us, Father. It has been dull as tombs around here with all of ye gone."

Crisdean laughed. "Has it?"

"Aye. Nae much talk, all of us were too worried to make much conversation. We did nae even celebrate Hogmanay."

"Ach, that is a shame."

"Did ye?"

"No, but we were in Glasgow trying to raise men and funds while keeping some of the clans from trying to burn it down and sack it in retribution."

"Sack it!" Emi said in surprise "Why would they do that?"

"There was great anger at Glasgow raising men for Hanover, so when we garrisoned the city, some wanted to make them pay. With the help of Cameron of Lochiel, we prevented that. I see Alasdair gave ye his gift," he said, smiling.

Emi touched it and then smiled. "Is it nae the loveliest thing ye ever saw? I still dinnae know how he afforded it, but it must have cost him dear."

"I helped him," Crisdean said, chuckling. "He was staring at it in the window, and I knew he was thinking about ye and wishing he could buy ye something so fine. He had more than earned the money I gave him, but I had to threaten to buy it and give it ye myself out of spite before he accepted it and went in to get it."

Emi laughed. "I thank ye both, then."

"No need, lass. As I told ye, he more than earned it."

"How so? Did everyone else get extra pay?"

"No," Crisdean said. "Alasdair ..." he began, then sighed. "Alasdair did some things outside of the main body, as he was asked to do. He also helped distract and draw off Wade's and Cumberland's armies. All of it was extremely dangerous, and he earned every bit of that money."

Emi looked stricken. Alasdair had been in more danger than the others, and the thought upset her.

"War is a fearful thing, my sweet lass, and none of it is easy."

"Of course," she said, shaking it off and changing the subject. "I took the liberty of taking stock of provisions and sending for more, so ye were ready when ye have to leave again. The reply from Inverness was that it would be here before the end of the week."

"Ye clever lass," Crisdean said. "Thank ye for seeing to it without even being asked."

"Ye dinnae need to thank me; it is my job, is it nae? I brought the books in case ye wish to see where we stand and if ye wish us to economize."

Crisdean took her hand with a smile. "I cannae say what a pleasure it is to see ye, Emilia. Come sit with me for a time and let us talk, then we can go over those accounts in due course."

***

"Men! Make ready!" Crisdean called out.

The regiment began to form up in their columns in the darkness before dawn, saying their final goodbyes. It had taken nearly six weeks for the order to march to come again, and this time they were ordered to Inverness, where they would join the rest of the army. Though they'd all known it would come, it seemed to come too soon, and there was fresh grief even as they moved into preparation to ready the regiment once more. Emi and the kitchen staff again worked long hours to bake bread and hardtack, though this time she was able to go home at night, as Alasdair was. Her final supply checks done, she hugged him a final time.

"I love ye, Alasdair. Be safe and come home to me, just as before."

Alasdair cupped her cheek and kissed her. "Aye, I will do my best. I will miss ye, and I love ye with all of me. Be wary."

"Aye," she whispered with a nod. "And ye."

Alasdair kissed her a final time and then forced himself away from her, mounting his horse and joining the other officers before Crisdean called the order to march, leading the Stewart men away from home and off to war once more.

Chapter 11

"Maman!" Emi called out as she drew her green cloak over her shoulders.

"Yes?" Bridgette asked as she stepped out of the kitchen office.

"I am going to take some things to Coira, if ye dinnae mind? I worry about her with Alasdair gone. On my way back, I will stop to check on Ealasaid and Arabella."

"You are a sweet girl, Emilia," Bridgette said, kissing both of Emi's cheeks. "Please give them my good wishes."

"I will," she said, giving Bridgette a hug. "I will be back in a while, Maman."

"See you then," Bridgette replied.

"Wait. Maman?"

"Yes?" Bridgette said, sticking her head back out.

"I love ye," Emi said.

"And I you," Bridgette said with a soft smile. "Off with you."

Emi hurried down the kitchen steps and out to the road. Taking a deep breath of fresh air as she walked, she took the time to admire the beauty of her surroundings as winter gave way to spring. The air was still cold, but the days were getting longer, and the bright yellow daffodils turned hillsides golden as they once more poked their heads up from the earth. She wondered where Alasdair was, what he was doing now. She prayed he was safe, that they all were, and she hated not knowing for certain. She touched the pendant and smiled, closing her eyes for a moment and letting herself think of his smile, his laugh, and how much she loved him.

"Coira?" she called out as she came into the clearing.

The door to the cottage opened, and Coira stepped out. "Emi, love! What are ye doing here?"

"I brought ye some bread I made this morning and some cheese as well. I also have tea and some other things."

"Ye did nae have to do that."

"I wanted to," Emi said. "Alasdair may nae be here to worry about ye, but I still am."

Coira smiled and embraced Emi before guiding her inside. Emi unpacked the basket as Coira shut the door. "Ye are looking well."

"I feel well," Emi replied. "I was nae for a little while, but that seems to have passed."

"Oh? I am sorry to hear ye were nae feeling well. Did ye eat something that did nae agree with ye or catch a bit of a fever?"

"No, at least I dinnae think so? It was the strangest thing. I would wake up nae feeling well, and sometimes I would even be ill, but then it would go away after a bit and I would be fine. Though sometimes it would come back, and I would have to go outside because the smell of the food just made me ill again."

Coira looked at her, an eyebrow raised in curiosity. "How long were ye that way?"

"A couple of weeks, perhaps? It started just before Alasdair left again, so perhaps it was just my being upset at his leaving or being exhausted from all the preparation. It still happens, but nae as often, so I must be getting past it."

Coira took a few steps toward her. "Emi, when was the last time ye shared a bed with Alasdair?"

"Just before he left, why?"

"But how long after he came home?"

"Two days."

Coira smiled, her eyes filling with tears. "I dinnae think ye will be getting past the illness anytime soon, sweet lass."

"Why do ye say that?"

"Emi, do ye really nae know?"

Shaking her head, she looked at Coira in confusion. "Know what?"

"Ye are with child, lass," Coira said, laughing in amusement at Emi's innocence.

Emi's eyes widened. "No! I cannae be! I mean … I dinnae feel different?"

"And ye will nae for a while yet. Oh, love, I am so happy for ye! He will be so excited when he comes home to find ye this way!"

As the realization sank in, Emi smiled. A child. Her hand covered her abdomen, and she looked down, thinking about how strange it was that a life was taking shape there and she hadn't even realized it.

"I suppose we should get ready to —" Coira began, but a loud sound cut her off and made both women jump.

"Was that a musket?" Emi asked, heart pounding.

"Aye," Coira replied.

The sound then came several more times, and Emi took a sharp breath in, backing away from the door and toward Coira. Something was wrong. That sound was out of place here, as no one would be hunting this close by and anyone who would have such a weapon was gone with the regiment.

"Coira," Emi said, fear making her voice waver. The bang came again, this time much closer, and Emi jumped and let out a small scream.

"We need to go," Coira said. "Now. Something is nae right," she continued as she threw the things Emi had brought back into the basket, along with some other things of her own. On top of it all, she placed Alasdair's new set of clothing, folded and wrapped in a length of tartan.

Coira threw the door open and grabbed Emi's hand, pulling the young woman out behind her but stopping short halfway across the clearing as a group of four men on horseback came off of the road and into it. Three of them wore the distinctive red uniforms of the English army.

"Well, good afternoon ladies," one of them said as he dismounted. It was clear, at least to Emi, that he was an officer. "I wish to inquire as to whether there are any men on the premises."

"No," Coira said. "At least nae here. They are all gone to —"

"Battle?" he finished for her, the smile that spread across his lips cold and malevolent. "I thought you might say that. That makes things far easier."

"What does that mean?" Emi asked, her voice tight.

The officer's eyes fell on her, and he looked her over, almost as if appraising her for her suitability to remain in his presence. "It means there will be no one to interrupt my task," he said, grabbing her hard by the arm.

"Dinnae touch me!" Emi shouted, pulling back against him. "He will kill ye when he finds out!"

"Whoever 'he' is, he can do nothing because he is very likely *dead*," the officer replied, his tone cold and efficient. "They *all* are."

Dead. They were all dead. The words felt like a knife in her heart. "No ..." Emi choked out. "No, he cannae be! Ye are lying!"

"I most certainly am not," he said before looking at another man with them. Emi knew him, he was one of their own, she hadn't noticed before because he wasn't wearing a kilt or anything he normally would be. "Do you know these two?"

"Aye. That one is an officer's lass; Emilia is her name. The other is his mam."

"Which officer?"

"Alasdair Stewart."

"And do you know his fate?"

"Aye. He is dead; I saw him cut down myself."

Coira wailed in anguish, and all color drained from Emi's face. She wanted to scream, but it felt as though there was no air left to breathe. Alasdair was dead.

"So, you see, pretty Emilia? Your precious Alasdair will not save you because he cannot," he said as he started to walk Emi backwards. "No one will."

Using their names made all of it worse than it already was, and Emi struggled against him to no avail. He stopped at the doorway, reaching out his free hand to lift the pendant from her neck before grasping it and yanking hard, snapping the chain, and causing her to cry out in pain and fear.

"This will make a lovely gift for my wife. Thank you," he said. "And *you* will make a lovely gift for *me*," he said as he shoved her forcefully through the door.

Emi stumbled and slammed into the table, but before she could make sense of it, he grabbed her and threw her onto her back on top of it. It was then that she realized what he meant to do, and she screamed again, louder this time, kicking at him, hitting at him, trying to keep him away from her. He delivered a slap so hard she saw double before pinning her wrists to the table with one hand as he shoved her skirts up with the other. He wasted no time in forcing himself on her, and Emi's scream erupted in a way that felt as though glass shards sliced through her throat before she began sobbing. Every move was painful, and she didn't understand why he was doing this, but it felt as though he were ripping apart everything she'd been, everything Alasdair had loved, and making sure that he'd never be there to welcome her when her time came. Why would he want to now? The man's hand suddenly came up to clamp around her throat, leaving Emi struggling to breathe as he tightened his grip. It seemed an eternity before he was done, and with his hand still squeezing her throat, she was beginning to feel lightheaded, her vision blurring.

"This is what we do to our enemies to completely crush them. *Especially* officers," he said into her ear, following it with a dark chuckle as he squeezed harder. He was still holding her wrists, keeping her from grabbing at him or shoving him away from her. "We breed them out. I am sure he would hate to know that one of us had you last, right here in his own home, on the very table where he likely had his last meal with you, but I do envy him having you in his bed when he did. How I do wish I had more time to spend with you, Emilia; I might even get you to enjoy it. What would he think then? I suppose we will never know, will we?"

He released her throat, and Emi gasped deeply for air, coughing as he dragged her from the table and shoved her outside where she collapsed onto the ground beside Coira, sobbing.

"Now, ladies, have you any final requests?" he asked as he came out, buttoning his breeches. "No? Very well, then. Put them inside, bar the door, and fire it," he directed the other two with him.

"Wait … ye cannae … they are women!" the Stewart man protested.

"Unless you want to join them, I suggest you remain silent!"

The man ceased speaking and looked away from them as the other two soldiers dragged Coira and Emi back inside, slamming the door shut. There was a loud sound as something was shoved into place to bar the door, and Coira cried out in fear, pulling Emi close to her. Emi could smell the acrid scent of pitch as they lit the torches outside, and she closed her eyes, praying for their souls, for Alasdair's, that he'd be there to meet her when this was all over despite what had just happened. There came a sudden commotion, loud shouting, and then silence before the door was pulled open.

"Coira!"

"Fergus!" Emi cried out as his familiar figure filled the doorway.

"Emi, ye too! Thank Christ! Come, quickly! I will get ye to safety!" he said as he helped them from the floor and ushered them out. Coira crossed herself and grabbed the basket, letting Fergus put her on his horse as he mounted behind her. "Emi, take that horse there and follow me!"

Emi stepped over the dead bodies of the three English

soldiers and their Stewart informer, grabbing the reins of the horse the English officer had been riding and mounting it. As Fergus took off, Emi followed him, speeding across the bridge and along the loch. She knew where they were going: the designated area in case of raids or other such emergencies. Any of the clan who could make it there would, and if Fergus were now here, it was likely any of the remaining regiment would also be there. The man who could've led the English to that place was now dead, but that didn't mean there weren't others so they wouldn't remain there long. The rain that had begun to fall would wash away any tracks they might make, and that would buy them time. As they rode into the clearing, it looked like a dead end, but it wasn't. Instead, they made their way into a ravine through a crevice hidden by foliage, and Fergus whistled. People appeared from where they'd taken shelter at the sound of approaching riders. Fergus dismounted and brought Coira down, who was taken in by those who knew her as she sobbed. Emi dismounted and looked around her. Exhausted and wounded men, frightened women, children, and elderly. In the faces of the men, she sought out the ones she was desperate to see. Where was Evander? Maybe Alasdair was there, and the informer had been lying.

"Emi," a soft, familiar voice said, and she turned to find Cailean.

"Cailean," she whispered in relief.

"Aye, it is me."

"Cailean," she said, grabbing hold of the arms of his coat, "Cailean, where is Evander? Where is Alasdair?"

The absolute pain in his face couldn't be mistaken. "Emi, I am so sorry."

"No," she said. "It is nae true. Cailean, please! Please ..." she pleaded through tears.

He said nothing, tears in his eyes, and shook his head.

"NO!" she sobbed out, turning to look for Bridgette. "Maman! Maman!"

All that met her were sad faces, but no response from

Bridgette. Emi shook her head vigorously in disbelief, the world spinning and causing her to stumble forward before her legs gave out altogether. Cailean caught her, and she buried successive screams against his shoulder, her crying hysterical as he held her in his arms and tried to comfort her. She'd lost everyone, her husband, her brother, the only mother she'd ever known, and she wasn't sure if she could survive it or even if she wanted to.

***

Cailean held Emi close to him as he closed his eyes, her raw grief shattering his heart more than it had already been. His own family had survived, and he was thankful for that. Fergus's sister and mother had also escaped. The main body of the English army was less than a day behind them, fanning out across the Highlands to deliver the brutal retribution ordered by Cumberland, and the remnants of the Stewart regiment had arrived in just enough time to clear everyone out as they approached the castle from this side of the loch. What they hadn't been able to do was reach the castle fast enough to prevent the scouts sent ahead by the English from killing everyone they found there.

"Cailean," Fergus said. "The chief wants to see her."

Cailean nodded, helping her up, though he knew she no longer understood what was happening. He guided her to where Crisdean sat, gravely wounded himself.

"Emilia," he said, opening his arms to her. To the surprise of both of the younger men, she went to him immediately, and he folded her against him as she wept. "I know, darling. I am so very sorry," he said to her before he looked up. "Fergus, thank ye for finding her. I owe ye a debt of gratitude for saving my Emilia."

Cailean and Fergus looked at him in confusion. *His* Emilia?

"She is my daughter, the only one of my children left here

135

in Scotland," he said, answering the unspoken question. "I am done with the secrets, done with hiding this. Doing so is pointless now."

The eyes of both men widened in shock.

"Alasdair," Emi sobbed out. "Maman … Evander …"

"Aye, sweet one. Ye will miss yer family and yer young man, and I will miss him too."

"Chief, he …" Cailean said, choking back a sob of his own as he decided it was now best to tell the truth. What was the point of lying about it? Who would it hurt now? "He was her husband. They married in the old way a little over a year ago."

"Why did he nae tell me? Emilia …"

"He had planned to when this was over. He wanted to make sure he was ready to go to ye for yer blessing."

"And he would have had it, with my whole heart, regardless of whatever position he would have been in. He was a good lad, one of the best I have known, and I would have worked with him had he told me."

Fergus slumped to the ground, covering his face with his hands and weeping, joined by Cailean. Their best friend, their brother, was gone, and to know he could've had all he'd desired without hiding it, even if only for a short while, was devastating.

Crisdean stroked Emi's hair. "Dinnae fear, Emilia, I will care for ye. As long as I live, ye are never alone."

Chapter 12

Emi cried herself to sleep, waking again to darkness and people murmuring around fires, confused for a moment before the realization returned. Alasdair, her beautiful Alasdair, was dead. Evander was dead, Bridgette was dead, and Emi wanted nothing more than to join them.

"They are burning the castle!" someone called out in a loud whisper, and people scrambled up the sides of the ravine to see for themselves, while Emi hung her head and curled up alone in a corner. She pulled the cloak Fergus had made for her tight around herself, thankful to have been wearing it along with both sets of gloves when she'd gone to visit Coira. It meant that at least she'd always have them, even though she'd lost everything else.

The next morning, someone shook her awake, and she recognized Fergus' mother Ealasaid through bleary, tear-swollen eyes. "Emi," she said in a soft voice, "Coira told me ye were ... that they ..."

Emi offered a single nod in wordless response as Cailean and Fergus looked at her in horror, and Crisdean's face darkened with rage.

"Ye poor love. Take this," she said, holding out a cup. "This will make sure ye are nae forced to bear a child from this."

"No, I cannae," Emi whispered, pushing the cup away from her.

"Why nae?"

"I will nae have any child from it because I already have one."

Cailean reached out to take her hand. "Emi, are ye carrying Alasdair's bairn?"

Fresh tears pooled in her eyes as her lower lip trembled, causing Ealasaid to gasp and cover her mouth.

"Sweet Christ," Cailean breathed. "Emi, did he know?"

"No, I did nae know before, but I do now and I —" she stopped, shaking her head. What did it matter now? She would never get to tell him.

"Natural or nae, at least ye have that," Ealasaid said.

"Nae natural, Mam," Fergus said. "They were married."

"Please, leave me alone," Emi whispered, turning her face toward the wall as she pulled her hand from Cailean's.

"Emi," Fergus said, taking her hand even though she wouldn't look at him and pressing something into her palm before closing her fingers around it. "This is yers."

Emi pulled her hand back and opened it to find her necklace, and she realized Fergus must've pulled it from the officer's body before he'd let them out of the cottage. She closed her hand around it, pressing it to her heart, her body shaking with fresh sobs at yet another reminder of all she'd lost.

She didn't move from where she sat, not wanting food or drink or conversation. She was willing herself to die, she heard everyone whisper, and perhaps they were right. Why should she want to stay when everything she loved was now gone, stripped from her in a few short and horrific days? There were others who cared for her, that was true, but they weren't the ones she wanted most. There was the baby, too, a little piece of Alasdair left with her, a gift from the same God who'd so cruelly taken him away from her. She should live for it, she knew that, but she couldn't find the will within herself to want to.

That night, as everyone slept, Emi sat awake, staring at

the fire. Reds, yellows, and oranges danced around each other in intricate patterns and allowed her to focus on something other than how her very soul hurt. Fergus and Cailean were taking turns sitting with and guarding Crisdean, and Emi remained there as well, not having the desire to go elsewhere. No one had pressed her about moving, and she knew it had everything to do with Crisdean's revelation to his two officers. Others had heard it said, and it spread quietly through the camp: Emi was Crisdean's daughter. It was so clear now, especially with them sitting near each other, and now that they knew and he'd publicly acknowledged her in front of others, Emi was under the same vigilant guard her father was. If he died, Emi would be the one the clan looked to until one of his sons returned to take his place.

From her place at the end of the camp, she saw someone stumble in, the movement bringing her eyes back into focus as she looked up. His clothing was filthy and torn, his skin caked with dried blood and dirt. He was clearly a Stewart soldier who'd somehow escaped, but how had he gotten past the lookouts unnoticed? They must've seen his uniform and not stopped him, she reasoned. Reaching out to shake Fergus awake, she stopped before she touched him, narrowing her eyes before she stood and took a few steps toward the stranger. He reached out for her, trying to move more quickly, and it only made him stumble and fall. As he hit the ground, she hurried toward him and knelt at his side, turning him over.

"Christ, are ye all right?"

"Emi," he croaked.

Her heart jumped into her throat, choking her, and she grabbed a ladle of water, dribbling it into his mouth before she grabbed a rag from a bucket of water set near the fire to warm. She smoothed it over his face, wiping away the blood and dirt.

"Alasdair?" she whispered in disbelief as his features became clearer beneath the grime. She was hallucinating; she had to be.

"Emi," he whispered in return.

"Alasdair!" she shouted, waking the others immediately.

Cailean and Fergus scrambled up from where they'd been sleeping, as did Coira, all three kneeling at the man's side.

"Mam," he said to Coira.

"Alasdair! Lord, this is a miracle!" she cried out before bursting into tears.

"Quick! Dr. Stewart!" Cailean called out.

Seumas Stewart, a clansman educated in medicine and Crisdean's personal physician who'd gone out with the regiment as its doctor, hurried over, his eyes widening in surprise. "Christ above, it is! Alasdair, lad! Everyone back up; let me see him."

Everyone did as asked, but when Emi went to move, Alasdair grabbed her wrist. "No, dinnae … leave … me …"

"Emilia, stay," Seumas said. "Keep him calm."

Emi held Alasdair's hand as Seumas stripped him down and examined him, hardly able to believe this was real.

"He took a shot from a musket, but nae in a place that will kill him or he would be dead already. He will live if he can make it through the fever coming his way. Looks to be a few nasty cuts from a blade, but those will heal. He needs water and rest; he is exhausted and probably ill already. I dinnae know how ye survived or how ye made it here, lad, but the Lord was with ye."

"Em …" Alasdair whispered, his eyes moving back and forth quickly beneath the closed lids. "I am … I am coming … coming … please wait … please …"

"Ye are here, my love, ye are here," Emi said, trying to reassure him.

"He is delirious," Seumas said. "Let us get him someplace comfortable and clean him up."

Alasdair groaned as the three men lifted him and carried him toward the back of the camp, placing him under an outcropping. Emi and Coira grabbed the buckets of warm water as a few of the other men hurried out into the darkness to fetch more water for both Alasdair and the camp. Kneeling beside him, the two women began to wipe the blood from his skin so that any other injuries could be seen. As Seumas cleaned the wounds, he allowed Ealasaid to place salves and poultices to draw the infection out and help the wounds heal, then began dressing them. Coira rinsed the dirt and blood from Alasdair's hair, and when there was nothing left to do, they turned him so they could place a plaid beneath him before covering him with another. Emi rested his head in her lap and squeezed a small amount of cool water into his mouth from a clean rag.

"Emi, love," Coira said. "Ye should see to yerself."

"No," she replied. "He needs me."

"Aye, but ye need to eat and drink yerself or ye will be joining him here soon enough. What good will ye be doing him then? I am going to bring something for ye, and I want ye to take it."

Emi nodded without looking up, stroking his face. Somehow, he'd returned to her, and she knew Coira was right. She needed to keep her strength up for him because he needed her now. Coira returned with bread and tea, and Emi took it. For a moment she felt like she might be sick as she ate, but it passed soon enough. She dozed off but woke again a short time later to feed him more water with the cloth. He didn't move or make a sound, but she could see his chest rising and falling and knew he was at least still alive.

Over the next few days, Alasdair moved in and out of consciousness, though he was never lucid during the brief moments he was conscious. He called for Emi, for Coira, for Cailean and Fergus, but never seemed to realize they were there. Once, a government raiding party came close, spotted by the hidden sentries in enough time for the fires to be smothered, and for everyone to go still and silent. The men lined the two walls, their eyes on the entrance, weapons drawn, in case anyone appeared. Emi placed a hand over Alasdair's mouth to stifle any sound he might make in case he woke up and called out again. The voices of the English soldiers could be heard remarking that it was a dead end and turning around, much to everyone's relief. There were reports back from small groups sent out at night to assess the damage and check the positions of the troops, keeping everyone apprised of numbers and the places they needed to be wary of. They'd return with scavenged supplies and goods from the homes of those here who'd told the groups where to find it. Wool, cloaks, gloves, stockings, shirts, flour, and other dried goods, all stored away in locations the raiders had missed. There were even goods pulled from hidden castle stores, thanks to Emi's direction. The castle was burned to the ground, but the underground stores had been spared, and it would make all the difference for their coming survival.

***

"We need to move," Crisdean said. "We cannae stay here much longer, or they will find us soon enough."

"Where should we go?" Fergus asked.

"There are plenty of places to hide in the hills between here and Inverness," Cailean offered. "As long as we keep away from any towns, that is a lot of land to search, a lot of hidden glens and hills; it is unlikely we would be found."

"Aye, good thinking, Cailean," Crisdean said. "The others will be safe if we can find an out of the way spot for them to hide for the next several months, at the very least. But I cannae remain here forever. It is too dangerous for me and for the rest of the clan because they will be set on finding me and bringing me to justice, along with the other chiefs. I need to get to France and join my family there."

"We will go with ye," Fergus said. "Ye need what officers ye have left."

"Aye," Cailean said, his face and voice just as resolute as Fergus'.

"What of yer families, lads?"

"They can come with us. Normally it would be a concern, but moving slowly and deliberately is key now. If we rush, they will find us, but if we take our time, the initial wave of retaliation can slow and let us slip through."

"Solid plan, Cailean," Fergus said.

Crisdean gave a nod. "I will accept yer coming with me. Ye are right; I need ye. I am still injured myself and cannae go far on my own or even quickly."

"Hopefully Alasdair recovers enough to wake soon. He cannae stay here," Fergus said. "Nae with the bounty on his head."

"Aye," Crisdean said. "He will have to come as well, and I will be glad to have the three of ye. Let us give it two more days, give everyone time to be ready to move and any other supplies we can gather to be brought here. Have the women take the wool we have and make breeches for as many men as they can since the tartan will need to be hidden. Let them all know."

"Aye, Chief," the two men said before dispersing to do as asked.

The clan wasted no time in obeying the order. Meetings were held to reveal any last locations of hidden supplies, and the women immediately set to making the required breeches. The first to get them would be Crisdean and the remaining officers, as they'd be the ones the English were searching for. If they ran out of wool for those gathered here, some would be scavenged from any extra clothing that was not immediately needed, such as extra skirts or old coats. Emi remained at Alasdair's side, though she made his breeches herself, and continued sewing for the rest, too. Cailean, Fergus, and Alasdair all had brand new coats and waistcoats, thanks to the winter work of their women, and it would only aid in shielding their true identities. The uniforms of all three men were destroyed because they could no longer be used nor have material salvaged from them, after any buttons and buckles were removed. This would also keep any pestilence or bugs from the rest of the survivors.

There was a quick hunt for any possible clan members hiding elsewhere, but none were found. All those at the camp could do was hope that they'd made a run for it and were safe somewhere even though they had been unable to get to the meeting point. It seemed likely, as a great many of them would've had far more warning than those closer to the castle, especially since the flames when the English set it ablaze were so high they could've been seen for miles. Any who lived too far out were likely warned by those fleeing and joined them. All that was left for them to do was pray for those not with them because no matter what else happened, they were leaving Stewart land in two days.

Chapter 13

Cold. It was so cold. Where was he?

Alasdair's eyes fluttered open to look into a gray sky and an eerie stillness. The sounds of battle were gone now, the ground no longer rumbling from cannon fire and the feet of men and horses. There was an odd sort of weight around him as well as on top of him, and in the next instant, he realized they were bodies. He shoved back his instantaneous urge to scream and shove them away, being of sound enough mind to realize they were likely keeping him from being seen. Every bit of him hurt and felt weak, but he knew he had to get away from here. By some miracle he was alive, and he needed to find a way to escape this moor, escape the notice of the English, and get home to his mother and his wife. They weren't safe anymore; none of them were. Emi. He closed his eyes as the thought of her drifted into the front of his mind, the way she'd cried when he'd first told her they were going to war and pleaded with him not to go. Why hadn't he listened? It was possible now that he'd be too late to save her, too late to save anyone, and tears slid from beneath his closed lids.

"I am coming," he thought. "Coming back to ye, Emi, just as I promised. Wait for me."

The sound of boots made him go still, barely breathing,

his eyes remaining closed as they walked past him. He then heard the distinct sound of a body being dragged across the ground. They were burying the dead, and if he didn't move soon, they'd discover he wasn't actually among those dead and make him that way. He opened his eyes a sliver and turned his head, able to see a group of men standing nearby before they moved away. Moving his head, he propped it up on a body to get a vantage of the field. At the moment, there was no one towards the woods; they were all on the other side, burying bodies and seeing to their dead and wounded. Ever so carefully, he eased himself out of the pile surrounding him, and once he was free, he remained on the ground unmoving and waiting to see if he'd been noticed. When he was sure he hadn't been spotted, he remained on his back so he could see, inching backward with painstaking and slow movements toward the woods, stopping for a long pause after each one to ensure he seemed like just another body on the ground.

After what seemed an eternity, he reached the trees at last, and when he felt he was inside far enough to avoid being seen, he sat up. The movement made him dizzy, but once it passed, he looked around him. There was no one here, but he could see the field from between the trees. The bodies of his fellow Scots littered the moor, and it made him feel sick. The battle had been disastrous for them, and they'd been like cattle to the slaughter. He had no idea who in his clan still lived, if any. Loud shouting got his attention just as he saw one of the cottages go up in flames. Alasdair looked at it with a mix of curiosity and fear, wondering why they were burning it, until the wind brought the screams to him. They were the screams of men they'd trapped inside before setting the blaze, and with the screams came the scent of burning flesh, causing Alasdair to retch, horrified by the scene.

The screams all at once changed, and it gave him pause. They were now women's screams, and he wasn't on the moor but in the woods at home. How? Panic instantly descended when he realized that the burning cottage was his mother's, and the screams were coming from inside. He scrambled up from the ground, pushing past any weakness or pain, and threw himself at the door. He had to get it open, but it wouldn't move.

"NO!" he screamed as he shoved at it, throwing his shoulder against it in an effort to break it down. "MAM!"

"Alasdair! Help!" Coira called from inside, even as she began choking on smoke.

"Alasdair! Please!"

The second voice stopped him for a split second, the horror washing over him along with the recognition. Emi. Emi was inside! Alasdair renewed his attack on the door with increased fervor.

"EMI!" he screamed out.

"Alasdair! Help me!" she called back between screams of pain and choking.

The flames had reached them now, he could smell it, and their screams intensified. Alasdair screamed with them in rage, pain, desperation, and fear as he fought the door, but it wouldn't budge. The screams became a deafening silence, and his heart felt like it stopped with them.

"NO! NO!" he screamed desperately as he pounded on the door with his fists. "MAM! EMI! ANSWER ME!"

All that met him was the crackle of flames, and he knew he was too late. They were dead. They'd died screaming for him, knowing he was there, just on the other side of the door and unable to get to them. This was his fault. He'd killed them as surely as if he'd lit the torch himself. The scream that welled up in his chest and burst from his throat felt like it tore everything in him asunder as he fell to the ground, staring up at the sky through the trees as he'd once stared at the gray clouds above Drumossie Moor. He closed his eyes, feeling as though he couldn't breathe, the pressure of the pain in his chest too great, and he gasped for air, but when his eyes opened again, he was somewhere else.

"Alasdair?"

Panting, he turned his eyes toward the sound of the familiar voice. "Emi …?"

Her beautiful face smiled down at him, and he felt her hand on his cheek. "Aye."

"What … how … I just saw …"

"Shh, ye are well. Ye have been asleep and unwell, but ye seem to have come back to us now."

Asleep. He'd been asleep. He closed his eyes for a moment and tried to calm his racing heart. His body still hurt, but he could feel her soft hand stroking his cheek and knew she was right. It had been a nightmare. She wasn't dead. "Where am I?" he asked, opening his eyes again.

"Home. Well, sort of. We are in the clan hiding spot now. Ye managed to get home to us."

"Home," he repeated.

The memories rushed back to him now. The battle, waking up in a pile of bodies, making his way home on foot even though it was some 60 miles and he was wounded. The pain, the fear, the determination. Alasdair groaned as the pain caught up with him along with the memories, but the sound of someone crying brought him back to present and he opened his eyes to find Emi covering her face with a hand, weeping.

"What is wrong?"

"I am so thankful ye are alive. Everyone said ye were dead, that they saw ye. Even the soldier said so."

Alasdair's heart seized, and he managed to sit up. "Soldier? What soldier?"

"A small group came. They found me with yer mam, and they had one of our men with them. He was trying to save himself and told them who we were; he told us he had seen ye killed. They were going to lock us inside and burn the cottage, but Fergus saved us."

Alasdair felt as though he might be sick. What he'd seen in his dream just now had almost happened. "Where is my mam?"

"Here. I will go wake her."

"No, wait," he said, placing a hand on her arm to stay any movement. Knowing his mother was safe allowed him time to talk to Emi first. Reaching out, he cupped her cheek and stroked it with his thumb. "I am so thankful ye are safe, my own love. I had to come home to ye, and I made sure I did no matter what. I promised."

"Aye, ye did, and I am thankful God saw fit after all to leave me at least one person I love."

"What?"

"Evander and Maman are dead," she whispered, her lower lip trembling. "I was told that the small party that got to us killed her when she was on her way to warn us, and Evander died in the battle."

It felt as though the words punched him in the gut, taking his breath away. Both Evander and Bridgette were gone. "Jesus, Em, I … sorry is nae enough."

She shook her head. "Ye are here, and that is what matters now. I thought I had lost all of ye."

"Never," he whispered. "Even if I had truly fallen, I would always be with ye."

"Aye, ye would. In more ways than one."

Alasdair looked at her, confused. "What does that mean?"

"I am … I did nae know when ye left, but …"

His eyes went wide. "Emi, are ye telling me that ye are with child?"

"Aye."

Alasdair was swiftly overcome, his chest heaving as he tried to stop himself from bursting into tears and failed. Pulling her into his arms, he held her close, resting his cheek against her shoulder and feeling her hand come to rest on the back of his head. A child. Somewhere in all of this death and destruction, there was life, hope, and he'd almost missed it. Lifting his head, he took her face in his hands and kissed her before resting his forehead against hers.

"I love ye," he said. "Both of ye, and I will do whatever I must to make sure ye are both safe."

"I know ye will."

He looked up and smiled at her through tears. "When do ye think?"

"Sometime after ye came back from Stirling, probably right after ye woke up."

"Perhaps that will be its name."

"Maybe," Emi said, chuckling. "I should let the others know ye are awake. They have all been worried about ye, even the chief."

"The chief is here?" Alasdair breathed a sigh of relief. "Thank the Lord."

"Aye. I will be right back," she said as she stood up and left.

Within moments, Cailean, Fergus, and Coira were there, along with Seumas. Alasdair felt like weeping again when his mother's arms closed around him, the nightmare still fresh in his mind. When she released him, the other two embraced him.

"Ye scared us all half to death," Cailean said. "Welcome back, little brother."

"Aye," Fergus said. "Dinnae do that again, ye wee bastard!"

"I will certainly try nae to," Alasdair said, following the words with an exhausted smile.

"Let us have a look at those wounds," Seumas said. "Back down with ye, lad." Once he was down, Seumas removed the dressings and nodded. "The cuts are looking good and should heal nicely. The wound from the musket ball will take a bit of time, though," he mused as he took Alasdair's arm and moved it, though he stopped when the young man hissed in pain. "Naught broken, though. Ye were very lucky. Coira, would ye help me redress these and see if Ealasaid has any more of the poultice and salve?"

"Aye, of course," Coira replied.

"Where is Emi?" Alasdair asked.

"She snuck off to have a wash while we were with ye," Fergus said.

"She should nae be alone!"

"Calm yerself, lad," Cailean said. "She is still here in the ravine, just in a place more private and set aside for those who wanted to go there for exactly that purpose. She has nae had the chance to wash that devil Englishman from her yet."

Everyone went still, with Cailean seeming to realize he'd said more than he'd meant to. Alasdair shoved Seumas' hands from him and sat up.

"What does that mean?"

"Alasdair —"

"No, ye tell me right now what ye meant by that, Cailean," he said, his voice calm in the way that frightened anyone who'd been stupid enough to challenge him. It was usually the last thing they ever heard.

"Alasdair," Coira said. "When they came, they …" she began before she sighed. "The officer amongst them stole the necklace ye gave her, ripped it straight from her neck. He said it would make a lovely gift for his wife … and Emilia would make a lovely gift for him."

"No," he whispered. That moment. He'd seen that moment in his dreams after Falkirk. He could've told her, warned her. Why hadn't he? "That … ye stopped it, right? She said ye saved them," he asked Fergus.

Fergus shook his head. "It happened before I got there, or I would have. I am sorry to her and to ye for nae being able to."

Alasdair's head spun, and he felt like he couldn't breathe. One of them had raped his wife. He hadn't been there to protect her, and this was what had happened. "I will kill him. I will hunt him down and cut this throat in front of his family after making him plead for her forgiveness as well as his own life."

"Dinnae fret, I did it for ye," Fergus said, his voice as dark as his expression. "Got her necklace back, too."

"Thank ye, Fergus. At least I know he is no longer walking

this earth even if it was nae me who ensured it. How dare he, how dare any of them," Alasdair seethed.

"This is war," Seumas said. "They dinnae follow our code, and women are targets just as much as anyone else. In fact, larger, because that is where they can hurt us the most. The point is that she survived it, yer bairn seems to have survived it and all of this, and ye are here instead of dead on a moor. The lass is strong, a survivor, and it seems yer bairn is, too. Focus on that."

Alasdair nodded, but he was still furious. "How is the chief?"

"Crisdean is recovering, and he will live. He wants to see ye if ye feel up for it."

"If he wishes to see me, then I will go to him."

"He was overjoyed when he heard ye had come back," Cailean said.

Coira fetched the breeches Emi made for him and helped him into them before he allowed them to redress the wounds. Alasdair reached out his good arm and Fergus ducked under it, draping the arm over his shoulders and helping him stand up. Wobbling, he was steadied by his friends, and Cailean wrapped an arm around his waist on the other side. He was still weak, his body tired, even if his mind wasn't. They guided him to where the chief was resting, and he smiled when he saw Alasdair.

"So, it is true after all," Crisdean said as Fergus helped Alasdair sit down. "Ye made it back."

"Aye, Chief," Alasdair replied. "I am glad to see ye did as well."

"It was close, to be certain, and if nae for these two, I would certainly be dead," he said, gesturing to Fergus and Cailean before frowning. "So many others were nae so fortunate, including our innocents here at home. I will feel the weight of their loss for the rest of my days and regret it."

"There is naught to be done now to change it."

"No, there is nae. How did ye survive?"

"I dinnae remember. I know I woke in a pile of bodies,

and I realized they were burying the dead. When I was sure they were nae near, I squeezed out, stayed on my back so that I could see them coming, and inch by inch slid my way to the woods. It seemed as though it took years; I stopped after every tiny move to make sure no one noticed me. When I was finally safe in the trees, I sat up and saw the moor littered with the dead, saw them fire a cottage full of Scottish officers."

"What!"

"Aye, it was horrific; I will nae lie to ye. I heard them taunting those men as they screamed, asking them if they liked being officers now, which is how I knew what rank those unfortunate souls were. I knew I was wounded, but I needed to get here because they would come for reprisal. I made my way back on foot, stayed off of the road. When I arrived, I saw the castle still smoldering, and I knew where everyone would have gone. I came here, and that is where my memory stops."

"Christ," Cailean said.

Crisdean sighed. "I am glad ye made it. Emilia was inconsolable."

"Aye, I understand why, believing she had lost us all. I did nae see what happened to Evander."

"I did," Fergus said. "It was … well, there was naught left of him to bury. Let us just leave it at that."

Alasdair closed his eyes and shook his head, his heart aching for the loss of his childhood friend. "I am glad he did nae suffer."

"Aye," Fergus murmured. "From yer mam and Emi, I know they heard the gunshots as the English opened fire on those at the castle, and from what I saw, it seemed as though they'd lined them all up for a firing squad."

"Bastard sons of bitches," Alasdair said through clenched teeth.

"Bridgette somehow got away, and based on where I found her, she was running to warn yer mam. She must have known Emi was there. I have nae had the heart to tell Emi that the final, close gunshot she told me she heard was the murder of her own mother."

Alasdair closed his eyes and ran his hands through his hair. "God rest her soul, for she is worthy of His kingdom and His care."

"Aye, indeed. We are moving soon, Alasdair, taking what remains of us to hide in the hills between here and Inverness," Crisdean explained. "I will join my family in France; Fergus and Cailean have agreed to come with me, along with their families. I want ye, Coira, and Emilia to join us. Ye cannae stay here, lad, nae with the bounty on ye, and they will kill ye if they find ye, along with the women."

"He is right, Alasdair," Cailean said. "None of us officers can remain."

With a sigh, Alasdair nodded. "Aye, I know ye are right. Even if just to keep my mam and Emi safe from further harm."

"There is naught more we can do here. There is nae enough of the army left to regroup and go back out, and even if there was, I am nae sure I would want to," Crisdean admitted. "We may be able to someday return, well, at least ye lads can."

"As ye wish, Chief."

"Is there something ye wish to tell me, Alasdair?"

Alasdair was confused for a moment before he realized that the chief must know about him and Emi now, that there was more than he'd been told. There was no way he couldn't. "Aye. Emi is my wife and has been for a wee bit more than a year."

"Why did ye nae tell me sooner?"

"I meant to. At first it was because I wanted to make sure that when I went to ye, I had everything together: money, a home, a plan. Then I realized war was coming, and it was nae the time to tell ye about it. I was going to do it afterward."

"It is afterward, lad."

Alasdair smiled and shook his head, laughing. "Aye, it is."

"So?" Crisdean prodded expectantly.

"I would like yer blessing to marry Emi officially."

"Ye have it, and happily so, for I cannae think of anyone better. Had ye told me from the start, we would have worked something out; I would have helped ye. Why do ye look relieved?"

"I thought ye may say no."

"Why would I do that, ye daft boy? This does nae have anything to do with her parentage, does it?"

Alasdair looked up in surprise.

"Aye, I know ye are aware of it. Coira told me, but ye should know everyone else here knows as well, including Emilia."

"A bit, aye," Alasdair admitted.

"Ye really are daft then. I will see the pair of ye married in the church in France when we get there. Now, get ye gone out of my sight, so ye dinnae pass on to me whatever has worked itself into yer mind to make ye an idiot," Crisdean said with a playful roll of his eyes.

Alasdair, Cailean, and Fergus laughed before the two men helped Alasdair up once more and led him back to where he'd been. By the time they returned, Emi had done so as well and smiled when she saw him. He could, however, see the bruises now. He hadn't noticed before, but they were there, marring the skin of her cheek, her throat, her wrists.

"Ye seem much more awake."

"Feel it, too," Alasdair responded as Fergus and Cailean helped him down before departing.

"Where were ye?"

"The chief wished to see me."

"Oh, of course."

"He wants me to go to France with him. Cailean and Fergus are going, along with their families."

"What did ye say?"

"That I would. It is nae exactly a choice; I am still one of his officers."

Emi's expression saddened. "Ye will leave me, then."

Alasdair frowned. "No, I would nae. Ye are coming with me."

"How? I am nae yer wife, at least nae as far as he knows."

"Aye, he does. I just told him, and he gives his blessing. He says we can marry officially in France when we arrive."

The smile that spread across her face was one of pure joy. "I suppose it is good I can speak French then."

"Aye," Alasdair said, chuckling as he moved himself closer to her. "I would never leave ye behind, my love, nae again. I would have refused to go until he agreed to let ye come with me if it came to that, but ye know it would nae because there is no chance he is leaving his daughter behind now that everyone knows about her."

"I suppose that is true; I had nae thought of it that way."

"Why would ye when such a thing is new to ye?" he asked, looking down in silence before he forced the words from his lips. "Emi, when were ye going to tell me."

"Tell ye what?"

"About what happened, about what that soldier who came did to ye."

Emi's expression darkened. "I was nae going to."

"Why nae?"

"What good would it do? It happened, and there is naught that will change it."

"Maybe nae, Em, but I could at least comfort ye and try to help ye heal from what it surely did to yer heart and yer soul. Ye should nae hide things from me."

"Maybe I was hiding it from myself, too. When I thought ye were dead, I begged ye for yer forgiveness, begged ye to come for me when they killed me."

"Why would I need to forgive ye?"

"Why would ye want me after that? I tried to stop him, but I could nae, and now I am damaged, nae yers alone. I was nae going to tell ye because I did nae want to see the betrayal in yer face, and I know ye will want to leave now that ye know."

Frowning, Alasdair reached out and took her hand. "Dinnae say that," he said. "Ye are my wife. Whatever happens we face it together, and this is just one of them. This was nae yer fault, Emi. Why would ye believe I would see it as a betrayal and leave ye? It was nae as though ye welcomed him into yer bed, and I know ye tried to stop it, did nae want it. The bruises on ye show it plain enough. Ye are nae damaged, nae to me, and I am sorry beyond words that it befell ye."

"So am I, but at least it was nae yer mam. I would rather it was me than her," she said.

The words broke his heart, though he could hear the relief in her voice at his assurances, and he kissed her hand, smoothing his fingers over the bruises on that wrist. "I would rather it was neither of ye."

"Let us nae speak of it again, please."

"As ye wish," he said, squeezing her hand. He had so many questions, but he would respect her wishes and not ask them. At least not of her.

"When they told me ye were dead …" she whispered, "I wished I could die right there on the spot."

"Did ye know about Bridgette and Evander by then?"

"No, I did nae find out until we got here."

"He did nae suffer."

"Did ye see —"

"No," he replied before she was forced to say the words. "I did nae, but Fergus did. He may tell ye if ye ask, but I dinnae think those are details ye need."

"At least I remembered to tell Maman I loved her before I left."

Alasdair drew her into his arms and held her close, his heart hurting for her. He couldn't imagine what she felt now and didn't want to. There had been days where she'd thought she'd lost everyone, when she'd lived his nightmare of knowing those she loved were beyond her reach, that she couldn't help them. Though she'd gotten *him* back, it could never and would never erase what she'd lost. He knew how much she'd loved Evander, knew that his quick death was cold comfort, but it was the only thing Alasdair could give her. He hoped it had been the same for Bridgette, that the shot that killed her had been true and she hadn't suffered in agony as he'd seen others do.

"Aye, at least ye have that," he said, running his fingers through her hair. It was loose now, drying, and it didn't seem to matter to anyone. There was an informality born out of necessity, decorum that couldn't be maintained under current circumstances.

"What happened to ye, Alasdair?"

"I can tell ye what I remember, though so much of it feels distant," he said. "It was horrible, Emi. When we arrived, it was already clear things were in disarray. There was no food for the regiments. The Camerons arrived nae long after us, and their supplies, combined with what ye sent, managed to feed all of us for a day. Without that, I dinnae know what we would have done. There was an overland march meant to surprise Cumberland, but we got lost and men were falling from exhaustion and hunger, dropping right to the ground. By the time we returned to Culloden House, it was all any of us could do to find a place to try and get some rest. When Cumberland's forces arrived, we were outnumbered, but we did our best. When the charge was finally called, we all ran together and I ..." He paused, trying to think. "I remember feeling blades cut me, but I honestly dinnae know if it was from the English or simply being too close together. Then there was this pain in my arm, blinding, and I fell to the ground."

"The musket shot."

"Aye. When I woke up, I was looking at the sky, and I realized the battle was over. I was surrounded by bodies, and they were preventing me from being seen. Some of them were my clansmen, some were nae. It became clear that the English were burying bodies, and I knew I had to get out of there before they realized I was nae actually dead. I slipped out of the pile, stayed on my back, and inched my way to the woods. After every move I would stop, waiting to see if they had noticed, and eventually I made it. As soon as I knew I could nae be seen, I sat up and tried to take stock of things. There were so many dead; the moor was covered in bodies. I saw them set one of the cottages near the moor aflame, and I could nae figure out why … until the wind brought the sounds of screaming and the scent of burning flesh." Alasdair stopped, closing his eyes as the vivid memory resurfaced, leaving him able to smell it and hear it once more. He took a deep breath to try and keep from being sick.

"Screaming? Why? What —" but then she stopped, suddenly understanding what he was saying. "They were burning prisoners alive?" she asked in a horrified whisper.

"Aye. Dinnae know who, but I am sure I would have been amongst them if I had nae gotten away. That or buried alive."

"Oh, dear God."

"I started to make my way back here on foot from Inverness, staying off the main road and traveling by night. I just wanted to get home to ye and to Mam, to warn ye and protect ye even though I knew I might be too late. I had no food, and my injuries pained me greatly, which only got worse the longer it all went untreated. I know I was delirious at times because I saw ye walking just ahead of me. I called to ye, asked ye to wait for me, but ye never turned around. I saw the castle in ruins when I arrived and knew where to find ye if any of ye still lived."

Emi sighed. "No wonder ye kept murmuring that ye were coming, to wait for ye, after ye collapsed here."

"Ye were what got me home, Em, what saved me and gave me the strength to keep going, even when I thought I had none left. If I just followed ye, it would all be fine. The last thing I remember is seeing ye standing here, finally facing me, and I knew I had either died or made it here."

Reaching up, she placed a hand on his cheek. "Ye were nae well, but we cleaned ye up and put ye here to rest. Ye seemed to wake up several times, but ye were nae really here, calling for us even though we were right here beside ye."

"I am past it now," he said. "Nae going anywhere yet."

"Good, but ye still need to be easy or ye will make it worse."

"Nae sure I will have much choice, but I will try."

"Emi!" two men called out as they came back into camp from one of the last runs to scout for supplies. "Look at who we found skulking about, eh?"

From a sack, the man produced a very confused, very dirty, and very frightened Lamb, setting the cat down on the ground.

"Lamb!" Emi cried out. "Sweet Jesus!"

Lamb turned to run but froze upon hearing Emi's voice. He turned and looked at her, unsure, before he ran toward her, yowling. Emi scooped him up, and he moved between purring and piteous meows as she cuddled him close to her.

Alasdair shook his head with a small smile. "I dinnae know how ye manage it, cat, and this must be the second of yer nine lives gone, but ye are a Stewart all right. A survivor, just like the rest of us."

Chapter 14

Alasdair spent the rest of the day sleeping, the first true rest he'd gotten now that the fever had released its grip on him. He'd need all the rest he could get, as they were to leave as soon as darkness fell. The idea was much the same as Alasdair had used to get here: stay off the main roads, travel by night, rest during the daylight hours. The stillness of the night would allow them to hear their pursuers far sooner and make them easier to spot by looking for the fires of their camps. They would find a good location farther into the hills, where there would be no reason for the government soldiers to go. When the time was right, after the patrols and retribution had died down, Crisdean and the others would leave for the Continent.

Gently shaken awake, Alasdair opened his eyes to find his mother beside him. "Mam? Is it time to leave?"

"Nae yet," she said, "but ye should eat before we step off, aye?"

"Thank ye," he said, pushing himself up with his good arm and trying to shake off the sleep. "Where is Emi?"

"Seeing to her father," Coira said. "Making sure he eats. She made his food herself, still seeing it as her duty."

"It must be strange for her to know."

"From what I understand, he told her before ye all left the

first time, wanting her to know in case he did nae return. It seems as though he is now tired of hiding it from anyone, and I cannae blame him," she said, handing him the spoon and holding the bowl for him.

"Mam," he said after taking a bite. "While she is nae here, I need ye to tell me something."

"What is it?"

"What happened? The bruises, tell me how she got them."

Coira winced. "Alasdair …"

"Please, Mam, I need to know what he did. I cannae help her if I dinnae know the things that will frighten her now."

With a sigh, Coira looked down at the bowl in her hands. "When they came, he asked if there were any men with us, and when we said no, he said that was good because there would be no one to stop him. Emi asked him what he meant and, oh, Alasdair, the way he looked at her. It was like he was sizing up some little tart in a doorway and salivating. He grabbed her by the arm — and there are bruises from that too that ye cannae see while she is dressed — and she screamed at him nae to touch her, that ye would kill him if ye found out."

"She is nae wrong."

"He told us ye were dead, ye all were, and he asked the Stewart man with him who we were. When he found out that Emi was an officer's lass, I knew right then her fate was sealed. The officer asked for a name, and the man gave yers, then said he saw ye cut down and knew ye were dead. That officer smiled at her so coldly, telling her that ye could nae help her now, no one could. He used yer name to hurt her, and I will never forget those words: 'Yer precious Alasdair will nae save ye because he cannae.' The pain on her face when he said it …" Coira said, stopping to regain her composure.

Alasdair could imagine it, knew the tactic was used on purpose because he'd heard of and seen it before after other conflicts, and it infuriated him.

"He took her necklace then shoved her inside. I could see

her, she was on her back on the table, screaming and fighting him until he struck her. Then he grabbed her wrists in one hand and pinned them to the table so that she could nae fight him. That is when he did it, and she screamed as I have nae heard anyone scream before," Coira said, pausing to again try and keep her composure. "That was when he started strangling her with his free hand. I thought he was going to kill her!"

Alasdair felt ill and now almost wished he hadn't asked. The bruises on her neck had come from the bastard choking the life out of her even as he humiliated her and took something from her that she could never get back. She'd always remember, always be able to see his face and hear his voice, always know that someone other than Alasdair had touched her in such a way.

"No wonder she did nae wish to speak of it," he said.

"Of course, she would nae. But she tried to stop him, Alasdair, she truly did."

Alasdair looked at her with a raised eyebrow. "Why do ye say that? As though I would think anything else?"

"Some men would."

"I am nae them, and ye should know that without it needing to be said."

"Ye can say all ye want until ye are there, but ye are proving ye mean it."

"Mam, I have seen men three times her size freeze in the face of battle. Even if she had been too frightened, too shocked to fight back, I would nae think less of her for it. Her fear would nae mean she welcomed it."

"Aye, ye are right."

"I should have been here," he sighed.

"But ye could nae be, and there was naught ye could do about that."

"Mam, I —" he closed his eyes, trying to force down the bile rising in his throat. "I saw it. I knew it would happen."

"What?"

"I had a nightmare, just after Falkirk, and in that nightmare was everything ye just said. I saw it before it happened and I should have told her, warned her. That way if she saw anything similar, she would know what was coming."

"Alasdair, even if that is so, ye had no idea this would actually happen. Why would ye tell her that?"

"I dinnae know," he whispered. "I just cannae bear that such a thing happened to her, and all because she was tied to me."

"No, he would have done it anyway; ye could see his intent quite clearly. The knowledge that she was an officer's lass only made it better for him, allowed him to inflict more cruelty. I dinnae know what he said to her; I could nae hear it."

"I am thankful Fergus came. I will never forget what he has done for us, and when I can I will repay the favor, but he will always be my brother."

"Aye, and just in time. They had barred the door and were lighting the torch when he got to them. Fergus has always been a good lad, and I have loved him like my own, just as he has always loved ye. He saved us both, well, three of us if ye count the bairn."

A small smile appeared on his lips at the mention of the baby. "Aye, at least I have that. Even in the midst of all we have lost, I am gaining something precious."

"I can tell ye that she had no idea," Coira said, chuckling. "Just thought she was unwell. It is all right, ye know, Alasdair, to be happy. To be excited about yer first bairn. It does nae make ye callous or mean ye are forgetting; ye are just choosing something bright to hold on to. It is what she is trying to do. That poor lass has lost so much so quickly, and we all saw what the thought of losing ye did to her."

"What do ye mean?"

"She could nae stop weeping but did nae want anyone near her. Would nae eat or drink, would nae speak, just sat against this wall with her face turned away. That lass was willing herself to die, and we all knew it. If ye had nae returned, she might have managed it. Cailean and Fergus did what they could even as they grappled with their own grief, but she wanted none of it."

Alasdair closed his eyes, tears escaping and sliding down his cheeks. "I hope I am enough. I cannae replace Evander or Bridgette."

"No one is asking ye to, least of all her. She will find her way, and that way may be pulling Fergus and Cailean closer to try to fill the hole left by Evander. I am almost glad Bridgette did nae have to suffer the knowledge that he had died. They are together now."

"Fergus said he did nae suffer, and I hope she did nae either."

"I dinnae know," Coira admitted. "I hope for the same. I am thankful to nae have to remain amongst the mothers whose sons never came home, for the time I dwelled there was more than enough. Mine did, and I will thank God every day for it."

Alasdair smiled and took another bite of his food. "It is strange, the knowledge that I will be leaving here once more, never able to return."

"Surely ye could if ye wished, once things have settled a bit."

"No, I cannae. Nae with the —" he said before he stopped, having said more than he'd intended to.

"With the what?"

"Naught," he said. "Nae with the chief in France and all. I will have to stay there."

"Ye just said ye could nae come back ever, and his eventual death would mean ye could," she said, narrowing her eyes. "Dinnae ye lie to yer mother, Alasdair Stewart."

Alasdair cursed inwardly. "I cannae come home again because there is a bounty on me, Mam. As long as it is out there, I cannae be here. The moment they find me, I am a dead man."

"What! How!"

"All I will say is that I killed someone important and the English were nae happy about it." Seeing his mother's expression, he quickly added, "Nae that I did nae have a reason to do it, I did, but they dinnae care about reasons."

"Christ, Alasdair!"

"Aye, I know. It is why I have to leave no matter what. If I stayed here, if ye stayed here with me, they would murder ye both as well as me when they tracked me down. I cannae let that happen, and so to France we go."

"I was hoping we could return."

"*Ye* can, Mam. *I* cannae."

"I am nae leaving ye in France, Alasdair."

He reached out and covered her hand. "It will be fine. I dinnae know what our life there will be like, but no one else will either. We will settle it out, and all will come out right, I promise. No matter what I have to do."

"I believe ye," Coira said. "Now, finish yer food so we can all be on our way. Will ye be able to walk?"

"At least for a while, aye. Cailean said we would be moving slowly, so I may be fine. If I am nae, I can ride in the cart or on a horse. I think we will only have to worry about getting caught by patrols this first night. The farther we go, the less likely it will be."

As dusk deepened, the cart was loaded with what supplies they had been able to find. One horse was assigned to pull the wagon, and any others would either be ridden or tied to the back. The English horse Emi had ridden was set free; the branding on it would give them away if they were seen. Small children or those unable to walk were put into the cart around the supplies, though there weren't very many of them, and Lamb was placed in a basket held by Cailean's children. Emi helped Alasdair dress himself, fashioning a sling for his wounded arm and draping one arm of his new coat over his shoulder. It was strange to be wearing breeches this way, but none of them could wear tartan now. It would be a dead giveaway even if the English didn't recognize the clan to whom it belonged.

Two riders went ahead on horseback — they'd be able to

ride back to warn the group if someone was coming — and the party stepped off behind them. As they left the ravine, Alasdair took Emi's hand in his own, walking with Crisdean, Fergus, Ealasaid, Coira, Cailean, and Anna. When they reached the head of the loch where it became a river, Alasdair took a moment to look behind him. It was to be his final glimpse of the place he'd spent his entire life, and he wanted to memorize it so that he could always call it to him. The horizon was tinged with pink, leaving the hills around them a deep purple. The water of the loch shimmered faintly in what was left of the light, and a gentle wind blew through the trees. He'd never imagined leaving this place; he'd had no reason to. Everything and everyone he loved was here. It was where he'd imagined living with Emi, raising their children here just as they had been. Hearing them laugh and run and shout through the woods as they'd all done together, another generation of Stewart children. He had no idea what his life would look like now, but those dreams had died on the moor with the rest of his clan. Emi squeezed his hand, and he turned his head to see her smiling up at him as if she knew what he was thinking. In the end, he knew that his life was wherever he ended up, as long as she was there with him.

Darkness fully descended as the Stewart survivors made their way north into the mountains. Staying off of roads, travel would be slow with the cart, requiring them to make sure it could get through where they were going as well as trying to be as quiet as possible. They would be on the move until it was nearly dawn, then find a place to stop, hide, and sleep until it was night once more. There was conversation in whispers, and though everyone was wary, they were also in good spirits. They were all alive, and for now, that was a good enough reason to be happy. A little over an hour into their journey, the warning call made Alasdair's head snap up, his mind immediately focused: a patrol had been spotted.

"Everyone, farther into the trees away from the road! Get that cart farther in, go! Now!" Crisdean ordered in a loud whisper.

The group scattered into the deeper darkness of the trees. Alasdair pulled Emi into his arms and behind a tree, pressing her back against it, covering her body with his own as best he could as everything went silent and still while they waited for the group to pass them. The sound of their horses and their conversation were loud by comparison, but when they stopped Alasdair swore inwardly. He knew it wasn't because they'd been seen or heard; it was something else. The sound of footsteps on leaves as at least one of them walked into the woods made Alasdair unsheathe a sgian dubh in the darkness, and as the footsteps continued to get closer, he pulled his left arm from the sling to clamp his hand over Emi's mouth to smother any sound from her. As he felt her start to shake in terror, he placed a silent kiss on her forehead before resting his against hers to try and ease her. The footsteps stopped right in front of the tree where they were hiding, and Alasdair closed his eyes before he heard the very distinct sound of the man urinating against it. Once he'd finished, he turned around and left the woods the same way he'd come in, and it was soon followed by the sounds of their horses continuing on down the road.

No one moved; no one made a sound, knowing that any sound they made at this moment might be heard for a great distance. Emi's sobs were stifled into silence against Alasdair's hand, and he removed it once he was sure it was safe. There was a gentle rustle as people started to emerge from where they'd hidden themselves, and Alasdair stepped away from Emi, re-sheathing the sgian dubh.

"Emi, ye are all right," Alasdair said, keeping his tone as soothing as he could. "They are gone now."

She couldn't speak, burying her face in his chest, and he wrapped his arms around her.

"I know," he whispered to her. "But that man is dead, and I am with ye now. I would have killed him before I let him touch ye."

"Alasdair," she whispered. "I just … I …"

"Ye will be frightened for quite some time. I know," he said as he stroked her cheek. "Ye dinnae have to say it or speak on it. Come, help me reset my arm and let us all get back on the move. The farther from here we are, the better we will be."

By the end of the first night, they'd put a good distance between them and the main road to Inverness, and each successive night allowed them to relax a little more, to sleep a little easier knowing it was increasingly unlikely they'd run into any soldiers. After four days they came to a glen with a loch surrounded by mountains that could hide any fires or smoke as well as be used to set up a watch on the road to warn of any soldiers coming in. The loch would provide water, there were plenty of stones and trees to build housing, and hunting would be plentiful, particularly deer. They'd have to hunt without muskets, of course, as the sound would draw attention, but that would be a small adjustment to make.

Crisdean looked around himself, turning a small circle, and then nodded. "Aye. I think this will be a fine spot. What say ye, lads?"

"Aye," Cailean said. "There is plenty of natural defense here, though it is nae as though I expect any of the English to come in this far looking for anyone, and there are no clan lands near here to draw them."

"Agreed," Alasdair replied. "We have nae seen a patrol since the first night, so I doubt we will see any now. With the weather getting warmer, there is nae such a rush to get stabling built as there might be. We can focus on the people and nae the animals."

Fergus gave a small nod. "I think it is the right spot for the clan to set down temporary roots while they wait to be able to return home. It is two days' ride to Inverness from here, maybe three, so it will nae be hard for them to get supplies if they need them."

"Then it is agreed. The Stewarts have found a new home

to ride out this storm. Let us tell everyone to begin unloading. We can discuss plans tonight and get started in the morning."

Chapter 15

Emi wove her way through the marketplace in Inverness, Coira by her side. The city was crawling with English soldiers using it as a base to patrol the upper western Highlands while Fort William took care of the lower part. There were other forts on the east coast handling the same patrols, all to ensure that the retribution on surviving clans was carried out per Cumberland's orders. Emi was sent with Coira and one of the other men to see if Mr. MacMillan was still in business and if he could or even would sell to them. Alasdair's protests were vociferous, but Emi understood and reassured him; MacMillan knew her and would be willing to talk to her rather than someone else, so she was the one that had to go.

Emi forced herself to stay calm, to keep her head up and not look at the soldiers if she could help it. Her heart was racing, though she knew they wouldn't recognize her. They were in search of men here, not women. Neither she nor Coira nor the man with them wore anything that might identify them as Stewarts, though they'd discovered upon arrival that the English had now banned the wearing of Highland dress, and anyone wearing it would be arrested. What was tacitly understood was arrested also meant *dead*. Emi breathed a sigh of relief when she saw the door to the shop opened and undamaged, but as they stepped inside, she stopped short. At the counter were several English officers, and though she wanted to run, she instead closed her eyes, took a deep breath, and squared her shoulders before taking a place behind them.

"Ah! My dear Miss Taylor!" MacMillan cried out when he saw her.

Emi looked at him in confusion for a moment before she realized what he was doing and smiled at him just as the soldiers turned around to see who he was speaking to. "Good morning, Mr. MacMillan. A pleasure to see ye, as always."

"I am *very* glad to see ye here. I had heard yer father had fallen gravely ill, and I was greatly concerned when I did nae see ye here, fearing the worst."

Her father! She wondered for a moment if he knew, but realized it was most likely coded speech. Her father would mean her chief to him. "Indeed, he had, but he seems to be on the mend. Well, at least enough that I could step out for a short while. I thank ye very much for yer concern and will tell him ye are asking after his health."

"And Mrs. Taylor," he said to Coira. "A pleasure to see ye are also well."

"Aye, well indeed, thank ye," she replied.

"Ladies," the officers said together, bowing to them.

Emi and Coira curtsied to them, though Emi prayed her smile was convincing.

"Mr. MacMillan, thank you for your time. We will be expecting delivery soon," one of the officers said.

"Of course," he replied, smiling, before the group departed. Once they were gone, he gestured for Emi and Coira to follow him, and when they were in the backroom and out of sight, he cast aside any propriety and hugged Emi. "Lord be thanked, Emi! I am so glad to see ye!"

Emi returned the affection, relieved to see someone else she knew in a world that seemed to be falling apart. "And I am glad to see ye!"

"When everything went to hell after the battle, I was so worried about ye and the rest! I knew they were sending soldiers and wanted to send word to warn ye, but I knew nothing I sent would get there faster than they would. All I could do was pray ye all got out of harm's way."

Emi's expression saddened. "Some of us did, and some did nae."

"Emi?"

"Maman is dead. They killed her."

"Oh, Christ, Emi," he said, crossing himself. "Bridgette was a good woman. May the Lord bless and keep her."

"My brother died in the battle, as did most of the Stewart men."

MacMillan sighed. "I was afraid of that. But ye said most, nae all."

Emi lowered her voice to a whisper. "The chief is alive. Fergus and Cailean also made it."

"Thank God. And Alasdair?"

Emi smiled. "Alive. Almost nae, but he made it."

MacMillan smiled, relieved. "At least there is that. And ye say some of the others made it?"

"A fair few," Emi replied. "This is Alasdair's mam, Coira."

"Good to meet ye, Mrs. Stewart. I apologize for earlier, but I did nae want them to know what yer real names were. If they did, they would have taken ye in on the spot. They have a list of names of clans present, and those on it are being picked up if they are found. Ye were wise nae to wear yer tartan."

"Lord help us," Coira said.

"Mr. MacMillan, we need yer help," Emi said. "We are desperate for supplies, and I was sent to see if ye could help us. The English burned the castle and either took or destroyed any supplies they found, so we have next to naught. We only have a little bit of money, but the chief promises to send the rest on to ye when he gets to France."

MacMillan paused for a moment and then nodded. "Aye,

I will do what I can. I will make up for it by charging the English more," he said, winking, and it made Emi laugh.

"Thank ye, ye dinnae know how much this means to all of us. We can only carry some rather than let ye know where we are, in case they are following any of yer wagons to try to find out where clans are. I have a feeling they will be watching ye."

"Aye, that is certainly a fair concern, and ye are smart to think of it. Ye always were a clever lass, Emi. We shall do it this way: ye take what ye can with ye now. When ye arrive, wait a day, then send yer cart back with a different man and he can take the rest."

"How will ye know him?" Emi asked.

"Have him tell me Miss Taylor sent him, and I will know it is yer man."

"Thank ye so very much, Mr. MacMillan. Yer kindness will be repaid, I swear it to ye."

"Yer clan were amongst my best and most trusted customers; I cannae help but repay the favor now. When will the chief leave for France?"

"As soon as he knows it is safe to slip through here and onto a ship. We dinnae know how long that will be."

"Nae long," MacMillan said. "I have a ship leaving soon for supplies, and he needs to be on it. If he is nae and they discover where ye are, none of ye will be safe. The sooner he is away from the rest of ye, the better."

"There are several of us going with him," Emi explained. "The three officers and their families."

"Fine. Have the lot of ye at the docks in two weeks. Come at night, and I will tell ye the name of the ship sent back with yer man on the next pick up."

"What! Mr. MacMillan —"

"Dinnae argue with me, lass. I want ye out of here and safe. I have been doing business with yer clan for as long as I have been in charge here, and my father before me as well as his. There will still be Stewarts here when ye are gone, and one day, the sons will return to take their rightful places. Even with ye gone, I will still provide goods to those left here, and ye can tell the chief I will send him invoices to pay for it. I trust him, and he is a good man. The world here is going to change, and I dinnae know what it will look like when it is over, but now is the time to hold together and nae let them destroy everything about the way we have all lived for God knows how long."

"Thank ye," Emi whispered.

MacMillan took her hand and kissed it. "Ye and yers would do the same for me if I needed ye, I know ye would."

"We would, and we will. Yer family will always find friends and protectors with the Stewarts, I promise ye."

"Bless ye, lass. We just might need it one of these days."

***

Emi looked around the cabin given to them on the ship that would be carrying all of them France. It was small, but they'd make do. This was a great favor being done for them, and none of them had any intention of complaining about it. She knew Crisdean hated that they were leaving at all, but there was nothing to be done about it now. Choices had been made, the repercussions of those choices had followed, and he knew he now had to do what needed to be done for everyone's safety. The trip here was stressful, but they were aboard now and leaving with the tide just after midnight.

"Prepare to be boarded and searched!"

There were gasps from all of them at the shout from the docks. The English were searching ships for fleeing Highlanders now, likely in the hopes of catching either chiefs or the prince himself. The children were ushered into the wardrobe and told to be silent and still as the door shut. The rest pressed themselves against the wall where the door was, hoping the searchers would just open it, see an empty space, and shut it again.

"Hobbs, search the hold. I will search up here," someone said.

"Ye cannae open that door!" they heard the ship's captain say near the cabin.

"And why not? I need to search your ship. Why do you not wish me to go in? What are you hiding?"

Emi shoved herself away from the wall and into the center of the room as Alasdair extended a hand to try and stop her, staring at her in wide-eyed horror, unable to do anything.

"Sir, there is naught there."

"Then you will have no problem with my going in."

As the captain stalled, Emi made quick work of unpinning herself out of the top portion of her dress, pulling the pins from her hair and shaking it loose just before the door was thrown open. Emi shrieked in feigned mortification at having her cabin barged into by a man as she was undressing and pulled her clothes around herself, staring at the officer in shock and embarrassment.

The officer immediately averted his eyes. "Begging your pardon, miss," he said as he shut the door just as quickly as he'd opened it and hurried away from the cabin.

"All clear, sir," the other voice called back as he came up from the hold.

"Thank you, Hobbs. You are free to depart, Captain."

There was silence in the cabin as they heard the fading sounds of boots down the gangplank and then nothing, before a slow, dark smile spread across Emi's lips. Alasdair began to laugh and slid down the wall to sit on the floor, burying his face in his hands. It wasn't long before the rest were laughing too, both at her ingenuity and their near capture. Anna opened the wardrobe to let the children out, and they hurried into her arms.

"Christ, Emi," Fergus said. "That was a brilliant bit of quick thinking."

"Aye," Crisdean said. "Well done, lass."

Emi laughed and covered herself up, pinning her dress again. "I am just glad it worked."

"As am I," Alasdair said, "even if ye did need to half undress yerself to pull it off."

"Needs must, aye?"

"Aye," he said with a smile. "Needs must."

There were no further inspections, though the captain was also greatly amused by Emi's ingenuity in stopping the officer from going into the room. As the tide rose, the ship was loosed from the moorings, and there was a slight jolt as the wind caught the sails and began to move them more than just drifting. Once they were given leave to do so, the children made their way onto the deck, full of excitement and reveling in the experience of being on a ship at sea, as well as the ability for the first time in weeks to laugh and be happy. Tensions eased, knowing they were safe now, and it allowed a sense of relaxation to settle on the passengers. Emi made her way to the back of the ship, placing her hands on the railing and watching the dark line of the Scottish coast as it grew smaller. There was an ache in her heart, knowing she'd never see it again, and she closed her eyes as tears made their way down her cheeks.

"It feels another lifetime ago when the pair of us stood on a bluff overlooking this same sea and wondering what it would be like to sail on a ship," Alasdair said, his voice soft as his hands covered hers on the railing while he stood behind her.

"It was," she replied. "A lifetime ended by a war."

"Aye." Alasdair sighed. "I am sorry for this, Em. Yer life never should have been this way, and ye never should have been forced to leave the home ye love. Had it nae been for me, ye would nae have. So many times over the last several weeks I have wondered if it would nae have been best if I had never said a word to ye."

Emi turned around to look at him. "Why?"

"If I had nae, ye might be safer and remaining in Scotland."

"Alasdair, I might still be in Scotland, but I would nae be safer, given who my father is."

"Ach, Em, no one would know that, and no one would tell them."

"Would they nae? What happens when people are frightened, when times are hard, and they know that turning me in would net them a reward? I have already dealt with one of our own trying to save his skin by trading our lives for his, and he did nae even know. How much more possible is that with people who all know? They are offering £30,000 for the prince's capture, and though the sums for the chiefs are nowhere near that high, they are plenty high enough to make it enticing. Turning me in would allow the English to use me as bait to try and draw my father out of hiding, and ye are a fool if ye think they would nae jump at the chance."

"Aye, ye are right, and I am surprised I did nae even consider it. Perhaps I was too focused on my own impact on ye to do so."

"All of that aside, I would likely be unmarried still, probably nae courting anyone, with a brother dead from war and a mother murdered. I would have no one. I never would have known what it was like to have someone love me the way ye do, never known what it was like to feel that love in return. Ye may never have come home, for ye would have been lost in the woods and dead without me to guide ye home as ye said I did, without the promise ye made to me pushing ye onward. I am nae sure that is a life I would want."

Alasdair kissed her forehead. "Ye speak true about all of it. I would have been miserable, and I am nae sure I could have kept it in no matter how I tried. It was already hard enough and getting harder by the day."

"That day on the bluff, ye wondered about seeing the wider world away from Scotland, and now ye will."

"Aye, I will, and ye will be at my side for it. I want to tell ye how proud of ye I am, how amazed. Ye have been so strong, caring for others and doing what needs to be done. It was ye who got us onto this ship, ye who saved us today by thinking quickly. Ye negotiated the delivery of goods that will save our clan. Ye survived all that has been done to ye. Ye are yer father's daughter, and ye have never shown it more clearly than ye have these last weeks."

"I am nae sure I could have done any of it had ye nae returned."

"But I have and ye did, and that is all that matters in the end. I am glad ye are my wife, glad everyone knows now what ye are to me and what ye meant, even if it was looking back at the previous year and seeing the signs."

Emi smiled at him. "Good. Ye are stuck with me now. No giving me back."

Alasdair chuckled at the memory of their handfasting. "Dinnae want to, thank ye."

She laughed and shook her head, then rested her head against his chest. "A new life is waiting, and as terrifying as the thought is, I can face it with ye."

"Aye, all of us on this ship are in it together. We are still in his service, so where he goes is where we go. I am nae sure what this will all look like, but whatever it is, we are a family more than we ever were before. Bound together by what we have all lived through, it is a bond stronger than blood, and that will get us through the new challenges we are sure to face."

Emi closed her eyes, stepping back from him to let the cool sea wind wash over her, taking back to Scotland with it all the pain, fear, and degradation of the last weeks, where it could remain. She took a deep breath and released it before opening her eyes and looking at him. "I am ready."

Chapter 16

"Crisdean!"

"Màiri," Crisdean said with relief as his wife rushed into his arms in the courtyard of the family home in France, and he embraced her.

"Oh, thank God!" she said as she wept. "When the news came, I feared the worst, and when I did nae hear from ye, it only made it seem all the more true!"

"Shh, I know, but I am fine. I could nae write, for it was nae safe to do so, and I was in hiding but I can tell ye about that in a while. Where are the boys?"

"Inside at their lessons. They dinnae know ye are here yet."

Crisdean nodded. "I have brought some familiar faces with me," he said, gesturing to the wagon where the others waited.

"Fergus! Cailean! Alasdair! Lord be praised!"

"Mistress," the three men said together with a nod.

"Oh, and Coira and Anna! Ealasaid!" she exclaimed, but then stopped short. "Emilia," she said.

"Aye," Crisdean said. "The lads could nae remain in Scotland, just as I could nae, so they pledged their service once more and came with me. That, of course, means their families also came."

"Of course," she said with a smile, but Emi could see it wasn't a true one. She wasn't happy to see Emi there amongst the living. "Come in, all of ye. I am sure ye are in dire need of rest."

Given permission, the small group got out of the wagon to join their chief. The arrival in Le Havre had been an experience, full of sights and sounds and people. Alasdair and Emi translated for everyone and, other than the chief, did the talking. The four-day journey to Paris was smooth with no need to worry about how, when, or where they traveled. Upon entering the city, the entirety of the group gasped in shock at the sheer size and scope of the place, and they'd all gawked at the churches and buildings that were seemingly everywhere. Ushered inside now, they stopped in the foyer to look around them, surprised by the opulence of the setting. Marble flooring, walls covered in varying colors of paint, some in colors they'd never seen before. Glass, chandeliers, and furniture covered in material so fine all of them were afraid to touch it, much less sit on it.

"Louis," Màiri said to a liveried man who appeared from another room and kept to English for the sake of the guests. "Would ye please show our guests to the servants' quarters, where they can stay for now?"

"No," Crisdean said, also in English, and Màiri looked at him in surprise. "Louis, see them all to rooms upstairs where they can get proper rest. Ask the kitchens to have water heated for bathing, as we all need it. Send for the tailor and dressmaker as well."

"Oui, monsieur," Louis said, departing to relay the orders and send a housemaid to show everyone upstairs. Màiri looked unhappy but said nothing as the small group was led upstairs. As they went up, they heard the voices of Crisdean's sons, Alexander and James, cry out with joy at their father's return.

"Would ye look at this," Coira whispered, and Anna nodded in the same sort of stunned surprise. The sounds of their footsteps were muffled by thick carpeting on the stairs and running the length of the hallway. Cailean and Anna were given a room with a smaller room attached to it that would usually be used by a valet or ladies' maid, and that was where the children could sleep. Fergus, Ealasaid, and Arabella were given the same sort of room, and Coira got her own next to that, with Alasdair and Emi having one to themselves.

Alone in their room, Emi turned a slow circle, not knowing what to think. This was even finer than the inn at Inverness, and that had been a luxury. In this room was a large bed made of beautiful, dark wood, with a canopy and curtains of blue velvet. There was a large wardrobe and a chest of drawers for holding the clothing they didn't have, a washstand, a fireplace, and two chairs of the same blue color sitting across from each other before the fireplace with a table between them. Crossing to the window, Emi looked out onto the gardens, though she could also see the townhouse next to them, which she found strange.

"I cannae believe it," Emi said in a quiet voice. "This does nae seem real!"

"Aye," Alasdair said, looking around. "Well, it at least does nae seem real that I am being allowed to stay here. We saw a lot of similar surroundings on campaign."

Emi looked at her clothing and frowned. "I am afraid to touch anything for fear of dirtying it."

"I assume that is why the chief sent for the dressmaker and tailor," Alasdair said, chuckling. "Ah, but love, ye belong in such a place as this. I always felt so."

"I dinnae know why."

"Well, I suppose that even though I did nae know the truth about ye, there was still something in ye that made me aware that ye did," he said as he came forward and took her hand. "I dinnae care what anyone says," he whispered in her ear. "This is yers, Emi; by all rights this should all be yers. Ye are the first child, and this is the world ye should have been kept in all along."

"Shh, dinnae say such things, Alasdair," she whispered back. "It is nae mine and never was. I am nae a legitimate child, so it does nae matter a whit. Besides, I am a woman and I cannae be chief, so it would have gone to Master Alexander anyway."

"Still," Alasdair countered. "Had he been able to marry yer mam, ye would nae have known any different."

"But he did nae. Please, ye cannae say that, nae here. The mistress is already displeased enough that I am here."

"What?"

"Ye did nae see her face when she saw me? She is nae happy about it."

Alasdair shrugged. "I did nae, but it does nae matter either. We are only here until we can be settled elsewhere, and I doubt it will take long."

There was a knock at the door, and Alasdair opened it to find a maid with a tray of food and tea.

"Hello," he said, stepping back to allow her in.

"Hello," she replied in response, bustling into the room and placing the tray on the small table between the chairs. "Monsieur asked for food to be sent up to all of you."

"Merci beaucoup. C'est très gentil," Emi replied. *Thank you very much. That is very kind.*

The maid looked at her in surprise. "You speak French?" she asked, switching to it.

"We both do," Alasdair replied in French.

The maid smiled at them. "That is unexpected," she said, keeping to French, as it was likely easier for her.

"Is it?" Emi asked.

"Well, you are not from here, so why would you speak it?"

"The woman who raised me was French; she met her husband here when he was with the former chief on a visit. She taught me."

"Oh! Well, that makes sense then."

"The chief required I learn," Alasdair said, "and I spoke it with her in order to keep in practice."

"Welcome to you both," she said with a nod. "Everyone is happy the chief managed to escape. I am Hortense."

"Emilia, and this is my husband Alasdair. He is one of the chief's officers."

Hortense blinked in shock. "Emilia? *You* are Emilia?"

"Aye," Emi replied.

"Oh, we have all heard about you, madame, though only in whispers here. There was talk of the son of the old chief having a daughter before he was married to the mistress, but no one knew for sure if it was true. Apparently, the old chief was heard speaking of you, which is how they knew your name. We younger ones heard about it as rather a shocking secret; though, when the war happened, we wondered in whispers if you would come to claim what was yours if you lived."

Emi shook her head. "Naught is mine."

Hortense gave a small smile. "Not so, madame, but that is not for me to tell you. If you will excuse me, I need to get back downstairs and make sure water is ready for bathing."

She gave a small curtsy and departed, leaving Emi staring at the door in shock before she looked at Alasdair. "What do ye think that was all about?"

"I dinnae know," he said, just as perplexed.

***

As the others began their baths, Crisdean finished with his, dressing and going down to the study. It had been a relief to bathe, and even more of a relief to put on fresh, clean clothing. Opening the door, he looked around with a small sigh before going inside. This had been his father's room, and he couldn't help but feel a bit like he didn't belong in it even though he was the chief now. His father had died in exile in France, and now so would he. He hoped that his sons would not suffer that same fate, able to go home to their lands and their clan one day.

"Crisdean," Màiri said as she stepped inside and shut the door. "Ye wanted to see me."

184

"Aye," he replied, turning around and hugging her close to him. "It is *so* good to see ye again."

"I have missed ye terribly," she said, returning the embrace. "But ye are here now and alive, and that is a cause for joy."

He smiled at her as he pulled back. "Aye, but ye dinnae fully feel it."

"What?"

"Màiri, I saw yer reaction when ye spotted her, and so did she."

Màiri sighed. "Crisdean, why is she here? I told ye I did nae want her here when ye sent us in the first place, and now ye bring her with ye?"

"Aye, I did. Aside from anything else, she is Alasdair's wife. What did ye want me to do? Tell him that he could come but she could nae? He never would have agreed to that, and I was nae going to leave that lad in Scotland, nae after all he has done."

"His wife? Since when?"

"Apparently for over a year. Done the old way, handfasting, but valid enough."

"Nonsense. It was nae done in a church before God. No register was signed, and ye did nae give yer consent to it. She has no business being here."

Crisdean frowned. "Ye have that little respect for our traditions? Or is it because ye dinnae want her here so badly that ye are willing to disregard it? Either way is unbecoming of ye, Màiri. I have given my consent now, they will marry here in church, but she is his wife even without that."

"And what about my feelings in the matter? We are exiled from our home forever, and now ye are asking me to allow yer bastard to live here while telling me to be happy about it!"

"Màiri!" Crisdean said, shocked. "Ye had no problem with her serving ye and living in the castle; why are ye acting this way?"

"Because she was easy to ignore there, Crisdean! It was a much bigger space than this house is, and she will nae be serving us here, will she? Unless ye are planning on replacing the cook? At least there she was in her *proper* place."

Crisdean shook his head. "I am shocked at yer behavior, appalled. Let me tell ye a few things, Màiri, so that ye can perhaps look within yerself and find some Christian mercy. That child has lost everything. Bridgette was murdered by the English. Evander was killed in the final battle. For a few days, it was even thought that Alasdair had died, though truly I am still nae sure how he survived. She was violated by the English in retribution. Yet ye have the nerve to complain about her being here? She is my daughter, and naught changes that. Did ye honestly think I would sit by and ignore it? Leave her there with naught, try to strip Alasdair from her — the one person she has left — just so ye can continue to pretend she does nae exist?"

"Ye owe her naught! I am sorry for the tragedies she suffered, but that is nae yer responsibility!"

"Nae my … ye cannae be serious? As members of the clan, they *are* my responsibility! Yers!"

"She is nae a legitimate child, Crisdean!"

"Aye, she is nae, but she is still mine. Ye can see it when ye look at her, just as I can. She is no threat to ye, so why do ye see her as one? Even if she was nae my child, she is still the wife of one of my officers. One who has served me faithfully, who saved my life more than once over the last nine months, and who has a bounty on his head because of what he did to protect me. He cannae ever return to Scotland even if the others could."

"So, what is it ye plan to do with them? They cannae all live here forever."

"No, they cannae. However, what I *can* do is find property nearby and make sure they have small homes to live in while they serve me. I owe them at least that."

"Which is why I suppose ye are also paying to clothe them?"

"They have no clothing, Màiri! For Christ's sake! Everything they owned was burned when the English set their homes on fire! When did ye become so unfeeling toward the members of the clan ye are mistress of? Or would yer attitude be different if Emilia were nae here?"

She said nothing and Crisdean just stared at her in disbelief as he realized that was exactly how it would be if Emi weren't there.

"Ye are nae going to like what I am about to say to ye next, but I cannae let that dissuade me: I am going to acknowledge Emilia. Publicly."

"What!" she shouted. "Crisdean, ye swore never to —"

"I swore never to do it when my father was alive. I swore nae to do it when life was normal, but it is no longer normal! I am tired of hiding! Tired of lying! She has the right to be known for who she is, and be assured that those in the clan who remain in Scotland are well aware of her lineage. It changes naught about what is due to our sons; they are still the rightful heirs to the clan."

"No! I refuse to let ye do this!"

"Refuse? Ye can refuse all ye want, but it will nae change a thing. I am going to do what I feel is right, Màiri, whether ye agree to it or nae. If ye are cruel to her, if ye treat her with anything other than civility, I will make ye regret it. Ye should try to welcome her as a mother should, as ye would if ye were my second wife and I already had a child."

Màiri gasped. "Make me regret it! So ye are threatening me now?"

"Take it as ye will, Màiri, but I am hurt beyond words at the way ye are behaving. I have always known ye to be kind and caring, wanting to help those below ye, and now, when ye have the biggest chance to do it, ye have become a hypocrite. Ye are showing me that ye are only willing to help those *ye* deem worthy of it."

"I will leave —"

"Then *leave!*" he shouted, slamming his hand on the desk in anger and frustration. "But know ye will get naught from me if ye do. The boys would also remain here in order to learn and prepare for the expectations placed on them in the future.

Ye can return to Scotland and live in hiding with the rest of the clan, return to yer own family, or figure out how to make yer way here in France. Ye will nae manipulate me, Màiri, and I suggest ye make yer choice carefully."

"You would nae …"

"Would I nae? I owe ye naught, particularly when ye are trying to single someone out and demanding they be treated with less compassion than ye would show a beggar on the street! All because ye dinnae like her parentage. If ye think ye would get any sympathy for it from me, then ye are wrong."

"Ye would nae say this if I was yer precious *Helena*!" she spat at him, tears in her eyes.

Crisdean's face darkened. "Dinnae ye *ever* speak her name to justify yer selfishness. Ye are right, I would nae say this, because she would have given me no cause to do so. She was from among my clan, a farmer's daughter, and had she been raised to a higher life, she would have understood her place to provide for those in her former station. But nae ye. Ye who were born to a chief and have never understood what it was like to live the way the rest of yer clan does. Ye have always had fine clothes to wear, fine food to eat, people to serve ye and make that life possible. Ye have never lived the way they have, while every day they see ye eating food they cannae have and wearing clothing they could only dream of. Perhaps it is time ye find out."

"Another threat! If ye loved me, truly loved me, ye would nae say such things or be so cruel as ye are to do any of this without a care for my thoughts and my feelings!"

"*If* I loved ye? How can ye nae see that it is *because* I love ye that seeing ye act this way upsets me so much? This is nae the woman I know! Nae the woman I married or was lucky enough to find love with! I expect more of ye, Màiri! Better! I am disappointed in ye. I had hoped that, after all that has happened, ye would be willing to look beyond yer own bias and let the past go to be kind to someone who needed help, someone who served ye gladly and still would if I asked her to. I did nae even know ye when this happened, and it is no reflection on ye. It is nae as if I left our marriage bed and fathered a child. I did nae and never have. All I have *ever* done for the last 20 years regarding her is have a care for everyone's thoughts and feelings but my own, and it ends now! I respected yer wishes then and watched my own daughter be relegated to a life of near poverty and service in my household, never aware I was anything to her other than her chief. I watched her serve ye with a smile while nae having any idea that ye hated her very presence. When is it enough? When have either of us paid enough penance in yer eyes?"

"Crisdean, I —" she said through tears. "She is a constant reminder that ye loved another!"

"And ye did nae? What about Andrew, hm?"

Màiri's face paled.

"Aye, ye did nae think I knew about him, did ye? Oh, love, I did. In the first year of our marriage, I cannae tell ye how many times I heard ye call for him in yer sleep, or the times ye said *his* name instead of mine when we were abed together. It hurt, but I understood ye, and after a time it stopped. I was nae going to be upset with ye over something I felt, too. Do ye think any other man would have done that for ye? Do ye think any other would have held his tongue when he discovered ye were nae a maid? I doubt it. And had ye come to me with child, I would have kept it to myself and claimed that child as my own. Dinnae act as though ye have loved only me when we both know that is nae so."

"Ye knew … I …"

"So, ye see? What I have forgiven in ye I have long allowed ye nae to forgive in me, and I am tired of it. The world we all knew is gone, Màiri, and it is nae coming back. The English burnt the castle to the ground and killed everyone they found there. They sent raiding parties hunting for survivors and killed them, too. I am asking ye to let it go now and let everyone cease living a lie. Let her have a father who can love her while still loving ye. Try to get to know her and ye just may find ye enjoy her company. Her birth is no fault of her own, and I am asking ye to stop punishing her for it."

Màiri sank into a chair, covering her face with her hands. "I did nae know I had done any of it."

"I know ye did nae," he said, his demeanor softening as he sat down across from her. "I never told ye, I did nae want to hurt ye or embarrass ye, but I have never in all our time together held it against ye. Having loved him did nae mean that ye would love me less forever, and ye did nae. Just as I have nae with ye. I love ye, I do and have. Ye are my wife and I would nae be without ye. Helena is dead, and though I remember my love for her, it does nae change or overshadow my love for ye. I can love Emilia and nae love the boys less, just as I have nae done their whole lives."

"I wish it were that easy!"

"Ye dinnae know it would nae be because ye have never tried. Instead, ye have chosen to hold on to an anger ye had no right to anyway, and I allowed it, but I will nae allow it any longer. I am nae asking ye to raise her, nae asking ye to do anything but be civil and accepting. She is a good lass, a kind lass, and ye know that to be true, for ye have seen it yerself. It is thanks to her that we are even here at all, for it was *she* who got us onto a ship and *she* who saved us from being caught during a ship inspection in Inverness. Ye have no idea what she has done nae only for me, but for ye and the boys. Please, try and understand my side. How long could ye go on seeing yer boys each day while they never knew ye were their mother? I have done it for 20 years, Màiri, and all I am asking is that I be allowed to stop."

Màiri sobbed softly. "Ye are right. I could nae have lasted a week, much less 20 years. Very well, I will do this, but promise me ye will nae put her above the boys."

"I cannae," he said. "She is a lass, she cannae take over the clan, only they can do that. She might get a sum when I die, as she should, but that will have no bearing on ye or on them. As ye surmised before, she will no longer be serving any of us. I cannae, in good conscience, ask her to do so. I want the set of clothing I provide for her to reflect her place and the staff to be instructed to treat her appropriately. Alasdair will still be serving me and the rest of the family, and I am sure Emilia cannae be idle, so we will come up with something for her to do."

Màiri nodded. "I can accept that, and if I find I cannae at first, I will try for ye."

"Thank ye," he said, taking her hand and kissing it. "I am glad ye will nae leave," he said, offering her a small smile.

Màiri sighed. "An empty threat."

"I knew it was," he said with a chuckle.

"I do love ye, Crisdean, and perhaps I am jealous of the love ye had for Helena, that ye still have."

"Aye, perhaps, but the love I hold for her and the love I hold for ye are different. That love for her resides in a young lad's heart that has long since been taken over by a man's. It is the man's heart that belongs to ye fully; ye have no need of the other. Just as it is for yer own heart. I know what is mine, and I am happy with that."

"I should try to think of it that way. Ye have always been faithful to me, never given me cause to feel shame or strayed from the vows ye made. Nae like so many others. I should remember that."

"I have never asked ye this, but who was he?"

"One of my father's junior officers. He was young and handsome, kind. Deep down I knew I could never keep him no matter how I tried to convince myself otherwise in the romantic dreams of a young lass' mind. I did love him, and he loved me, but after ye and I were married for a time, I realized it was nae as deep as the love I had come to have for ye. I had long ago released him without even realizing it."

"One of his junior officers!" Crisdean exclaimed before he laughed. "Ach, ye were courting danger, were ye nae?"

"A bit, yes," she admitted, laughing with him and drying her eyes. "Perhaps that is what made it even more intoxicating."

"Oh, probably. The romance and the danger of it all, the things the young love most," he chuckled as he reached out to wipe stray tears from her cheeks. "But I dinnae doubt ye loved him, nor he ye, for if he had nae, he would nae have risked his neck to court ye."

"Aye, well, that is long done now. I saw him some years later and he had married a lass from the village, but I was past it being able to hurt me by then."

"That is fortunate."

"Ye speak from experience."

"Aye, I do. I was forced to be there to watch Helena wed the man that would claim my child as his own, a final bit of cruelty by my father to make sure I understood it was all over. It was still fresh, and I hated every moment. It hurt more than ye can imagine."

Màiri frowned. "Ye never told me that."

"Ye never asked."

"I am sorry I did nae. Had I been strong enough to do so, things could, perhaps, have been different."

"But ye were nae. Yer heart was broken, and ye were angry over all ye thought ye lost; ye had no space to consider that our circumstances may have been similar. All ye knew was that I had once loved another lass and fathered a child with her, but ye did nae want to know the full story."

"No, I did nae; ye are right. I will admit that it felt as though taking away something that meant so much to ye was retribution for having had something taken that meant so much to me," she said, frowning. "Now that I have said it out loud, I realize how utterly ridiculous that is, how unfair. Ye did nae take that from me, my father did. Life and circumstance did. Ye tried yer best to make it up to me, and ye saw the pain in me that I refused to acknowledge in ye, letting me blame ye for all of it with grace and understanding. Ye allowed me my fury at Helena even though there was no cause for it, because ye felt it was what I needed from ye."

"Aye, I did. Ye are right about all ye just said. I did nae try to explain my relationship because I knew ye did nae want to hear it and would nae. It would nae have helped. I wanted ye to be happy, to love me, and if this was what ye needed to do so, then so be it."

"God forgive me," she whispered. "Crisdean, I am … sorry is nae enough. I never should have let this go on; I should have asked ye once I felt sure of my place in yer heart, but to even consider it came too close to my own pain, and by the time I could have done it, it was so ingrained in me that I could nae change it. I should have acted with the same grace and compassion ye showed me and let ye take Emilia when Helena died, and I will forever regret nae having done so. Ye are right that ye have earned the chance to stop lying to everyone. It will no longer matter, nae here."

"Precisely. Ye have the chance to make it right now, and ye should take it. She is going to need care, Màiri. She is expecting her own child and will no doubt be fearful without a mother."

"She … oh Lord, nae from —"

"No," Crisdean said quickly, not letting her finish because he couldn't bear to hear the words spoken aloud again. "The bairn is Alasdair's, conceived before we left for the final battle. That is without doubt."

"Thank God for it. What will ye do with the others?"

"As I said, I will search for a property for them, a house they can share. We would be hard-pressed to install them in the servant's quarters here. Except —"

"Except for Emilia. It is yer wish that she remains here."

"Aye, as she is entitled to do as my child."

"All right. We will need to think of positions for the rest of them."

"We will figure it out. Thank ye, my love."

"Crisdean, did ye hear anything of my brother and our clan?"

He sighed. "Aye. Hamish was killed at Falkirk and his son has taken his place. I know the lad immediately pulled the clan from the conflict and retreated. He was wise to do so, and I am sure they all still live because of it."

Màiri began to weep, and Crisdean moved to sit beside her, holding her close.

"I know, love, and I am sorry for it, but yer nephew and yer people are safe. Ye will see them again."

"Aye," she whispered, wiping her cheeks. "It will take time to have clothing made. I instructed the staff to immediately take the clothing they arrived in when they got to the bath and put it out to wash. For now, they can stay in their rooms in the underclothes we provided, and food can be sent up."

"A good plan."

"I still have *some* sense."

"Aye," he chuckled. "Far more than ye give yerself credit for."

"There is something I need to see to. Ye stay here, and I will join ye for tea, shortly."

"As it pleases ye."

Màiri stood and left the study, wiping tears from her face as she went up the stairs to her room. Opening her wardrobe, she searched through and removed a dress and petticoat before going to a chest of drawers and pulling out a large square of white fabric, followed by stockings and shoes. From her dressing table, she picked up a jar of pins and left the room. Stopping outside of a door, she took a deep breath, released it, and knocked.

"Mistress!" Emi said as she opened the door, dropping into an immediate curtsy upon seeing Màiri standing there.

"Hello, Emilia. May I come in?"

"Aye, of course!" Emi said, stepping back to let her inside. "I apologize for nae being dressed properly, but they took our clothing away downstairs."

"Aye, I instructed them to do so in order to have them cleaned for ye. Is Alasdair nae here?"

"It was his turn to bathe."

"Ah. Emilia, I —" she began, then paused to collect herself before going on. "I would like to apologize to ye for the way I greeted ye this morning."

"No need," Emi said, her smile reassuring. "I am sure ye were overwhelmed with all of us just appearing on yer doorstep."

Emi's smile and her ready forgiveness, her decision to explain away the behavior rather than let her feel bad, felt like a knife made out of pure guilt thrust into Màiri's heart. It only proved Crisdean correct, that Emi would still serve them if asked and think nothing of it.

"Aye, but I think we both know that is nae the reason, though I thank ye for yer kindness in trying to excuse me."

Emi fidgeted, looking down at her hands. "I know my being here makes ye unhappy, and I am sorry for it. I want ye to know I will nae be here any longer than I must be."

Màiri's eyes filled with tears upon hearing the young woman speak those words. "No," she said. "There will be no need for that. I am the one who should be sorry, but that is a discussion for another time. I am here to help ye because yer father wishes to see ye downstairs."

Emi gasped, looking up. "Mistress, I —"

"Hush ye now. Dinnae fret about it, aye? Come along," Màiri said, ushering her toward the dressing table and setting things down. "Put this on," she said, placing a small set of pocket panniers around Emi's hips and then tying them closed.

They were followed by a petticoat of a deep green silk damask, and the square of white fabric was draped around her shoulders. The over gown came next, made with the same fabric as the skirt. Màiri arranged the white fabric to cover the front of Emi's stays, and then tied the bodice closed with three ribbons. This left the bodice open wider at the top and smallest at her waist, showing off the fine white material as well as her figure.

Emi stared in shock, and Màiri realized she'd likely never even touched silk, much less worn it. She watched as Emi reached out with one hand and touched the delicate lace edging the three-quarter sleeve. Lace. Another thing seen from a distance but never touched or even dreamed of.

"Mistress, why are ye doing this?" Emi asked, fighting tears.

"Ye certainly cannae go down to tea in yer shift, can ye?"

"Well, no, but —"

"Precisely. Sit please."

Emi did so dutifully, and Màiri placed silk stockings on her legs, tying them with garters that matched the dress fabric. Taking a pair of shoes, she slipped them onto Emi's feet and nodded, then stood and picked up the comb from the table.

"A good thing ye and I seem to have feet nearly the same size," Màiri said, smiling as she ran the comb through Emi's hair. She styled it quickly but simply, though even this simple style was far more elaborate than Emi had ever worn before. The finishing touch was a ribbon of green velvet tied around her throat. "There. Ye look a proper young lady now. Come with me."

Emi stood and followed Màiri toward the door and out, the dress rustling as she walked, and it was clear she felt entirely out of place in it.

"Louis," Màiri said as they reached the bottom of the stairs. "Please tell my sons to come into their father's study for tea."

"Yes, madame," he said with a bow.

Màiri led Emi to the door of the study and opened it, letting Emi inside and then following behind her as Crisdean stood.

"There ye are, my darling, I was starting to wonder if —" but then he stopped as he caught sight of both women. "Emilia," he whispered before he stepped forward and took her hand. "Ye look lovely."

"Thank ye, Chief. The mistress brought a dress and said ye wished to see me."

Crisdean looked at Màiri and smiled. "Thank ye, my dear," he said to her. "That was very good of ye."

Màiri smiled in return, happy to have at least pleased him, though it didn't begin to make up for 20 years' worth of silent suffering, and she knew that. "Emilia, ye can …" she stopped, finding the next part difficult to say. "Ye can call him what he is to ye now … yer father."

Emi looked at her in wide-eyed shock. "But —"

"Aye," Crisdean said. "There is much to discuss."

The door opened once more, and Alexander entered with James behind him.

"Father," Alexander said, bowing, as James did the same. "Wait … Emilia … is that ye?"

"Aye, Master Alexander," Emi said with a smile and a curtsy.

"Ach! It is grand to see ye again, and I am so glad ye are here and safe!" Alexander grinned. "Dinnae ye look a fine lady!"

"Aye," James said. "I like it!"

"Lads, there is something I wish to tell ye," Crisdean said. "Ye have a sister."

"What?" James asked, confused. "Since when?"

"Is there a bairn coming here?" Alexander asked.

"No," Crisdean said, chuckling. "She is already here."

"One of the wee ones that came with ye? I thought those were Cailean's children and Fergus' sister?"

"Alexander, James, meet yer older sister: Emilia."

Their jaws dropped, and they stared at her, while Emilia stared at Crisdean.

"Are we adopting her?" James asked.

"No, she is yer natural sister, James. It has just been kept quiet all of this time."

"Whatever for?"

"It was yer grandfather's wish."

Alexander scoffed. "It is about damned time someone finally admitted it out loud. Dinnae know why it took this long or why grandfather wished it. Why does it even matter? If she is our sister, then she is and no amount of quiet will change it. Besides, none of that ever stays buried."

Crisdean raised an eyebrow. "When did ye become so wise, Alex?"

Alexander shrugged and smiled before he stepped forward and hugged Emi. "It is nice to meet ye for who ye are," he said.

"Thank ye, Mas … I mean … I dinnae know what to say now?"

Alexander laughed. "Alex or brother is fine by me."

James followed suit and smiled. "Ye can call me the same. Well, except James and nae Alex."

Crisdean laughed and shook his head. "I am proud of the both of ye for taking it this well. All the same, I want ye to know that this changes naught as far the two of ye are concerned. The both of ye are still where ye were before as pertains to the clan."

"Of course, Father," Alexander and James said.

"How did ye even know, Alex?"

"Because I am nae blind? She looks just like ye, Father."

"Right. Emilia, I would like ye to know that Lamb is currently making himself at home in the kitchens, charming the staff."

Emi laughed. "Aye, that sounds like him."

"Now, let us sit down and have tea," Crisdean said.

"Ch … I mean, Father, Alasdair does nae know I am here and will be wondering where I am," Emi said.

"Oh, I had nae thought of it. Alex, be a good lad, would ye, and fetch a set of yer clothes to lend to Alasdair, then bring him down."

"Aye, Father," he said, standing and swiping a tea cake from the tray as he did so.

"Alexander!" Màiri said, exasperated. "Where in the world are yer manners!"

Alex laughed, stuck it in his mouth, and departed as Emi stifled a laugh in her hand. Clearing her throat, she reached out and picked up the teapot, pouring tea into the cups without thinking.

"Emilia, what are ye doing?" Crisdean asked.

"Serving tea?"

"Christ, child, sit ye down. Ye serve no one now. They serve ye."

"Wait, but I —"

"Ye will find something else to do," Crisdean said.

Emi sat down, looking a bit bewildered and folding her hands in her lap to keep from fidgeting, studying the damask pattern on her dress until James slid a plate into her field of vision.

"Thank ye," she said, taking it in her hands before almost immediately giving it back and standing up, walking to the desk across the room.

"Emilia?" Crisdean said, concerned.

"Forgive me, I dinnae …" She swallowed hard. "The smell of the food."

Màiri's expression softened in understanding. "Ye poor thing. I had a terrible time with that when I was carrying Alexander. It does go away even though it does nae ever feel like it will." She stood up and picked up a cup of tea, bringing it over to her. "Here," she said. "The tea will at least help ye."

"Thank ye," Emi said, taking it from her. "And thank ye for the dress and the kindness. I know ye dinnae have to and it is hard for ye, but I appreciate all of it."

Màiri offered a small smile. "It is hard, and I thank ye for recognizing it. However, I do need to, and I will adjust. We all will. It is as strange for ye as it is for me," she said, patting Emi's hand before returning to her seat.

"Emilia," Crisdean said, turning his chair so he could see her. "What became of yer necklace?"

Emi winced and placed her hand at the back of her neck. "Fergus got it back for me and I have it, but the chain that held it is broken. The man who … he snapped it when he yanked it from my neck."

Crisdean frowned. "We will see it having it repaired for ye."

"Thank ye. It means so much to me still. I dinnae know what I would have done if I had nae gotten it back."

"I know it does," he said. "All the more reason to have it fixed."

The door opened and Alexander came in, followed by Alasdair. Now that he was cleaned up, he looked very near his former self. In Alexander's fine frock coat and breeches, he made quite the picture, and Màiri saw Emi's immediate smile, recognizing in it the love she felt for her own husband.

"Chief," Alasdair said, bowing. "Ye called for me, sir?"

"Aye. Emilia was concerned ye would return from yer bath and be worried to nae find her there."

"Aye, sir, she was in our room when I went down, and I am nae sure where she has gone."

Crisdean raised an eyebrow, and Màiri almost laughed because Alasdair hadn't recognized her in those clothes. "She is right here, lad," he said, gesturing to Emi.

Alasdair's eyes followed the direction and then widened when they landed on Emi, and Màiri could see he was stunned at just how beautiful she was in the borrowed frock. The green of the dress set off the green of her eyes, which was precisely why she had chosen it.

"Emi," he said in an awed tone, making his way to her to take her hand in his and kiss it. "Ye look … I dinnae even have the words."

The young woman's smile was shy over his reaction, and the sweet innocence in it touched Màiri's heart. She remembered as though it were yesterday the first time a compliment from Crisdean had made her feel the very same way, the moment when she'd realized she'd begun to care for him in a way she'd never expected to be able to do. The first step away from her childhood love affair. To see it between Emi and Alasdair made her regret what she'd said earlier about their marriage not counting because it hadn't been done in a church. They were married in all of the ways that mattered, and the pure love between them was obvious. She'd been so wrong about so many things, and now she had the chance to do as she should've always done.

"Ye look quite handsome yerself," Emi replied.

"She looks as she should," Crisdean said, "as her station requires."

"Sir?" Alasdair asked, looking at him quizzically.

"Everyone here knows, lad. My sons know they have a sister, and soon enough the household will know as well. There will be no more service for my Emilia as she takes her proper place in this family. It means naught as far as her marriage to ye goes, and ye still have my whole-hearted consent."

Alasdair smiled. "Thank ye, Chief."

"Now, come and sit ye down. There is business to discuss."

Chapter 17

Emi could hear the excited chatter of the others as they neared the dining room for breakfast the following morning. While Alasdair was back to wearing the clothing he'd arrived in, Crisdean had insisted on Emi wearing the borrowed dress in order to make her station clear to anyone who saw her. Hortense had helped her to dress, something for which Emi was quite grateful. There were far more pieces to this gown than anything she'd worn before. She'd still felt terribly out of place while studying her reflection in the looking glass, wondering who this person was and who she was expected to be. It wasn't Emi, and she felt lost, like a child playing at being an adult.

The door to the dining room was opened by a footman as they approached, and Crisdean entered first, followed by Màiri, Alexander, and James. When Alasdair entered with Emi on his arm, the already gathered group looked utterly shocked.

"Good morning to ye all," Crisdean said.

"Good morning, Chief," they all replied together, though distractedly because they were still staring at Emi.

Alasdair pulled her chair out for her and then pushed it back in once Emi had taken her seat before sitting beside her, and Emi dropped her eyes to the table, uncomfortable under the weight of their stares.

"Emi, why are ye dressed like a fancy lady?" Arabella asked as the rest took their seats once the family had done so, and her mother shushed her.

"Because, wee Arabella, Emilia is my daughter. She *is* a fancy lady, and now she is dressed like one," Crisdean said, a bright smile on his face brought on by being able to speak those words.

Coira looked at Alasdair across the table, and Emi saw him give her a wink and a reassuring smile as the breakfast was brought into the dining room. The children looked perplexed as the china plates and the silver were set before them, followed by the large silver trays filled with food.

"I can see my face in it!" one of Cailean's sons said as he held a shiny silver spoon in front of his face.

Alexander and James were laughing in an instant, not in the way of finding the child stupid or ridiculous, but in absolute amusement at watching these children experience things for the first time that they'd always taken for granted. The two of them picked theirs up and started making faces into them, which only spurred the younger children to do the same until the entire table was laughing so hard they were in tears.

"Before ye kill us all with laughter, will ye eat?" Crisdean got out between laughs.

"Aye, Father," the two of them said, trying to stifle laughter but failing.

"I dinnae know what any of this is," Arabella said, looking bewildered.

"Oh," James said from his place near her. "These are sausages, and some toasted bread. Eggs, and here are some crepes. Ye can put jam on those. Ye can put it on yer toast, too, like Alex does. Ye know the berries, and there is some porridge there if ye dinnae like anything else. In fact, here," James said, cutting a piece off of his sausage and putting it on her plate. "Ye try that piece to see if ye like it."

Arabella looked at his hands, then picked up the fork the same way he had it. Spearing the piece with the fork, she brought it to her nose and sniffed it, then looked at it curiously before putting it in her mouth. Moments later, she clapped her hands together excitedly and nodded.

James laughed. "Aye? Here ye are then," he said, putting one on her plate.

The other children clamored for one, and each had one placed on their plate by James or Alex, who'd gotten out of their chairs to serve them and help them to understand varying foods. Coira, Ealasaid, and Anna watched with tears in their eyes, touched by the behavior of these young men who were stepping down to help the youngest of their clan, the ones who would one day be serving them, instead. It only proved that either of them would make a fine chief when their turn came.

"While the lads are helping the children," Crisdean said, preparing his own plate. "I want to tell ye what my plans are."

"Aye, Chief," the rest responded.

"First, starting this morning, the children here will be attending lessons with Alexander and James. The tutor is aware of their ages and lack of formal education and is more than willing to work with them. They will learn French, reading, writing, numbers. It will give them a better chance in life, as the system they would have spent their lives in no longer exists."

"Are … are ye sure, Chief? I know that does nae come cheaply and —" Cailean began.

"I am sure," Crisdean said, cutting him off. "I owe them at least that. Today I will be going out to look at several nearby properties. I am looking for a place large enough to hold all of ye so that ye have a roof over yer heads while ye still serve me. There is nae room in the quarters here, so ye will have to live out, as ye have always done."

"Aye, Chief."

"As far as service goes, lads, naught has changed. Ye go where I go, same as always. Yer wage is the same. Anna and Ealasaid, I would like for ye to join the household staff here. More hands to help with the work of running the house is always helpful. Coira, I would like for ye to serve my wife, as her ladies' maid has only just recently departed. She knows ye well, and I think it should work out fine."

"Aye, Chief," the three ladies replied.

"In the meantime, yer measurements were taken yesterday, and two sets of clothing will be provided for ye by me: a daily set and a Sunday set. Anna, Ealasaid, and Coira will get a set of livery to match the others in the household. Is this agreeable to everyone?"

"Aye, Chief," they all replied.

"Good, now let us get on with our breakfast."

Once breakfast was concluded, the children eagerly ran off to their very first lessons, while the three women were shown to their areas of work so that they could start learning how things were run here. Crisdean departed with the three men, leaving Emi entirely on her own with no direction and nothing to do. She stood in the foyer at a loss, never having had a day in her life where she didn't have some task to take care of. With a sigh, she decided to explore instead. Opening one door, she stepped into what seemed to be a small ballroom, and she smiled. She'd never seen what a ballroom looked like, but this seemed right with its golden walls and chandeliers, though they were now covered in dust sheets. Closing her eyes, she tried to imagine what it might look like full of people, with music playing and laughter floating through.

"It is pretty, is it nae?"

Emi jumped and opened her eyes to find Alex in the doorway. "Aye, it is."

"Sorry, did nae mean to startle ye."

"It is fine. I was just looking around, as I have naught else to do."

"Aye, that has to be quite an adjustment for ye."

"Ye have no idea."

He laughed and walked into the room. "What were ye thinking of?"

"I was just trying to imagine what this might look like if ye were having a party."

"Ah! We had one nae long after we came, so as to raise money for the cause. It was probably as ye would expect: a lot of people milling about, having boring conversations. How people can make seditious talk somehow boring is beyond me, but they managed."

Emi laughed. "But surely there was music?"

"Aye. Music for the dancing," he said, taking her hand and starting a pavane she did her best to follow. "Nae as lively as a proper ceilidh."

Emi grinned "All the beautiful clothes, though!"

"If ye care about such things."

"I am sure there were more than a few young ladies with their eyes on ye."

"Maybe," he said, drawing the word out with a sly grin as he suddenly hooked her around her waist and lifted her off of her feet, turning them to face the other direction, which only made her laugh more.

"Surely ye are thinking of such things."

"Did I say I was nae? Come now."

"Are ye nae supposed to be at lessons?"

"Aye, but they dinnae need me right this moment and I saw ye here as I passed."

Emi began to pick up the steps, moving along with him more easily. "Are ye really all right with this, Alex?"

"With what?"

"Me. My being here."

"Of course," he said, then started laughing. "As ye saw yesterday, it was nae like we did nae already know."

"It did nae upset ye?"

"Why would it? The only thing that upset either of us was having ye wait on us. There were so many times we wanted to tell him we knew but did nae. I am glad it is out now and ye can be as ye should be, as ye should have always been. I wish ye had been there from the start, my sister, where everyone knew."

"He promised our grandfather."

"Aye, but that was a ridiculous promise. It makes no sense, but I cannae change it and neither can ye."

"I probably would nae have been allowed to wed Alasdair."

"Now, that is probably true and would be a great shame, for I like Alasdair a great deal."

"So do I."

"Ye married him, so I hope so."

Emi laughed. "Ye have a quick wit."

"Sometimes a good trait and sometimes nae."

"I think it is a fine trait all of the time."

"Ye are getting the hang of the dance! Perhaps Father should hold a ball to introduce ye before ye get too big to wear a ballgown," he said, tapping her stomach.

"Is that so? Well, maybe I will wear one right at the end and perhaps I can make it a fashion."

Alexander stopped moving, laughing. "I almost want to see that now."

"I bet ye would."

"Emi," he said, his face becoming more serious, his eyes anxious and sad. "I ... what was it like?"

"What?" she asked, confused by the switch.

"At home. What happened?"

"Oh," she said.

"If it does nae hurt ye too much."

"No, ye should know. It is yer clan, too. There was no warning. A group just came and ... I was visiting Coira, and we heard the muskets as they killed everyone at the castle. We hurried out to get away, and there was already a group there. They told us all of the men were dead," Emi said, her expression distant. "They had one of our men with them, he told them who we were to try and save himself, and he said he had seen Alasdair die. Then the Englishman, he —" but she stopped, unsure if she ought to tell him. Alex, however, seemed to understand immediately.

"No … oh no … Emi …" he whispered, his face pale and his expression horrified. "Please tell me it was nae —"

"I cannae tell ye that," she replied.

Alex closed his eyes and lowered his head. "Jesus, I am so sorry."

"They had locked us in the cottage and were going to burn it, but Fergus saved us. We went to the clan spot, ye know the one, in the ravine? We hid there. I found out when I arrived that Maman had been murdered by the English and Evander had died in the battle. A couple of days later, Alasdair stumbled in nearly dead, but he had made it home somehow. He had been shot, and the way he escaped, well, ye should have him tell ye."

"It is even more horrible than I imagined. And they burned the castle?"

"Aye. If ye ever return, ye will need to rebuild it."

"Oh, I will," Alex said, determined. "That land is ours, and I *will* get it back. But all of ye are safe here, and the rest of the clan is safely hidden away. We can be thankful for that. Thank ye for telling me."

"I am glad ye left," Emi said. "If ye had nae …"

"Aye, I know. Ye remember the day we left? I told ye to be safe, and I meant it as yer brother. I wanted to tell ye right then, tell ye that I knew, in case I never saw ye again, but I could nae bring myself to say it. I started to, started to tell ye I would miss ye."

"I remember, and I thought then that ye had meant to say something else but changed yer mind."

"Now ye know what it was. I did nae say it because I knew it would upset my mother and she was upset enough already. I heard them argue when she was asked to bring ye with us." Alex sighed. "I was so angry that she would nae do it, thought her selfish and still do."

"She had her reasons, Alex. It is none of it that easy, and she is doing her best to fix it now."

"It was that easy to me."

"But ye forget about Alasdair. I would have been leaving my husband behind, and in the end, knowing I was waiting for him is what kept him alive long enough to get home. The others needed me, too. I organized the supplies and provisions for the regiment. I had to stay, but I am touched by yer concern."

Alex reached out and took her hand. "Aye, ye are right; I had nae thought of those things. I just wanted ye to be safe with us here. Ye are my sister, and I love ye, I always have, even if I could nae tell ye out loud. Ye have never been half-blood to me. Nae ever."

Emi's eyes filled with tears at his emotional declaration. "Thank ye, Alex. That means more than ye know."

"I am sorry about Evander, I know he was a brother to ye as well, but just know ye still have brothers left. All any of us can do now is go forward. We are Stewarts; we dinnae give up so easily and are nae so easily defeated. They can take from us now, but we will come back stronger."

"Ye sound like yer father."

"*Our* father."

"Right. It still feels odd to say."

"I am sure it does. I should get back," he said, kissing her hand before squeezing it. "Take a chance to rest for the first time in yer life. Ye know how to read; ye should go to the study and pick a book."

"Aye, that is a good idea."

Alexander smiled and left the room. Emi looked around once more before following him out, crossing to the study and going inside. One of the housemaids was tidying up but stopped her work to curtsy to Emi, who was taken aback by the gesture.

"Madame Emilia," she said.

"Hello," she said, recovering herself and switching her

speech to French. "Dinnae let me keep ye from yer work."

The young woman smiled and curtsied again before resuming her task. Emi went to the shelves of books, looking them over, stopping when a book on the history of Scotland caught her eye. She pulled it from the shelf and went to the settee, sitting down as she opened it and started to read. The next thing she was aware of was someone giving her shoulder a gentle shake, and she opened her eyes to find Alasdair smiling down at her.

"Alasdair?" she murmured, groggy.

"Aye."

"Ye were nae gone long."

He raised an eyebrow. "We were gone most of the day. It is just past dinner now."

"What? How?"

Alasdair chuckled and sat down beside her. "Looks as though ye fell asleep reading."

"I must have."

Reaching out, he stroked her cheek. "It is good that ye are resting. Ye have nae had much of it since everything happened."

"I suppose nae."

"Ye may want to stay in bed tomorrow. I know it is nae yer way, but it can be yer way now and ye should take the chance. No one would begrudge ye a day of rest, nae in yer condition."

"Maybe," she said. "Did ye know there is a ballroom here?"

"I did nae! Did ye find it?"

"Aye. Alex came and danced with me, and we talked."

"Ye danced?"

"Aye," she said, following it with a sleepy smile. "He is very funny, rather like ye."

"He is a good lad," Alasdair said, "and I will be happy to serve him as I have served yer father."

"My father. It still sounds so strange to me."

"I can imagine."

"One of the lasses called me Madame Emilia and curtsied

to me. I have never in all my life been referred to that way or curtsied to, and I did nae know how to react."

"Well, ye ought to get used to it. The chief insists ye be treated as they would treat any of his children. It is a different life for ye now, Emi, a life ye deserve."

"A new life for ye, too."

"Aye, I am married to the chief's daughter, which is nae how I thought I would end my days, but there ye have it."

Emi laughed and sat up, kissing him. "I am glad ye are safe here with me."

"Aye, so am I."

"Alasdair …"

"Aye?"

"Why cannae ye go back?"

"What?"

"Ye said before that ye cannae ever go home. Why?"

He looked conflicted before he sighed. "Em, there is a bounty on me. I cannae go home because I am a dead man if they find me."

"What! Alasdair! What did ye do?"

"I killed a man, someone important, but it was nae murder as they claim. He would have killed yer father had I nae killed him first, and almost did. I found him just in time."

"Oh, dear God."

"I did my job, no matter what the English try to say about it."

"How much?"

Alasdair faltered for a moment. "£100."

Emi's eyes widened. "£100! That is a fortune!"

"It is, is it nae? In the end, it is good we left, for if anyone found out, it might be hard to resist turning me in for that sort of money."

"None of the Stewarts would have turned ye in!"

"Dinnae be so sure. As ye said to me on the ship, when times get hard and people are desperate, they will do a great many things ye once never thought them capable of."

"Aye, that is true. All the more reason to be glad we are here."

"Would ye like to have yer dinner and then go for a walk with me? There is a lovely park nearby; I saw it when we were out."

"Aye, that would be wonderful, thank ye."

"Come," he said, standing and taking her hand to help her up.

As they entered the dining room, those sitting there stood, though Cailean and Fergus bowed to her as the young men serving did the same. She looked at the two men in confusion for a moment before realizing it was something they had to do now, and it made her uncomfortable.

"Please, dinnae do that, Cailean and Fergus."

"Why nae?" Cailean asked.

"Because it just does nae feel right. I dinnae like it."

Both men looked to their chief, who gave them a small nod. "As she asks ye, lads. I can understand why it would be hard for her to make such an adjustment after spending her whole life as yer equal."

Emi sighed in relief. "Thank ye, Father. I dinnae think I can really take it from anyone who came here with us," she admitted. "I have known them all my life and I just … I cannae." The thought of Coira curtsying to her made her cringe.

"I will allow it for the adults, Emilia, but nae the children. The rest of the household is also nae exempt, as ye have nae known them."

Emi nodded, finding it a reasonable compromise. Alasdair pulled out her chair for her, and she sat down. "Did ye find what ye were in search of?"

"Aye, I did. We found a nice property less than a mile from here that will serve everyone well with plenty of space."

"So, everyone will be nearby. I am very happy to hear that."

"The children can come for lessons each day and things will settle themselves out."

"Father," Emi said, toying with her spoon. "I need something to do."

"What do ye mean?"

"I cannae sit here this way, being idle. I never have been, and I dinnae know if I can start now."

Crisdean smiled and shook his head. "Just like me. What is it ye want to do?"

"I miss cooking."

"Emilia, that is … ye cannae go back to the kitchens. There are people here to do that already, and I cannae cast them out so that ye can be there."

"I know, and I would nae ask ye to, but perhaps I could help? At least with bread, which I always enjoyed. Or desserts. I could teach them how to make Maman's tarts so that the recipe does nae …" She closed her eyes for a moment, realizing what she was going to say and forcing herself to go forward. "Die with her," she finished in a whisper.

There was an uncomfortable silence before Alasdair spoke. "And no one can make a venison pie like Emi does."

"Aye, that *is* true," Fergus agreed. "Best I have had."

"Let us do this, Emilia: when I want a venison pie or am having guests, ye can make it, just as ye have always done. On special occasions or holidays, ye can make desserts. I had a more specialized task in mind for ye," Crisdean said.

"Oh?"

"I was thinking that perhaps ye could take over the accounts. Màiri hates to do it, and ye have a great deal of experience there in managing it while we were away. I was also hoping ye could handle my schedule and write letters if needed."

Emi looked at him in surprise. Managing the household accounts was a very important task, and while she had done it during the war, that seemed different from doing it now. "Aye, if ye wish."

"Good," he said. "Ye can start next week. For now, I want ye to rest."

"Have ye been speaking to Alasdair?"

Both men laughed. "No, but ye do need some rest, Emilia. Ye have been living on a knife's edge for weeks."

"So has everyone else."

"They are also nae with child," Crisdean countered.

Emi opened her mouth to retort but shut it again and pressed her lips together when she realized there was nothing to say to that.

"Aye, precisely."

"May she have leave to go on a walk in the park after dinner, Chief?" Alasdair asked.

"Aye, that is something altogether different," he replied.

Once dinner concluded, Emi rose from her seat to go on the promised walk with Alasdair, looking forward to getting outside, but as they went to the door, a sharp gasp stopped them.

"Madame Emilia!" Hortense said, hurrying toward her. "Where are your hat, gloves, and parasol? No, no, no! You cannot go out without them!"

"I cannae? But I never —"

"It is different here. Perhaps in the country but not here."

"Oh," Emi said. "I dinnae have any of those things."

"You stay here, I will fetch them," Hortense said before dashing upstairs and returning with the items borrowed from the mistress of the house. "Here, put out your arm," she continued, pulling the gloves onto Emi's hands and arms. She then handed Emi a hat and hatpin and handed the parasol to Alasdair. Emi made quick work of putting on the hat, and Hortense nodded. "There, now you are ready. Enjoy your walk, Madame Emilia and Alasdair."

The pair watched her bustle off back to her duties, and then Alasdair grinned and opened the door to pull her outside, waiting to laugh until it shut behind them. "I did nae know a lady required so much to simply step outside," he said as he offered his arm.

Emi threaded hers through his and let him lead her toward the park. "Nor I. I am nae used to such things; before we would just go outside."

"Aye," he said with a chuckle before he opened the parasol and held it for her as they walked.

"There are so many people and buildings. I thought Inverness was busy."

"It is a large change, to be sure."

"I am glad that I am at least allowed to nae have all of ye bowing to me. I cannae stand the thought of yer mam doing so."

"Aye, that would be odd to me as well."

"And yet when we officially marry, they will have to."

"I think, like ye, I will insist on those we have always known nae doing so. Especially my mam."

"What would they call ye, I wonder?"

"Monsieur Alasdair or Monsieur Stewart, I would imagine."

"Hm," she said, quiet.

"All I know is that I am happy to be out of doors with ye once more, with ye all to myself, where we can pretend as though the last months never happened and dinnae need to fear seeing soldiers."

"Aye, me too. Happy to be out with ye, I mean."

Alasdair laughed. "I knew what ye meant."

As they stepped into the park, Emi smiled. The late spring flowers were a riotous display of color and scent, and the fresh new leaves rustled in the late afternoon breeze. If it weren't for all of the noise around them, she could close her eyes and imagine herself being home for a moment. The river, the loch, and the sounds of the birds in the quiet of a Highland afternoon were all things she knew she'd miss the most.

"I did nae get the chance to properly tell ye yesterday how beautiful ye look in this dress."

"Thank ye," she said. "It was very kind of her to lend it to me."

"Aye, indeed it was, though I am sure yers will be just as fine when they arrive."

"Nae sure if I want them to be."

"Why nae?"

"It just feels *strange*, Alasdair. I am suddenly in this life I dinnae know, where those I love and have known my whole life are supposed to be below me, where I have fine things they dinnae, and I am nae used to it. I would be happy in my normal dress, back in the kitchens with everyone, preparing supper for the chief and his officers or walking to the loch with ye."

Alasdair sighed. "I know, love, but it cannae be. Even if ye were in those clothes, that world is gone. Those kitchens are gone and all of the smiling faces that used to sit in that hall have gone with it. We cannae go back to it."

"Sometimes I wonder if I would nae have been better off, had I been one of them."

Alasdair stopped short and turned to look at her with a concerned expression. "Why would ye say that?"

"Because then I would be there forever instead of here, trying to make sense of a world I dinnae understand."

"Emi," he said, placing a hand on her cheek. "Ye cannae say such things. Ye cannae leave me here alone without ye, for if ye cannae make sense of it, how will I? I know ye miss home and our friends and family, I do too, but we can only go forward, and looking back does nae help us."

"I just want to be myself! When I looked in the glass this morning, I did nae know who that person was looking back! What do they want from her? From me?"

"Then do it! Be who ye are! No one can stop ye, and ye dinnae have to become something ye are nae to please people who dinnae even know ye! Fine frocks dinnae change that Em; it cannae change what is within ye. What it *can* do is make ye more visible so that ye can use this new life to make things better for others. Lighten things up, Emi, just as ye always did at home. Yer spirits are low now, everyone can see it, but ye can come back. Emi, *my* Emi, did nae die back in the woods that day. She persevered, she took care of me, took care of her father. She took care of her clan by securing them a supply line, and she got all of us here safely by getting us on a ship and making sure we were nae caught. Somewhere between the North Sea and Le Havre, she disappeared. Where is she? Where has she gone?"

Emi closed her eyes and pressed his hand to her cheek with one of her own.

"I need her; we all do. I need the woman I married, the one who boldly stood in front of me one night and asked me for what she wanted. I need the lass who can always make me smile, who has been my very best friend from the time I could understand what friends were. I dreamt of coming home to her, and I did, at least for a little while. *She* would nae say what ye just did; she would take what she was given and make something brilliant and beautiful out of it. She would nae be afraid of anyone, and ye *are* afraid. Dinnae let them win, dinnae let that bastard Englishman succeed in killing ye while yer body goes on living. Please, Emi."

"I am so sorry," she whispered. "Ye are right; I *am* afraid. What if I displease him? What if I do or say the wrong thing and shame him?"

"Ye cannae displease yer father by being who ye are because that is the only way he has ever known ye."

"What should I do?"

"Ye should rest, as we have all said. It will do ye a world of good and set yer mind to rights again. When ye rise, then ye will be the Emi ye have always been before all of this. Ye will accept the service to ye, but ye will treat them kindly because ye *were* them once. And when ye come down, ye will be our Emi with a fine dress, and that is all. Ye can do it; I know ye can."

Emi nodded and turned her head to kiss his palm. "I will try."

"Ye will do better than that because ye are Emilia bloody Stewart, and if ye survived a war, ye can certainly survive this."

Emi laughed and shook her head. "Aye, fine."

Alasdair kissed her forehead and smiled. "There ye are; I was wondering when ye would come back. Now, let us finish our walk, shall we, Madame Emilia?"

Chapter 18

Emi sat in the study at the writing desk, working her way through the account books and familiarizing herself with the way the household was run here. What were the staples for the kitchens, how much was purchased, and for what reason? Could there be economies made even though it wasn't necessary they do so? She put the quill down and lifted her eyes from the page, looking out onto the street in front of her. She still wasn't used to all the noise and bustle, but she was getting closer to being able to tune it out.

The week of rest had done wonders, Alasdair had been right about that, and she was feeling much more herself than she had since they'd arrived. He'd also been right about being unapologetically herself. When she'd gotten up again, she'd put on her normal dress and taken herself to the kitchens despite what Crisdean said. It was where she felt the most comfortable, and she needed to work her way into this life instead of just being dropped into it. The kitchen staff was surprised to see her, unsure of why she was there even when she announced her intentions. She'd shrugged it off and familiarized herself with the kitchen stores before deciding to make some bread as they'd had daily at home. She was very excited to find lemons and used one to make a different loaf flavored with lemon, garlic, and rosemary. A tray of tablet followed that, and there were enough supplies to make individual meat pies for each person for dinner.

The reaction of everyone in the kitchens when they'd seen her working would have been funny if she'd noticed it. It was clear she knew what she was doing and wasn't some pampered princess who wouldn't know an honest day's work if it slapped her. Emi doled out the tablet and enjoyed watching their faces as they tasted it for the first time. She'd shared a meat pie with the cook, who tasted it and then let everyone else do the same. After that, she'd told Emi she was welcome in the kitchens any time she felt the need to be there. Hurrying up the back stairs, she changed her dress and made her way down to dinner just in time for the food to be brought out. The looks on everyone's faces when the trays were uncovered had been worth the work. Seeing the foods they were normally used to eating was a joy, and the familiar bread and its taste were a calming reminder of many past dinners and suppers.

"I will have to commend the cook on learning these recipes!" Crisdean said as he happily tucked into a meat pie.

"She did nae," Emi said. "I made them this morning."

He froze, his fork halfway to his mouth, and the others looked up from their plates. "Ye what?"

"I made them," she said. "I wanted to and so I did. It made me happy to be doing something I so loved. Dough does nae care what yer station is, it rises and falls all the same."

Across from her, Alasdair smiled into his wine glass. *This* was the Emi he knew.

"But Emilia —"

"I will nae do it all the time, but there will be times where I want to for reasons that are my own. I will nae be in anyone's way, and no one outside of the house needs to know. Now, Father, try the other bread and let me know what ye think? I added some flavors, and I think it turned out well."

Crisdean smiled at her and then shook his head. They all

knew it was a battle he wasn't going to win, and it wasn't worth it to even bother trying. As directed, he took a piece of the bread and took a bite, then stopped and looked at her.

"Lord in heaven, Emilia, that is grand." Those words immediately spurred everyone else to take a piece, and the unanimous decision was that she should make it again.

The memory made her smile before she looked to the books again. The sickness, too, had passed, it seemed, and she was grateful for that, though she now had to loosen her stays just a little in order to be comfortable. The new clothing for all of them had arrived, with fine breeches, coats, and waistcoats made of Stewart tartan for the three officers for their daily wear, and a finer set for Sundays. The children were all clad in comfortable suits and dresses for general wear, and the three women had fashionably cut but functional dresses, with both groups also having Sunday clothes. Emi's clothing was different, as she'd been told it would be. For her there were several dresses, so she wouldn't be wearing the same one every day of the week, all made of silk or some other rich material and cut with her current condition in mind so that they could be adjusted as needed. Hats to match, gloves, a fan, and two sets of shoes. There were fine lawn shifts, a dressing robe, and slippers. Though she'd been a bit surprised by all of it, she was becoming more accustomed to wearing them, having taken to thinking of them as a uniform she was expected to wear and nothing more.

The door to the study opened, and Emi looked up to see Alexander breeze in. He danced around her, placing a bunch of flowers on the desk in front of her before kissing her cheek and twirling around to sit in a chair near her. "Sister," he said, smiling.

Emi laughed and picked up the flowers. "Mmm, thank ye Alex, how sweet of ye."

"Are ye nae even going to ask me why I am in such a good mood?"

"It had nae occurred to me since I have never seen ye in a bad one."

"Hmm, touché. So then perhaps why I am in an extra good mood?"

"Very well," she said, chuckling. "Why?"

"Because there is to be a ball!"

"Here?"

"No, silly! At the palace! The king is throwing a masquerade ball, and we have been invited!"

Emi's eyes widened. "Have ye! How splendid for ye, Alex! What do ye think ye will wear? Ye will have to tell me all about it when ye return."

Alex looked at her as though she'd lost her wits. "Ye realize that means ye are going ... right?"

"*Me?* Whatever for?"

"Last I checked ye were my sister, so that means ye are going. The family was invited."

"Oh, Christ," Emi whispered. "I dinnae know the first thing about balls or how to behave with a king!"

"I am sure ye will get some lessons before then, but ye should be ready, as mother has called in the dressmaker to be sure both of ye have suitable attire. The lady should be here any moment, I would think."

Emi stood and marked her place in the book. "Thank ye for the warning."

"Ye are welcome. Could nae let ye be ambushed with that one. Oh, and by the way," he called out as she was hurrying from the room, "Alasdair will be there, too!"

The house was a flurry of activity by the late afternoon, with dress designs and measurements, fabric choices, and all manner of trims. The next two weeks seemed even busier, at least to Emi, as she was schooled in etiquette, court rules and expectations, varying dances, and primers of who might be there and who she might see. It was all enough to make her head spin, and by the end of it she was no longer sure she wanted to go. There was hardly time for Alasdair alone, and when she came to bed, she could hardly keep her eyes open. He voiced his concerns that they were pushing her too hard, but she convinced him it was all fine and would be over soon enough.

When the evening of the ball arrived, Emi sat before the mirror of her dressing table as Hortense dressed her hair and wove a beautiful silver ribbon through it. A string of small drop pearls was pinned into the front of her hair to act as a circlet, and they stood out against her dark hair. Once her hair was finished, a lace mask was tied over her eyes, and Emi went to stand.

"Not yet, Madame Emilia," Hortense said, opening a box to reveal a triple strand pearl necklace, with earrings and a bracelet.

Emi gasped and touched them with a gloved hand. "How beautiful! It is very kind of the mistress to lend them to me."

"They are not Madame Stewart's; they are yours. Monsieur Stewart told me they were a gift to you from him."

Emi did her best to hold her tears in as Hortense fastened the necklace around her throat and affixed the earrings and bracelet. "Thank ye."

"You look beautiful Madame Emilia. You will be the talk of court; I am sure of it."

"Let us hope not," Emi said with a small smile as she stood and left the room.

She could hear the others downstairs waiting for her, and she hurried to the stairs. The rustle of her skirts caught the attention of the others, who all stopped and stared at her as she descended them. Coira, Anna, and Ealasaid all gasped to see the fine material and to see Emi in it. The dress was made of ivory silk with flowers brocaded in silver all over it, with half-sleeves ending in a ruffle of the same material behind her elbows with lace in the front. Fergus and Cailean couldn't look away from her, and Alasdair seemed at an utter loss. Alex and James smiled brightly, and even Màiri looked pleased.

"Emi is a princess," Arabella breathed, her hands clasped together. "Just like in the stories."

"Thank ye, Arabella," Emi said, blushing.

Crisdean held out his hand to her and kissed hers when she placed it in his own. "My darling, ye look magnificent."

"Thank ye, Father, and thank ye so very much for yer lovely gift."

"It looks well on ye," he said. "Come, or we shall all be late."

The five of them got into the waiting carriage, while Fergus, Cailean, and Alasdair mounted horses to ride guard alongside it. Emi very much wished Alasdair was inside with her, but he had a job to do and it didn't stop just because his wife was going to a party. Though everyone else was chattering in excitement, Emi was watching the landscape from the window, curious to see how it changed, though she breathed in sharply when the palace came into view. She'd never in her life seen something as large as this, the building seeming never-ending while surrounded by massive lawns and gardens.

When the carriage stopped in the forecourt, footmen immediately met it, opening the door. Crisdean stepped out first, followed by James and Alex, then Màiri. Emi was the last out, assisted by Alex, while Alasdair, Fergus, and Cailean fell into line behind them, and Emi forced herself not to gawk at her surroundings as they walked in. At the entrance to the ballroom, they stopped, waiting for their turn to be announced even as the officers slipped inside.

"Monsieur Crisdean Stewart, Chief of Clan Stewart, and his wife, Madame Màiri Stewart," the herald announced before the two of them walked in and down to the front, where Crisdean bowed and Màiri curtsied to the king and queen.

"Masters Alexander Stewart and James Stewart, sons of Monsieur Stewart and Madame Stewart," the herald called out, and the two young men followed their parents' lead.

"Mademoiselle Emilia Stewart, daughter of Monsieur Stewart," the herald announced.

Emi pushed away the irritation at being referred to as an unmarried woman, knowing that here she had to be, because what she and Alasdair had done wouldn't be recognized. With a deep breath, she forced herself to take a step forward, hearing the whispers around her. She knew they were wondering who she was and where she'd come from, but she tried not to think of it. Instead, she kept her eyes forward, focused on the two people seated on the thrones at the end of the long carpet. When she reached them, she curtsied elegantly and waited for the king to bid her to rise. Instead, he stood and made his way from the dais to where Emi stood. Holding out his hand to her, he waited for Emi to place her hand in his and kissed it.

"Yer Majesty," she said in French. "It is an honor."

"And it is an honor to me to have such beauty brought into my court, mademoiselle. A shame we have not seen you here before now."

"I am only just arrived, Yer Majesty."

"Indeed? From where?"

"Scotland, Yer Majesty."

"How intriguing. I did not know you had a daughter, Stewart."

"She was always in Scotland, Yer Majesty," Crisdean replied.

"I do believe I would like to take the first dance with you, mademoiselle, after I dance with the queen."

"It would be a privilege, Yer Majesty," Emi said with another curtsy before he released her hand and allowed her to join the rest of the family.

***

At the back of the room, Alasdair's hands tightened into fists behind his back, and his jaw was tighter. How dare they announce her as though she were unmarried! She *was* married. To *him*. He didn't care if it wasn't in a church, it was still done, but here it didn't seem to matter a bit. When they'd arrived at the palace, Alasdair had needed to force himself not to shove the footmen aside so that he could help her out of the carriage himself. The way they looked at her bothered him, but there was nothing he could do and he knew it. He wanted to be beside her, stepping out of that carriage and then helping her out, just like some fairy story. Instead, he was here to guard them all, and while that was important, he longed to be near his wife. It felt as though he hadn't seen her in days, even though she slept at his side each night. What was worse was the way the king so brazenly flirted with Emi in front of the entire court, and it was quite clear to Alasdair what he was thinking. He'd kill him, king or no, before he let that happen.

"Easy Alasdair," Cailean whispered.

"She is my wife, and he needs to take his hands *off* of her," Alasdair whispered back.

"He is a king, and he can put his hands wherever he pleases."

"Aye, and kings can bleed the same as anyone else."

"Ye should hold yer tongue before the guard overhears ye."

Alasdair pressed his lips together in supreme irritation as the last of the guests were announced. The space cleared to allow for the king and the queen to dance together and then, as promised, the king held out his hand to Emi, who took it and allowed him to lead her out to the floor. The others seemed to know which dance it was and lined up behind the king with their chosen partner. When the music began, she curtsied to him while he stood still, though the other men bowed in response to the curtsies of the ladies. Alasdair watched her glide effortlessly through it, the lessons over the last weeks bearing fruit, and it almost didn't seem real, didn't seem like it was her, but it was. His wife was dancing with a king. Had anyone told him a year ago that this would be happening, he would have laughed and called them a fool. She was so beautiful in this moment, a picture of elegance that she would deny she ever was. To see her in the silk and ribbon and lace he'd long imagined her in only proved what he'd always suspected: she was made for such beautiful things and now, at least, she got to wear them. She didn't miss a step, the light reflecting off the silver in her dress and her hair, and he was more than pleased to watch her deftly avoid the more intimate touches the king attempted to make while seeming as though she wasn't.

"Alasdair," Alex said, appearing at Alasdair's side out of nowhere.

"Aye, Master Alexander?" he replied, pulling his eyes away from Emi.

"Come with me. Hurry."

"Why? What is wrong?"

"Naught, just come on!"

Alasdair looked to Cailean, who shrugged, before he turned and followed Alexander.

***

As the dance came to an end, the couples bowed and curtsied to each other, and the king once again kissed Emi's hand. "Thank you, mademoiselle. I shall call on you again later, I think me."

"Yer Majesty," Emi said with a curtsy before he released her.

"Ye did beautifully, Emilia," Crisdean said, his smile proud.

"Thank ye, Father," she said, her relief showing in the smile she returned.

"Though, I would take care if I were ye, as he tends to have an eye for pretty ladies."

"What?"

"I think ye get my meaning."

"Father! I am married," she whispered.

"Do ye think he cares?"

Emi looked at him in shock. "Really?"

"Oh, aye, but dinnae worry now. A new dance is starting. Go, have fun."

Emi smiled, having to admit to herself that the dancing *was* quite fun. As she was about to turn around to see if she could find Alex, someone grabbed her hand, pulling her toward a set. As they lined up across from each other, her breath caught as she saw her partner. Before her stood her husband, dressed in elegant court clothing she knew wasn't his, but he still looked amazing in them. He now had a mask across his eyes, and he lifted her hand to his lips.

"Alasdair?"

"*Madame*," he murmured against her fingers, purposefully stressing the word before he released her and bowed.

Emi grinned and curtsied, letting the livelier dance carry her. She didn't know where or how Alasdair had learned it, but she didn't really care at this moment. She laughed as she put her left arm across his shoulders and placed her right hand in his left as he held it in front of him. Using it as leverage to balance her against his hip as they spun with all of the other dancers, she heard him laugh before he set her back down. As they slid past each other, the dancers all clapped twice in unison, then slid back the other way to clap twice again. They danced a square around each other and then came back together again, where he once again lifted her onto his hip and spun her about. All of the dancers were laughing now, moving nimbly through the steps, coming together for one last spin before the men set the ladies down and bowed as they curtsied.

"How did ye get these clothes?" Emi whispered as he kissed her hand.

"A mysterious benefactor," he said with a wink that made her laugh.

"I see."

"Could nae let the king have all the fun, now could I?"

"Mmm, I suppose nae. But now I wonder how ye know these dances."

"Ye were nae the only one learning."

"Is that so?"

"Aye, it is."

"Then ye had best dance another with me to be sure."

"As Madame commands," he said.

This dance was far slower but daring in how close the dancers had to be to each other for the whole of it. Emi followed Alasdair through it, her eyes on his, finding it easy to forget anyone else was even there. They were so close and yet not, a game to play as if they were not together even though they were, just as they'd once done what felt like so very long ago now. Moving through the figures, she let herself sink into the moment, let herself pretend to be some noble young woman dancing with a secret lover even though she was promised to another, and Alasdair played the lover's part to perfection. The air of danger in the game, of a seduction through dance and the barest of touches was heady, and when the dance came to a stop, they were inches from each other, close enough for her to kiss him if she wanted to … and Lord did she want to. They looked at each other in silence for a long moment, both seeming to weigh the desire to do what they knew they shouldn't. The applause from those watching the dancers parted them before either of them could act on it.

Alexander took Emi's hand with a grin when she returned from the floor with Alasdair. "Surprised?"

"It was ye!"

"Of course it was," he scoffed. "Could nae let ye go to the ball without yer husband, could I?"

"Alex, I could kiss ye!"

Alex turned his cheek toward her, and she kissed it, which made them both laugh. "Do I get a turn now? If Alasdair does nae mind, of course."

"For ye, Master Alexander? Never. Go on," Alasdair said, smiling.

As Alexander led Emi out to dance, Crisdean stepped up beside Alasdair. "Well, dinnae ye clean up nicely, hm?"

Alasdair chuckled and bowed.

"It looks good on ye, lad, and the pair of ye looked quite the picture together. I think most of the young women were thinking things they should nae of ye by the time that was over."

Alasdair laughed. "They can think it if they wish, but that is all they will get."

"Indeed," Crisdean said.

"Ye are nae angry then?"

"Angry? Why would I be?"

"Well, I am playing a bit of a part. I dinnae belong here this way, and certainly nae dancing in front of a king even if Emi is my wife. I am supposed to be on duty guarding ye, as always."

"Nonsense," Crisdean said. "Ye had better get used to it, Alasdair, because this is exactly where ye belong now. Those clothes are yers, made for ye at my order. Ye may be one of my officers, but at functions like this where Emilia is present, ye are my daughter's husband first."

"Chief —"

"Are ye planning on arguing with me? It will nae go well for ye, so I suggest ye dinnae try."

"Aye, sir," Alasdair said, amused by how alike father and daughter were. "However, I am nae her husband here."

"Nae yet."

"Aye, nae yet. We have nae gotten to that part."

"About that," he said, looking at Alasdair with a mischievous smile. "Come with me."

Alasdair looked at him, wary, but followed Crisdean after casting a final glance back at Emi.

As the dance ended, Alexander bowed to Emi as she curtsied, and they both laughed, a bit breathless. "Come," Alexander said. "I think I saw everyone go out to get some air."

"A good idea," Emi said, letting him lead her through the crowd and out, but when they turned away from the doors to the outside, she frowned. "Alex, the doors are that way."

"Aye, but we are going a different way."

"But —"

"Dinnae ye trust me?"

"Aye."

"Then come on," he said.

When they came to a small set of doors, he knocked on them, and they opened to reveal a beautiful private chapel. At the altar stood Alasdair, resplendent in his court clothing, with Cailean and Fergus at his side. Anna and Ealasaid stood to the other side, waiting for her and smiling. Coira, Màiri, James, the children, and the rest of the household sat in the pews. Emi stood staring in shock and confusion. What was happening?

"It is time to make it official, Emilia, love," Crisdean said as he stepped up beside her and offered his arm. "Are ye ready?"

"Aye," she whispered, her eyes full of tears.

"Then walk with me."

They progressed down the center aisle to where Alasdair waited for her, and it hardly felt real. These were things that didn't happen to women like her. Women from the Highlands who worked in kitchens didn't get married in the king's private chapel at a palace in France. They certainly didn't do it in a ball gown that she now understood had been designed to also be her wedding gown. Yet here she was.

As they stopped at the altar, the priest smiled. "Who gives this woman to this man?"

"I do," Crisdean said, "as do her sainted loved ones who are with God: Helena, Bridgette, Andrew, and Evander."

Emi almost burst into tears at hearing their names in this way, and Crisdean placed her hand in Alasdair's, who kissed it. She scarce noticed the readings as the priest went through them; they didn't matter to her.

"Do you, Alasdair Stewart, take Emilia as your wife, from this day forward?"

"Aye," Alasdair said, giving her hand a gentle squeeze before he pulled her glove from her left hand and slipped a dainty gold band onto her finger.

"And do you, Emilia Stewart, take Alasdair as your husband, from this day forward?"

"Aye," she said as Ealasaid pressed a thicker band into her

hand for Alasdair. It wasn't common for men, but it didn't surprise her that someone involved in this knew it would be what he wanted regardless of fashion.

"Then by the power given to me by God, and with the permission and approval of His Majesty, King Louis of France, I pronounce the pair of you wed. May God in his mercy bless you and keep you. Amen."

"I wish to see the young man kiss his new bride after that earlier dance performance," boomed a voice from the royal box above them.

Emi and Alasdair looked up to find the king and queen in the box, having been present for the entirety, and Alasdair bowed as Emi curtsied.

"Go on, I am waiting," he said, shooing at them with his hands.

Alasdair laughed, cupping Emi's face in his hands and pulling her into the kiss he'd seemed on the verge of giving her just after the aforementioned dance. There was an amused cheer and applause, and the two of them parted, laughing.

"Well done, well done," the king said. "Now, let us celebrate! This ball has just turned into a wedding celebration!"

Chapter 19

The rest of the ball was a bit of a blurred dream, lasting until nearly dawn as Emi and Alasdair became the unofficial guests of honor with an entire court celebrating their marriage. It became clear that the only people who hadn't been in on the plan were the two of them, with even the king volunteering to be part of the secret. He gifted them a pair of golden wine goblets, along with a day and night in one of the royal suites with instructions to remain inside and enjoy their "wedding night," with all food being brought to them. Their stay began when they woke the following afternoon in a bed so large it could easily fit ten or more people in it, and Alasdair wasted no time in claiming her back from English officers and French kings, from tragedy and danger and heartbreak. It was something emotional and cathartic for them both, allowing them to both start to heal.

They were returned by royal coach the following afternoon, but not before they were given the full benefit of a longer journey to let people cheer them. Certainly, anyone in a royal coach must be important, and it was fun to imagine themselves always fit for such things as people came out into the street to wave to them, the entire adventure leaving Emi floating on air for days afterward. From the moment they'd returned, Alasdair was recognized by the household as Monsieur Alasdair even though he also served the chief, an acknowledgment of his elevated position as the chief's son-in-law. As he'd told Emi he'd do, he eschewed being bowed to by any of the adults who'd come with them, just as uncomfortable as she was by such courtesies coming from those he'd known and been on the same level with for the whole of his life.

Life settled into a routine, with Hortense assigned to Emi as a ladies' maid, a task the young woman had been quite excited and honored to receive. Emi took over the household accounts, making adjustments where needed and saving them money in the process. Those who had dealings with Crisdean quickly became accustomed to going through Emi to make appointments to call on him or be called upon, to the point where their footmen or pages were instructed to ask for her directly. All letters passed through Emi's hands, though anything indicated as personal by the person delivering it went to him unopened to be dealt with at his discretion. They met each morning to go over requests and schedules, with Crisdean admitting to her that he was relieved to simply be told where to go, who he was meeting, and why. Emi took down his replies to correspondence and then sat down to write them out fully once he departed for the day.

Through all of it, Emi's pregnancy progressed easily and without much discomfort to her. Alasdair enjoyed talking to the baby at night when they retired, and the first time he'd felt it move against his hand had surprised him. It made him emotional in a way that touched Emi's heart, and both were looking forward to meeting this child, the one who'd survived so many odds, just as its parents had.

The summer was a long one, drawing on into September, allowing for more walks and later evenings out of doors. As Emi entered the house with Alasdair after one such walk, both of them laughing, Crisdean stepped out of the study, his face a mask of seriousness that ceased the pair's laughter with immediate effect.

"Father? What is the matter?" Emi asked, frowning.

"Emilia, Alasdair, I need ye to freshen up and come into the study, and I need ye to be quick about it."

"Aye, Father," Emi said.

"Aye, Chief," Alasdair replied.

As Crisdean disappeared back into the study, Emi looked to Alasdair to find the same concern on his face. "What do ye think is going on?"

"Dinnae know, but whatever it is seems serious. Let us nae keep him waiting," Alasdair replied, taking her hand in his before heading for the stairs and hurrying up them to their room.

Emi removed her hat and gloves, checking her reflection in the mirror and smoothing any hair mussed by the hat, while Alasdair straightened his clothing before running a comb through his hair and retying it. As soon as they were done, they left to go back downstairs, Alasdair holding her hand and walking sideways just in front of her, so she didn't fall. At six months pregnant, she found them a bit more difficult to navigate now. At the door, Alasdair opened it for her and stepped aside to let her through as a footman might do, then followed her in and shut it behind him.

"Ah, there ye are, Emilia. Thank ye for making such quick work of it," Crisdean said.

"Of course, Father, is every —"

Emi's words were stopped by Alasdair's sharp intake of breath and wide eyes before he went into a deep bow. "Yer Highness," he said.

Emi looked at Alasdair, shocked, before following his gaze to see a young man sitting in a chair near Crisdean. He looked exhausted and gaunt, his expression haunted. She had no idea who he was, but she curtsied all the same based on her husband's reaction.

"Ah! Captain Stewart!" the young man said. "Please rise. I am glad to see I was able to keep my promise to at least one person and get you home."

Emi looked back at Alasdair, confused.

"Aye, ye did, Yer Highness, and I am grateful to have made it in spite of the best efforts of Cumberland."

A sardonic smile spread across the young man's lips for a moment. "Yes, are not all of us who escaped grateful? Some more than others, I suppose."

"Yer Highness, may I introduce my daughter, Emilia," Crisdean said, and Emi curtsied again.

"The fabled Emilia at last! You certainly were speaking the truth, Captain, when you said she was uncommonly fair."

"Emilia, meet His Royal Highness, Prince Charles Edward Stuart," Crisdean continued.

"Yer Highness," Emi replied. "A great honor and pleasure to meet ye, and my sincere apologies for nae having recognized ye."

"I dare say I do not look as one might expect now."

"On the contrary, Yer Highness, I have nae ever seen yer likeness and have naught to compare it to."

"A fair point, madame."

"I am glad to see ye have escaped and returned safely to France."

"Whether I am glad or not depends on the day."

"I am sorry to hear it, for ye should know that many of those who support ye will rejoice to know ye still live."

The prince raised an eyebrow in interest. "Do you believe that to be so?"

"I do. I know it to be true for this house."

"Then it is good to be amongst those who would wish for my health and safety, and I thank you for your assurances."

"His Royal Highness will be residing with us for a short time while a more permanent arrangement is made. Like us, he went through a great ordeal to get here, and it is our honor to be of service to him in this hour of need," Crisdean said. "Emilia, I desire for ye to help him in the way ye do me while he is with us."

"Of course, Father, it would be my honor to do so."

"Alasdair, I want ye on duty with him if he leaves the house.

He is safe within these walls, but ye will wait on him all the same in case he desires to step out. I still have Fergus and Cailean to accompany me, and yer skill is best served with this task."

"Aye, Chief, as ye wish. It is my honor to once again serve His Royal Highness, though in a different capacity," Alasdair replied, bowing.

"Good lad, thank ye."

"Thank you indeed, Captain, and thank you, Emilia. It will be nice to be amongst friendly hearts and faces for a time. Would you mind, gentlemen, if I spoke with Emilia alone?"

The request took all of them by surprise, with Crisdean and Alasdair looking at each other and then back at the prince. Emi remained silent, her eyes on a portrait behind him so that she might avoid staring at him.

"As ye wish, Yer Highness," Crisdean said. "Come, Alasdair, let us discuss a few things about what will be needed."

"Aye, Chief," Alasdair said, and Emi could hear the reluctance in his voice, knowing he didn't like this without even needing to see his face.

When the door shut behind the two other men, there was a heavy silence, the ticking of a clock and the sounds of the street outside the only things to be heard.

"You may look at me, you know. I do not bite," the prince said.

Emi lowered her eyes to his face to find a gentle smile there. "I had no wish to stare, Yer Highness. It is impolite."

"If I were perturbed by being stared at, I would have been a wreck long ago, my dear girl," he said, chuckling. "And, please, no need to use the honorific in a personal situation like this one."

A smile crept across her lips before she could stop it. "I suppose that is true, aye. I dislike being stared at a great deal."

"It is my understanding you lived a life where such a thing was not a concern," he said, looking her over. "Sit, please. A woman in your condition ought not be standing for long periods."

"Thank ye," Emi replied as she took a seat in the chair her

father had occupied moments ago. "I will admit I find it hard to do so now."

"How much longer are you to go?"

"A few months now, nae long."

"I wish you the very best of luck when the time comes, and please know that the prayers of the House of Stuart go with you."

"Thank ye, that is very kind."

"You seem surprised I would say such."

"Forgive me, but ye are a prince, so I would nae expect ye to have a care for anyone like me."

"Like you?" he asked before he shook his head with a gentle laugh. Sitting up, he leaned forward, resting his arms on his knees. "Had we been successful, you would have been one of my father's subjects, and our care should be with every being under our rule. Aside from that, we are family, distant as it may be."

Emi raised an eyebrow. "I dinnae understand."

"Clan Stewart and its varying branches are descended from the original High Stewards of Scotland. Your branch is most closely aligned with my own, and given who your father is, we are distant cousins several times removed, I believe. All the same, I have always considered Clan Stewart my Scottish family and still do. Your father and the other Stewart chiefs were vital in their support of me and the cause."

"What a strange thing."

"Yes, it is, is it not? How small our worlds are? I think for you it must be more so, for you have only recently taken your place here."

"Aye, ye are correct."

"We are the same now, you and I. Both of us trying to make sense of a world we feel outside of, part of us still stuck in a world stolen forever by unspeakable violence."

"Unspeakable violence," Emi repeated. "Murder ye mean."

"Yes, there was much of that as I understand it. I saw some of it myself, saw what was done to the home of Cameron of

Lochiel and the members of the clan that remained, what was done to Macpherson and the rest."

"Closer than that for some of us."

"How so?"

"What has my father told ye?"

"That ye are his daughter by a young woman he loved before his marriage, you were kept by others, and he was able to acknowledge you before he departed."

Emi closed her eyes for a moment. "All of that is true, aye, but I served him. I worked in his kitchens while never knowing he was my father until the war came. I was there through all of it. I provisioned our men while I sent my father, my husband, and a brother to war. Evander was the son of the couple who took me in and raised me."

"Where is he now?"

"Buried with the rest on Drumossie Moor."

Charles closed his eyes and sighed. "I am sorry for it."

"So am I. When the soldiers came for us, I was away from the castle, otherwise I may have shared the fate of the others found there, lined against the wall and shot. Bridgette, the woman who cared for me, escaped and tried to warn me, but they shot her on the road. One of their officers decided that, as my husband was an officer and was now dead, he was free to do to me as he pleased."

Charles opened his eyes and looked at her, and the pain she saw there surprised her. "I ... the barbarism astounds. This is not ..." he trailed off, reaching out toward her stomach for a moment before pulling his hand back.

"No," Emi reassured him. "This one was already in place by then."

"Thank God for small favors. Emilia, I am sorry for what you lost, and if I could change it, I would. If I could bring them back to you, I would do so in a heartbeat. If I could bring them all back ..." he said, resting his head in one hand as he began to weep.

Without hesitation, Emi reached out and took his other hand. It was a liberty, but she wasn't thinking of that. Another person needed comfort, and that was all that mattered. "I know ye would, but ye cannae, and ye must remember ye did nae do this all on yer own. Aye, ye were in charge, but there were others there, too. As my father said to me once, war is a fearful thing, and those men died fighting for what they believed in."

Charles couldn't stop his tears now that they'd begun, turning his hand over to clasp hers. He seemed desperate for that contact, just as Alasdair once was, and desperate to release the pain in his heart and mind. She wondered if this was the first time he'd truly been able to let it out, though she wouldn't dare ask him.

"I have spent so long running from them, months, that it hardly feels real to me that I no longer have to look over my shoulder. It is nothing to what you suffered or what those still there suffer now, I know, but I still wake in fear."

"No suffering is ever naught," Emi said in a gentle voice. "All suffering is suffering, no matter how small it might be, and while it might seem small to another, it was nae small to ye. I would never tell another that they did nae suffer because what they went through would nae be suffering to me. Ye have every reason to wake frightened, every reason to see danger everywhere and wonder if ye will ever be safe again. I understand what that feels like, for I still feel that way. So do Alasdair and Cailean and Fergus. I am sure my father does as well. Alasdair wakes from night terrors often."

"No suffering is ever nothing, no matter how small," he repeated in a whisper. "What a beautiful thing to say."

"I hope it helps ye. I know ye feel lost now, we all do, but wishing ye had nae survived helps no one."

Charles looked up at her, shocked. "How —"

"How did I know? Ye said that some were glad they escaped more than others, and then ye said whether ye were glad ye escaped to safety depended on the day. Ye wish ye had nae, ye wish it all the time, but each day ye wake up and God has nae answered yer prayer. Ye may have lost a war, but that does nae mean there are nae still many who support ye and thank that same God for yer survival. Yer guilt is heavy, but ye cannae let it succeed in doing what Cumberland could nae."

"It is as though you are speaking my very soul," he said. "Bless you, Emilia. I think I needed to hear such from someone who would have every reason to hate me."

"I dinnae hate ye, nor would I have done. Ye are a man like any other, no matter yer title. I know that no one could hate ye more than ye hate yerself, could nae loathe the sight of ye more than ye loathe the sight of yerself in the looking glass each day when ye wake up amongst the living."

Charles broke down for a moment at her words and shook his head. "I see my failings and mistakes writ large each day, hear the whispers telling me how worthless I am, how all of this suffering is my fault. What do you do when you have failed at the *one* thing you have been raised for?"

"Now that ye are free of the burden of it, ye find something else to live for."

"It is not easy."

"Is it nae? What is stopping ye?"

"I … well …" he stammered, searching for an answer to her question. "I do not know. I suppose you are right; nothing is."

"Ask God for peace and ye shall have it. Ask Him to help ye find a new path, and it will present itself. One world may have ended, but there are still so many more open to ye. Life is nae over, nae for either of us. I found a way and so will ye. If a kitchen lass can do it, a prince certainly can."

He laughed softly and wiped his cheeks with a free hand before he took her hand and kissed it, then closed it in both of his. "You mean if the daughter of a Stewart chief can manage it, then surely I can overcome this."

"Aye, for one of us has led an army for nigh on a year and it was nae me," Emi said, flashing a wry smile that made him laugh harder.

"No, but you have kept command over a Stewart chief as well as a husband who is a natural leader himself and a strong warrior with a reputation. That is almost as difficult."

It was Emi's turn to laugh now. "Somehow I dinnae believe that to be true, but I will take yer word for it."

"You have no choice, do you? I am a prince, so I am right about everything. Always."

The two of them looked at each other before they started laughing together.

"Ye cannae even say it with a straight face!"

"Because I know it is a damned lie, that is why!"

"And I thought Alasdair could be ridiculous."

"I hate to be the one to tell you, but *every* man is ridiculous."

"Lord, if that is nae the truth."

He chuckled and squeezed her hand. "Thank you. I do not think I have laughed that honestly in months. I needed that."

"I am glad I can help in my own way."

"More than. I am glad I came here and glad I met you. I think your sweet spirit and your kindness is just the balm I need to soothe my heart and mind so that I may start again."

"I will do my best to help ye in any way I can."

"I do believe you will. Chief Stewart!" he called out.

"Aye, Yer Highness?" Crisdean replied as he opened the door and stepped inside with Alasdair just behind him, his eyes widening at the sight of Charles holding Emi's hand.

"I am most grateful for the gift of a few moments alone with this beautiful soul who has helped to begin to clear away some of the darkness. It is an honor to know her, and you are a most lucky man indeed, Captain Stewart."

"Thank ye, Yer Highness," Alasdair said, smiling as he bowed. "I whole-heartedly agree with ye."

"And she is a great asset and credit to you, Chief Stewart."

"Aye, she is," Crisdean replied. "I am a fortunate father to have such a lass."

"I hope you do not mind my saying this, Emilia, but to me

you are distant no more. You are, and ever shall be, a cousin to me, as close as blood if not more, for only family can see so plainly into one's heart as you did into mine."

"It is an honor, Yer Highness," Emi said, moving to stand, spurring Charles to stand and help her up. "I will go ensure a proper meal awaits ye."

Chapter 20

The prince's time with them had lasted only a few short weeks before he moved to a more permanent residence. He was not, however, a stranger to the household after that, returning to visit with Crisdean or have tea with Emi whenever he felt desirous of doing so. Emi noted that his visits to her coincided with his feeling in low spirits, but he'd almost always gone away laughing and smiling in the end. She'd found she quite enjoyed his company, and they conversed about any number of things, from Emi's life back in Scotland to the latest court and society gossip he brought her, and she knew he got a great deal of amusement out of her often shocked reactions.

As the weather turned colder and Emi grew larger, she had far less of a desire to walk anywhere or do anything but rest. Alasdair, James, and Alexander all doted on her as much as they could, with Alex taking great pleasure in sitting in the study with her and reading aloud if she wasn't already occupied with a task for their father. When Alexander returned home one early afternoon toward the end of November and walked into the study where Emi sat working, she could immediately tell something wasn't right.

"Alex?"

He turned his head to look at her, but his eyes were glassy, his cheeks were flushed, and he didn't say anything in response. Emi stood up and walked over to him, sitting him down on the settee and taking his hand.

"Alex," she said, frowning. "Are ye well?"

"Emilia," he said, his voice weak. "I dinnae think so."

"What is wrong?"

"I dinnae know? I just feel … I am here but nae here. Everything is so slow, and I can scarce hear ye."

Emi placed a hand against his cheek and pulled it back in the same instant, finding his skin hot to the touch. "Stay here," she said, hurrying to the door. "Ealasaid!"

Ealasaid appeared at the top of the stairs from one of the rooms she'd been working in, her expression concerned. "Aye? Emi, are ye well?"

"Aye, but … but Alex is nae. He is burning up!"

Ealasaid's eyes widened, and she hurried down the stairs, following Emi into the study to find Alex hadn't moved and was staring into the space before him. "Master Alexander," she said, patting his cheek. "Look at me."

Alex turned his head slowly and tried to focus on her but seemed unable to do so. "I cannae. Am I?"

"Jesus," she whispered. "Emi, I need ye to tell the kitchens we need cool water. Go quickly."

Emi swept from the room to deliver the instructions, and as she was returning to the study, Crisdean came in along with the three officers. Emi wanted to weep in relief to see them, and Crisdean could instantly tell something was amiss.

"Emilia, what is the matter?"

"Alex —" she said, pointing to the study.

Crisdean turned and hurried into the room to find Ealasaid trying to cool the young man off. "What is going on?"

"He is burning up, Chief," Ealasaid said. "A fever of some sort, but he is nae well."

"Father," Alex said, his voice sounding weaker to Emi now than it had when he'd come in, pushing Ealasaid's hands away from him as he tried to stand. He didn't get far before his eyes rolled back and he collapsed onto the settee.

"Alex!" Crisdean called out. "Ye lads! Get him upstairs!"

The three men wasted no time obeying the order, with Fergus throwing Alex over his shoulder as the other two hurried ahead of him to move people and open doors. Fergus placed him on his bed while Cailean and Alasdair proceeded to undress him. Ealasaid brought the water up and handed the basin to Emi before she left to send someone for Màiri, who was calling on a friend. Emi took the cloth and smoothed it over the young man's face and neck, the sudden cold causing him to moan but not wake.

"Where is James? Pull him from lessons, now!" Crisdean called out.

Emi paused, her heart dropping. James. He'd said he felt unwell the night before after supper and went upstairs to retire early. She hadn't seen him at breakfast, and she'd assumed he'd had his food brought to him. Standing, she shoved the cloth into Cailean's hands and ran from the room.

"Emi!" she heard Alasdair call out, but she ignored him.

Reaching the door to James' room, she opened it and saw him in bed, sighing in relief as she went in to check on him. "James?" she called out softly, not wanting to startle him, but there was no response. "James?"

Emi placed a gentle hand on his shoulder to shake him but recoiled upon feeling ice-cold skin under her fingers. Breathing heavily, her heart pounding, she shook her head. Surely that wasn't right, and she was mistaken in what she felt. Her hand was shaking as she reached out once more, her eyes full of tears, praying she was wrong. When the coldness registered again, it brought a soft sob from her.

"No," she whispered through tears. "No, please, James. Dinnae do this, please …"

Forcing herself to move, she turned him toward her, only to be met with cloudy eyes and purple lips telling her what she'd already known deep down. Emi broke down in a silent scream as she backed away from him, the sound following it soon after and bringing the others running. They all stopped just inside the door, as it was clear to them that the boy was dead.

"James!" Crisdean wailed in anguish, hurrying to the bed and taking the body of his youngest son in his arms. "James!"

Emi's legs gave out beneath her, but Alasdair was there before she hit the floor, holding her against him as she wept with the same anguish her father was displaying. Fergus, Cailean, and Ealasaid crossed themselves and whispered a prayer for the soul of the chief's youngest son, dead at 15.

"I know, I know my love," Alasdair whispered in her ear. "I am so very sorry."

"Alasdair," Ealasaid said. "Ye should take her back to yer rooms. She should nae be around this in her condition."

Alasdair nodded and pulled Emi up from the floor, leading her from the room. They were halfway to their own before she realized and stopped walking, pulling back against him. "Emi, love —"

"No!" she shouted, shoving him away from her before she ran back into Alex's room, where she sat on his bed and took his hand even as she wept. "Alex, ye have to get well, ye have to," she pleaded with him as she took the cloth and bathed him with cold water as Alasdair looked on helplessly from the doorway.

Crisdean was downstairs to meet his wife when she arrived, the sound of her scream when he told her about James echoing through the house. Emi sobbed when she heard it, placing a hand over her heart as if she could somehow make it stop aching, though she remained beside Alex. Màiri's shattered wail as she reached James' bedside reverberated with Ealasaid, Coira, and Anna, all mothers themselves and able to understand that grief. It was the same sound Coira had made when the English officer told them Alasdair was dead.

Màiri eventually joined Emi in Alex's room, and Emi relinquished her place beside him to let Màiri take it. "My baby," she wept as she smoothed his damp hair back from his forehead. "Oh, my Alex. Yer mother is here, my darling, I am here. Wake up for me, Alex, please."

Emi sank into a chair and buried her face in her hands as she listened to Màiri whisper soothing words to Alex, remembering how many times Bridgette had done the same for her or Evander when they were ill. What she knew was that she couldn't leave him and wouldn't. He would recover from this; he was young and strong. Emi rose again and went to the other side of the bed, taking his other hand in hers and stroking it.

Crisdean joined their vigil after making arrangements for James' body, and in silence Emi did the things Ealasaid had taught her. Giving him small amounts of water, rubbing his feet vigorously to try and draw the fever downward, wiping him down with cold water. The hours blended into each other, and Alex's breathing only grew more labored. Coira came to tell them that it was a fever that seemed to be sweeping through the city, as she had seen many others in mourning on her way home before she turned back, and it hardly registered with Emi. Her singular focus was Alexander and doing all she could to get him through the illness that had already claimed his brother.

A priest was called in to give him last rites, as they'd been unable to do for James, though they all hoped it would be for nothing. That hope was dashed less than an hour later when the young man's breathing slowed and then stopped altogether. Màiri's cry of utter anguish was the only sound as Emi stared in disbelief. Crisdean wept, both of his sons now dead within a day of each other, his heirs and the heirs to the clan lost forever. Emi sank to her knees and sobbed, pressing the back of his hand to her forehead. This couldn't be happening. It couldn't be. How could Alex, beloved Alex, be gone? His laughter swirled about her memory, his smile, his beauty. The moment in the ballroom here, the flowers, dancing with him at the ball and the part he'd played in her surprise wedding, the love and care he'd shown her these last months, all the little moments that would never come again. The unfairness of it washed over her. That these sweet young men should be dead while murderers lived seemed the greatest injustice she could imagine.

Crisdean knelt beside Màiri, and they cried together before he took a sharp breath in as though something had just occurred to him. Standing up, he strode to the door. "Louis! Alasdair!" he bellowed, and the two men made quick work of answering the summons. "Louis, I want ye to get the carriage around and do it now. Tell the driver he is going to The Garden. Hortense!" The young woman hurried up the stairs and looked at him expectantly. "Get ye to Emilia's room and pack her things!"

As Hortense nodded and hurried to do as requested, Alasdair bowed. "What did ye need from me, sir?"

"I want ye to take Emilia, and I want ye to leave."

"What!"

"Dinnae argue with me or question me, lad, just do as I tell ye!" Crisdean shouted. "Ye will take her to the country house, and ye will keep her there until ye are told otherwise. The driver will know where to go and a cart with yer trunks, as well as food and supplies, will be just behind ye and bringing Coira with it in case Emilia ends up needing her."

"Aye, sir."

Crisdean made his way to Emi, pulling her up from the floor and away from Alex even as she fought him. "Ye are leaving."

"No! I cannae!"

"Ye can, and ye will. I know ye are shattered, we all are, but it is more important than ever now that ye are safe. I need ye to be safe," he said, his voice thick with emotion. "I cannae lose all three of ye. Please dinnae fight me; there is naught left for ye to do here. It will nae be forever, but I need ye to go. Please."

"No, Father, please," Emi pleaded. "Who will take care of the others if they get ill, or ye? I have to stay!"

Crisdean heard the carriage pull around to the front and sighed, kissing her forehead and then closing his eyes. "Alasdair, take her and go. Go now."

Before Emi could protest, Alasdair scooped her up into his arms and hurried out. "No!" she screamed out. "Put me down! ALASDAIR, PUT ME DOWN! FATHER, PLEASE! NO!"

The front door was opened for Alasdair, and Emi screamed frantically as he bundled her into the carriage. As he let go of her to try and get inside himself, she made an effort to get past him and back out, only for him to catch her and push her back inside as he got in. Shutting the door behind him, the driver pulled out as soon as he heard it close. Knowing there was no chance of her getting away from this now, all Emi could do was cry as Alasdair held her close to him.

***

Emi's grief compounded his own, and his body shook with sobs as the realization that both boys were dead washed over him. He'd known them from their earliest days; they were good young men, the future of their clan. Now, like the other young men they'd left behind for their own safety, they were gone.

She cried herself to sleep, her head resting in Alasdair's lap as the carriage made its way down darkened roads. He had no idea where they were, where they were going, or even for how long, but he wondered if there would ever come a time again where they could be happy for a long stretch, as things used to be. It felt as though the war had poisoned everything, its reach long in making sure that those who had dared to rebel would always suffer for it. It didn't matter who the person was or what their reasons were for being there. Whether they were there willingly or whether they were there because it was their duty to be, they'd pay just the same, and not even their innocent loved ones were to be spared its wrath.

There was a fear he could barely admit to himself, though he knew it was there. Would this curse take Emi from him, ripping away the person he loved most in the world in the ultimate act of vengeance? Was it already too late to save her from the fever that seemed to have swept so quickly through the city? They'd all been together, and there was no telling if any of them had gotten it from the two young men before they died, but of anyone it seemed Emi was most at risk because she'd found James and tended Alex. Then there was the birth of the child and the dangers of the childbed lurking in the shadows, equally ready to claim her. The very thought of it made his chest ache. He neither could nor wanted to imagine a world without Emi in it; what would he do without her? She'd always been there for as long as he could remember, and the thought of that ending was terrifying.

Closing his eyes, he rested his head against the back of the seat. In his mind he was back at the ball again with her, dancing and laughing. Alex and James were alive once more, and for a moment everything was as it should be, with everyone happy. Emi shined in her gown, resplendent in her joy, just as she'd been that night. He turned a circle in the dance and when he came to face her again, he froze in terror. A blackness wrapped around her, becoming a figure in a ragged black cloak, the face beneath the hood obscured by pure nothingness.

"Alasdair!" she called out, reaching out for him in her terror.

Alasdair lunged toward her but found himself unable to move, no matter how he willed himself to do so, and a malicious laugh emanated from the wraith as he realized it was preventing him from getting to her. A dirk appeared in its shriveled, blackened hand, and Alasdair's eyes went wide.

"No," he choked out. "No, no ..."

The wraith's other hand locked around her wrist, and Alasdair watched with dread as blackness began to snake through and up the arm it held, an intricate lacework of darkness as it flowed through her. It continued up to her shoulder, and when it came to her throat, she coughed and struggled to breathe, her green eyes turning entirely black as it spread across her beautiful features. His panic only grew as it worked its way through her, and the dark, menacing laughter drew his eyes up once more. Before Alasdair could register the movement, the dirk was plunged into Emi's heart, and he screamed. Her beautiful dress became not red with blood but black from whatever had overtaken her as the wound released it, taking the blackness from her eyes with it. She stared at him in terror and confusion, the accusation that he'd done nothing to help her lingering in her eyes as a line of black liquid seeped from one corner of her mouth. In the next moment, the malevolent spirit was gone as quickly as it had appeared, releasing Emi's body, and Alasdair screamed as she sank to the floor.

With a start, a small shout, and a pounding heart, Alasdair's eyes flew open as he gasped for air. He looked down to find Emi still resting on his lap, and he put a hand against her ribs. When he felt them rising and falling as they should, he breathed a sigh of relief and tried to shove down the rising desire to be sick. It had been a nightmare, a horrible nightmare, and he whispered his thanks to God while praying it wasn't a foretelling of things to come, just as his nightmare at Falkirk had been.

It was near midnight when the carriage turned off of the main road, and when they came to a stop, Alasdair eased himself out to avoid waking Emi. Taking a lantern from the coach, he and the driver made their way to the door, the man handing the key to Alasdair. Once inside, they both made quick work of getting fires started in the sitting room, kitchen, and two of the upstairs bedrooms, as well as lighting candles that had been left behind for the next time someone came here. Alasdair pulled the dust sheet from one bed before he went down to collect Emi, still lost in the sleep only exhaustion could impart. Carrying her upstairs, he placed her gently into bed, removing her shoes and covering her with a blanket the driver handed to him from the wardrobe. He placed a kiss on her forehead and left her there, retreating back below stairs.

"Thank ye for yer help, Philippe," Alasdair said, his voice and his manner betraying how tired he was.

"Of course, Monsieur Alasdair," he said, quiet, and Alasdair could tell that he, too, was brokenhearted about the deaths of his master's two sons. "Madame Emilia will be well, I hope."

"Aye, so do I, but only time will tell. Where are we?"

"The country house, about two hours outside of the city. It is small, and mostly used for hunting parties, but it is named 'The Garden' for all of the flowers here."

"Small," Alasdair mused with a gentle chuckle. "This place is larger than my home and Emi's combined, probably bigger."

"What those with money think of as small and what the rest of us think of are entirely different, no?"

"Aye, very true. Please, get some rest before ye head back."

"Thank you, Monsieur," he said before he made his way to one of the rooms near the kitchen the servants used.

Alasdair rubbed his face gently. Now all they could do was wait.

Chapter 21

Coira arrived within an hour and sent Alasdair up to bed. When Emi woke in the morning, she wanted nothing to do with food, with conversation, with anything. She was mourning deeply, and there wasn't much to be done for it. Coira helped her undress and put her into a nightshirt before Emi crawled back into bed and retreated into sleep. It was safer for her there, Coira explained to Alasdair, a place where she couldn't feel the pain of her grief, a place where Alex and James could still live. To gain two brothers only to lose them was more than anyone could be expected to handle in a stoic and graceful way. The following day she'd at least been persuaded to eat and talk to them, but she still slept more than she was awake, and the rest of the week passed in the same manner. Coira and Alasdair kept an eye on her for signs of the fever but were relieved to find none and knew that those here had escaped it.

Alasdair was jolted out of sleep at the end of the week by feeling Emi suddenly grab his forearm in a tight grip and squeeze it as she let out a moan of pain beside him. Sitting up, he lit a candle. "Em?"

She looked at him with tears in her eyes, breathing heavily. "Alasdair … help …"

"Mam!" Alasdair shouted before he turned and brushed

some hair away from her face. "Aye, I am here, right here, my love. Everything will be fine."

Her back arched from the bed and she cried out. "Help me … please …"

Coira hurried into the room, taking stock of the scene. "Alasdair, get ye downstairs and boil water. Gather all of the toweling ye can find and bring it here, along with a basin of cold water. Hurry."

Alasdair leapt from the bed to gather the requested items, and when he returned, he found Coira sitting on the edge of the bed, holding Emi's hand as she panted with pain.

"Aye, I know sweet one, but it is time to bring that bairn into the world. I know ye can do this, ye are strong, and it needs ye now," Coira said, her tone calm and gentle.

Emi gave a weak nod before she cried out again. "Maman," she sobbed.

"I know. Ye want her and ye are afraid, but I am here with ye."

"How long …"

"What?"

"How long … until …"

"Ye are likely just at the start, poor dear."

"Get … get Màiri … please …"

"Ye want us to fetch her here?" The request surprised Coira, and she couldn't hide her expression, nor could Alasdair.

"Aye," Emi whispered. "Please."

"As ye wish, child. Alasdair, love, ye need ye to get yerself back to Paris. It is only a two-hour ride and ye can take the horse they left with us. Go now and bring Ealasaid back with ye. This is her first, and it may take a while; we will need her if things go wrong."

Alasdair paled. "Wrong? Mam —"

"Alasdair, ye cannae think of that, nae now. Ye know this is a dangerous business; ye have seen it yerself plenty of times when a lass does nae make it through. Get ye on the road; the sooner ye go, the sooner ye are back to her."

With a quick nod, Alasdair dressed as fast as he was able before going out and saddling the horse. Once done, he returned upstairs, leaning over and kissing Emi's forehead. "I am going for Màiri and Ealasaid. I love ye with all of my heart."

"I love ye," she whispered in return.

He kissed her hand and forced himself away from her, mounting the horse and taking to the road for Paris. As a single rider, it would only take him a couple of hours, as Coira said, but they were among some of the longest hours he felt he'd ever experienced. The relief that flooded him when he rode into the courtyard was indescribable, and he pounded on the door, knowing it was locked and barred for the night. He continued pounding on it until he heard the bar pulled back, and Louis opened the door. His eyes went wide to see Alasdair there, but he stepped back to let him inside.

"Chief!" Alasdair shouted as he hurried up the stairs, not caring about waking the rest of the house. "Chief!" he called again as he knocked on the door to Crisdean's room.

The door opened in almost an instant. "Alasdair? What are ye … oh Christ, is Emilia —"

"No," Alasdair said. "She is safe from that, but the bairn is coming and she sent me for the mistress."

"What?"

"She has asked for Madame to come; I dinnae know why."

Crisdean hurried from the room and knocked on the door to Màiri's room, only to have her temporary ladies' maid answer it, but he brushed past her. "Màiri," he said, going to her bed and giving her a gentle shake. "Màiri."

"Crisdean?" she mumbled. "What is wrong?"

"I need ye to wake up. Alasdair is here. The bairn is coming, and Emilia is asking for ye."

"For me?" Màiri asked as she sat up in a swift movement.

"Aye. Will ye go?"

"Jacqueline! Quickly!" she called out as she scrambled out of bed.

One of the other household was sent for Ealasaid, and Philippe was roused to ready the carriage. In less than an hour, Alasdair was back on the road with the two women in the carriage, while he and Cailean rode guard. As soon as they arrived, they heard Emi cry out, and both Ealasaid and Màiri ran to the stairs and up. Alasdair looked after them as they went, not sure what to do now.

Cailean settled a hand on Alasdair's shoulder and smiled. "Come on, lad. All ye can do now is wait."

***

Upstairs, the two women made their way into the room, and Coira smiled. "Look ye, Emi, they have come, just as ye asked."

Emi's face was pinched with the pain she was in, her hair wet with perspiration, and her breathing deep and heavy. As soon as she saw Màiri, she began to cry and reached out a hand to her. "Mam," she sobbed out, and both Coira and Ealasaid gasped and looked at each other.

Màiri, however, didn't hesitate to take her outstretched hand in both of her own. "Aye, lass. Ye will be all right."

"It hurts and I —" but her words were cut off in a pained cry.

"Aye, it does, and every woman in this room has been where ye are now. All of the pain will be worth it when ye hold that wee bairn in yer arms," she said, her eyes welling with tears at what all of them knew was the memory of holding her own sons, both only a week gone from the earth forever and only days in the ground.

"She is nae far off," Ealasaid said in a quiet voice as she rinsed her hands in the hot water. "She is moving quickly for it being her first."

"Then I will sit right here every moment," Màiri said to Emi. "I will nae leave ye. Look at me, Emilia," she said, and then smiled when Emi focused on her. "Let us speak of happy things. Yer father is safe, hm? We all are. He has been so worried about ye even though he knew he did the right thing in sending ye away."

"Father is safe?"

"Aye, as is everyone else. Our household was spared any other losses. That silly cat of yers has been looking all over for ye, and I know he will be happy when ye return."

"Lamb," she said with a weak smile.

"Aye, and though he gets plenty of attention, he does nae have yers, and that is all he wants."

Emi chuckled before her whole body tensed and she cried out once more.

"Emi, sweet one, ye have seen this all before when ye have assisted me," Ealasaid said. "I am going to check where ye are now, aye?"

Emi nodded, but her silence lasted only a moment before another wave of pain hit her. Ealasaid pulled the blanket back, followed by Emi's nightdress, before she, too, gave a nod as if some suspicion had been confirmed.

"Good thing we arrived when we did, or the bairn would have been here already. We need to get her up."

"Come on, Emi, love," Coira said. "Time to get out of bed."

"No!" Emi said through tears. "I cannae!"

"None of that now," Màiri said. "The Emilia that has survived all she has would never say such a thing. Up with ye."

The three women helped to pull Emi from the bed and brace her. Màiri helped her to place her hands on one of the bedposts, but she and Coira had to hold her up as the change in position brought a new kind of pain that buckled her knees as she screamed. Ealasaid took a tub Coira had put nearby and put it underneath Emi to catch the blood and any other fluids.

"Mistress," Ealasaid said. "I want ye to come take my place here."

"But —"

"Everything is fine, and she will have no trouble. Rinse yer hands in the hot water there, and yer hands will be the ones that bring yer grandbairn into the world," Ealasaid said.

Màiri nodded and did as asked while Ealasaid took up a position with Coira where Màiri had been.

"Now, Emi, listen to me. When ye feel the pain, ye push with all yer might, and when it eases, ye stop," Ealasaid explained.

Emi nodded, but the pain was there in the next second and she screamed as she did as Ealasaid instructed. When it eased, she was sobbing, but she had very little time to rest before it came again and brought another scream. The pain came and went for several minutes as Emi pushed with it until she suddenly felt blessed relief as a weight seemed to lift. In the next moment, the sound of a baby's cries filled the room.

"There ye are, lass! Ye have done it!" Ealasaid said.

There was a gentle sobbing from Màiri. "It is a wee lad!"

Coira joined her on the floor as they both marveled at the squirming, crying baby. "Let us clean him up," Coira said, placing a gentle hand on Màiri 's back.

Emi cried, exhausted and relieved as Ealasaid helped Emi finish her labor. The women then worked together to clean her up and help her to another room where the bed was clean before departing to give Emi some peace and deliver the news to Alasdair. In her first moment alone with him as he had his first feeding, Emi stroked his tiny cheek as he nursed, scarcely able to believe he was finally here, a tiny miracle amidst all the grief. Alasdair was finally allowed up, and she could hear him running up the stairs, practically sliding to a stop and catching himself on the door frame. He stared in disbelief as she looked over at him with a weak and tired smile, before he slowly approached the bed, sliding onto it beside her.

"This is …" he began before he was momentarily overwhelmed with emotion.

"Yer bairn? Aye. Meet yer son," she said.

"Son! I have a lad!" Alasdair said with a mix of shock and excitement.

"Aye, ye do. Did ye wish to hold him?"

"Please," he said in a near whisper before Emi passed the baby to him. "He is so tiny," Alasdair said through tears as he held the boy in his arms. "But, ach, Emi he is beautiful."

"He is ye."

"He is both of us. But tell me, are ye well?"

"I think I could sleep for days, but aye, fine now."

"I felt horrible when I heard ye screaming."

"Ye should have," she said, offering him a wry smile.

Alasdair responded with a quiet laugh. "Fair enough. Cannae promise it will nae happen again."

"Oh, I know, and for ye to promise that I would need to banish ye from our bed and that will nae be happening any time soon."

Alasdair grinned and then kissed her forehead. "I am so proud of ye," he whispered.

Emi sighed and kissed his cheek. "I think I know just what I want to name him, but I want ye to fetch everyone here before I say it."

"Of course," Alasdair said, handing the baby back to her before going to gather everyone.

Once they were all present, Emi looked up at them. "I wanted ye all to be here to witness his naming. It is important to me."

"What have the two of ye decided, lass?" Cailean asked.

Emi looked down at the face of the sleeping newborn and smiled. "Alexander James Evander Stewart, welcome to yer clan."

Màiri covered her mouth to hold in a sob, and Alasdair smiled. "I think it is perfect, love," he said.

"May I speak to Madame for a moment alone?" Emi asked.

"Aye," Alasdair said, kissing the top of Emi's head and leaving with the rest, shutting the door behind him.

"I just … I want to thank ye for coming here. Ye did nae have to."

Màiri made her way around and sat down on the edge of the bed. "Aye, I did. Ye asked for me. *Me*. In this most precious of moments, ye wanted me here with ye, and I could nae say no to that."

"Aye, but I … well … I am …"

"Ye *are* my daughter, Emilia," Màiri said. "Just as I should have treated ye as all along. It was selfish of me, but ye bore it so gracefully. Ye are a good lass, and as the months passed since ye got here, I softened toward ye more and more. I saw how happy it made yer father to finally be able to *be* yer father. The way he beamed with love and pride as he walked ye down the aisle to Alasdair. Now, ye are all he has left, and that is why he sent ye away. He could nae bear the thought of losing ye, too, and I found I could nae either. And in those horrible moments, ye were there, tending to Alexander with as much love as any true sister could. Ye loved him so much, and watching ye there, seeing how shattered yer heart already was from James, I knew how wrong I had been. When ye were pulled from the house and I heard ye screaming for yer father in yer grief and yer fear for his safety, that sealed it."

Reaching out, she brushed a tear from Emi's cheek.

"The boys loved ye just as much as ye loved them, Alex most of all. I had never seen him happier than he had been since ye came here, and making ye happy in any way he could filled his heart and spoke to his soul. The two of ye were kindred spirits born of the same man, and if ye wish me to be, I am yer mother as sure as I was Alex's and James', and a proud grandmother to this wee one in yer arms. Thank ye for giving him their names so that they may live on. I know they are here with ye and with him, and they will look after him every day of his life, just as Bridgette and Evander will."

"I do wish it," Emi whispered through her tears.

"Then so it is," Màiri said, kissing her forehead. "Now, get some rest, for as soon as ye wake, we will return ye home. It will be the best place for ye, so we can care for ye, and I know a grandfather who will be delighted to meet his new grandson."

***

"Monsieur!" Louis called out. "Monsieur, Madame has returned!"

"She has?" Crisdean said, hurrying out of the study as Louis opened the front door for him. Stepping out into the courtyard, he was just in time to help Màiri step down from the carriage. "My love," he said, kissing her hand. "I am so glad ye are back safely. How is she?"

"Why dinnae ye ask her yerself?" Màiri said, smiling as Alasdair stepped out of the carriage and helped Emi out.

Crisdean gasped when he saw her. "Emilia! Praise be to God!" he said as he hurried forward and embraced her. He held her for a very long few moments before he kissed her cheeks and her forehead. "My sweetest lass, I am so glad to see ye are safe."

Emi smiled, placing a hand on his cheek before she turned around and reached into the carriage, where Coira put the baby into her arms. Turning back around, she brought the baby to Crisdean.

"We thought ye might wish to meet yer grandson sooner rather than later."

"My … oh …" Crisdean said as he gathered the baby into his arms. "Look at him, how small he is! I am sure ye were too, and the boys, but it is hard to remember. He is a beautiful wee lad, just like his mother and father. What have ye named him?"

"His name is Alexander James Evander Stewart," Emi said as she stroked his little cheek.

Crisdean looked up quickly. "Ye named him after yer brothers?"

"Aye," Emi said with a smile. "The names of the angels watching over him."

Crisdean became overwhelmed with emotion, hugging

the baby just a little closer. "Emilia, ye cannae understand what this means to me," he whispered.

"Aye, I can," she said, placing a gentle hand on his arm.

"Let us get him inside and out of the cold air," Màiri said.

"Aye, of course. Of course," Crisdean said, turning around and walking in with the rest following him. "Louis, tell the household to come meet the newest member of the family."

"Yes, Monsieur," Louis said, departing.

"Welcome home, my wee lad," Crisdean said, going into his study. "What a life ye will have! We will make sure ye have fine tutors, the best of anything I can give to ye will be yers. Ye shall have it all, for I only have ye left to give it to, and I will do so with the gladdest of hearts."

As the household arrived, they were all smiles to welcome the new baby, a bright spot in the darkness of mourning. When they learned his name, some of them wept, touched by the gesture. Fergus had nearly done the same upon learning one of his names was Evander, a piece of a friend that would live on in this new child. Little Alexander was a beacon of hope, the first of a new generation of Stewarts, and when Crisdean saw Màiri hug Emi, he knew any rift was gone, washed away by loss and rebirth. It pleased him more than he could say, and he knew it would help Màiri to feel as though she hadn't lost everything, that there was one child left who could and would call her mother. It would fill a space in her heart, as would watching their grandson grow.

"Now that we are all here," Crisdean said as he stood with Emi, Alasdair, Màiri, Coira, Fergus, Cailean, Anna, and Ealasaid, still holding the baby in his arms. "There is something that needs to be done." Dipping his thumb into his dram of whisky, he used it to draw a small "S" on Alexander's forehead. "Alexander James Evander Stewart, as the chief of our branch of Clan Stewart, I anoint thee the next chief of the clan, as is yer birthright."

All of them made a small sound of shock. All except Màiri.

"Father, are ye sure?" Emi asked.

"Aye," Crisdean said. "With yer brothers gone, this bonnie wee lad is next in line by descent. If something happens to me before he is old enough to take my place, then ye and Alasdair will run the clan in his stead until he reaches a proper age. I will send the news on to the clan via a letter to Mr. MacMillan so that he can send it with the next shipment he takes to them."

Alexander made a small sound, and Crisdean smiled. "Aye, ye like that, do ye? Good, good. We will teach ye to be a fine chief, and when it is yer time, ye can go back home and reclaim what is ours, just as yer uncle meant to do."

"He meant to rebuild the castle," Emi said. "We had better start saving now."

Crisdean laughed. "Aye, that is true."

"Emilia," Màiri said. "Why dinnae ye go on upstairs and rest. Ye should nae be out of bed yet anyway, but I wanted to get ye back here so that ye were home with yer family and comfortable."

"Aye," Coira said. "The wee one is safe here. Alasdair, ye go up with her and get some rest yerself."

"Aye," Alasdair said, bowing to Màiri and Crisdean before taking Emi's hand and leaving the room. Once they were upstairs, he helped Emi undress and get into bed, watching her wince and knowing she was still in pain, though she'd hidden it from her father.

When he climbed into bed beside her, she was already asleep, and it made him smile. She deserved the rest after everything, and it was nice to know that this sleep was because of something happy instead of hiding from grief. Perhaps Alexander was the beginning of that new period in all their lives where they were finally free of the long shadow of an ill-fated rebellion that had cost them all so much more than they could've ever imagined it would.

Epilogue

The sound of benches scraping across the stone floor was what greeted him as he strode confidently into the hall. A wave of bows and curtsies rolled just ahead of his steps, and he smiled at those giving them if they met his eye. Stepping up onto the dais, he took a moment to himself while his back was to the hall, a moment to center himself. His eyes fell on the portraits of his grandfather and the uncles he'd never known, and he smiled through the sadness. How he wished they were here! How he wished they could see this! In a way they were, but not in the way he truly wished they were.

"Please sit," he said after he turned around to face the crowd. "It is my honor and my privilege to welcome ye home to Stewart lands after over 20 years away from them," he said, pausing for the thunderous applause he hadn't quite expected. "It was a long and arduous process, but I have reclaimed all that was taken from us and from ye. From the memories of those who once lived here: my grandfather, my grandmothers, my mother, my father, and my beloved kin, I was able to re-build this castle and restore it to its former glory. It was a dream inherited from my uncle, and one I gladly took on for myself as I was raised with the importance of what once was. As a clan we have persevered, thrived, grown, and now the next generation of Stewarts have returned to the land whose soil runs through our veins as blood and whose echoes sound in our very bones. As yer chief, I am determined to follow the example of my forebears, the great Stewart chiefs, and help our people to prosper and grow here in peace."

Lifting a golden goblet from the table — a gift to his parents from King Louis for their wedding — he held it out in front of him.

"I, Alexander James Evander Stewart, the chief of Clan Stewart, pledge my life and my service to ye, my clan and my kin. May I never give ye cause for disappointment or heartache and may ye find health and happiness under my leadership. To Clan Stewart: slàinte mhath," Alexander said before drinking from the goblet.

"Slàinte mhath! God save our chief!" rang out in response, followed by more applause.

***

From the back of the room, Emi smiled at her son. He was a natural, born to this, and trained for it from his earliest days. She was so very proud of him and all of the hard work he'd done to make this dream a reality, to bring his family home and make things right again. In this moment she could see his grandfather shining through even though he looked just like his own father. At 21, he was the same age here as his father had been when he'd talked his chief into letting her go with them to Inverness, the start of the road which led him to his moment. Beside her, Alasdair squeezed her hand, beaming with pride as he watched his son mark the return of the clan and the start of a new life here. Twenty years on, there was little worry about the bounty, such things were long buried, and they'd never come searching for him, so he'd been able to finally return to the land of his birth.

It saddened her that her father hadn't lived to see the day where he might do the same, though Màiri, Coira, Ealasaid, and Anna had, and they all stood to the other side of her. Hortense was also with them, having married Fergus about a year after they'd arrived. Cailean's and Fergus' sons stood on either side of the dais with their fathers, the loyal officers of the new Stewart chief, just as the two older men still were. To Alasdair's other side stood Helena, five years younger than her brother Alexander. She was a beauty like her mother and absolutely adored her brother with all her heart. Emi and Alasdair had been happy to remove her from France and bring her back to Scotland before the French court could get its hands on her, though they'd promised her that any marriage for her would be one of her choosing. They wouldn't make the same mistakes her great-grandfather had.

When Crisdean died, only then did Emi discover the meaning of what Hortense had once said about claiming what belonged to her. Unbeknownst to Crisdean himself, his father had left property in France to his granddaughter, should she ever come to France to seek it out. It was the proceeds from the sale of the property to the crown that had rebuilt this castle.

"Mam," Alex said as he made his way to her and kissed her cheeks. "How was it?"

"Wonderful," she said, smiling at him. "Yer grandfather would have been so pleased and so very proud of ye."

"And ye?"

"I am always proud of ye, Alex, ye dolt."

Alex laughed. "Aye, I know ye are," he said, hugging her.

"Very well done, Son," Alasdair said, his grin wide. "Could nae have said it better myself."

"Thank ye, Da," Alex said with a matching grin, such words coming from his father meaning more to him than most anything else. It wasn't that Alasdair wasn't free with them, he was, but it was always what Alex strove for.

"I thought ye looked very regal, Alex," Helena said. "Like a prince."

"Ye would say that even if I walked in with a chicken on my head, Helly."

"I would nae!" she said indignantly before she paused. "Well, what kind of chicken?"

He laughed and kissed the top of her head. "Ye are ridiculous in the best way, and I love ye for it."

Helena grinned and then laughed. "I think I must make ye a chicken hat."

"Dinnae ye dare," Alex said.

"But it would be fun!"

"Absolutely nae."

"A rooster hat?"

"Helly!" he said in exasperation, which made her laugh, before he rolled his eyes. She could always get a rise out of him. "Come on, call the first dance for the ceilidh."

"Really!" she exclaimed in delight.

"Aye, ye always pick the right one," he said, taking her hand and walking back toward the front as she hurried to keep up with him.

Alasdair laughed. "The pair of them."

"Aye," Emi said, laughing with him. "But they have always been this way. Thick as thieves in spite of their age difference."

"Very true," Alasdair said, slipping an arm around her waist. "Just as ye were with his two of his namesakes."

"I wonder if it will be the same with the new one."

"New one what?"

Emi looked at him with a sly smile.

"Wait … are ye saying …"

"Mmmhmm. Seems we were nae done yet and God saw fit to give ye and me a bairn born and bred on Stewart land."

Alasdair grinned with excitement. "And when shall we expect this surprise gift?"

"Hogmanay, if ye can believe it."

He laughed. "How fitting. A new bairn for a new year."

"A new life for a new life."

"Even better," he said before he smiled. "Emi, the weather is too fine to be indoors. Care to go out for a time?"

The memory he purposefully called her back to made her smile. "I thought ye would never ask."

ABOUT THE AUTHOR

A California native, Eilidh Miller, FSAScot, has a BA in English and studied history as an undeclared minor to better inform her literature studies. A Fellow with the Society of Antiquaries of Scotland, Eilidh is very active within Southern California's Scottish community, spending a great deal of time volunteering with the charitable organization St. Andrew's Society of Los Angeles.

A long-time historical reenactor, Eilidh loves research and educating the general public about historical events, as well as entertaining them with tidbits no one would believe if they weren't documented. She extends this same energy to her work, extensively researching the historical periods she includes in her writing to ensure that the information she presents is correct, even going so far as to travel internationally to access archives and scout locations.

She resides in Southern California with her husband, daughter, and her feisty Shiba Inu sidekick.

You can keep up with Eilidh on Twitter, Instagram, TikTok, or her website www.eilidhmiller.com. You can also join her reader group on Facebook, Eilidh Miller's Reading Lodge, to keep up to date on the next release, get exclusive content, teasers, and enter contests!

OTHER BOOKS BY THE AUTHOR

The Watchers
The Watchers Series: Book 1

Enemies of the Mind
The Watchers Series: Book 2

Echoes of the Rising
The Watchers Series: Book 3

The Gathering
The Watchers Series: Book 4 - Coming Fall 2021

Captain Merrick